Hearts of Clover

Half My Heart
&
Change My Heart

Book Bundle
Books 1 & 2 of the Clover Series

By Danielle Stewart

Copyright Page

Half My Heart
A Clover Series Novella

At nineteen, Devin Sutton lost his first love, his freedom, and his hope. Years later, the only thing he has on his mind this holiday season is finally settling the score back in Clover, North Carolina.

That is, until the girl he thought he'd lost forever crosses his path. Rebecca Farrus is supposed to be off living the life of her dreams, not tending bar in some dive.

When faced with the choice, will Devin decide to celebrate what he's finally found or keep seeking retribution for everything he lost?

Chapter One

I enjoy screwing with people. I know that makes me twisted, but I don't care. Fighting a smirk, I lounge back in my plush leather office chair, fingers laced behind my mop of messy hair. I keep it long as a form of protest against the business world I'm living in. I get sideways looks from all the stuffed shirt executives I have to meet with, but I couldn't care less.

I'm getting comfortable, preparing for the show that's about to unfold. Any second my office door is going to fly open. After the move I just pulled, it's inevitable. And just like clockwork, in charges my right-hand man, Luke Miller. Luke's normally even-keeled face is blood red and the vein in his forehead is throbbing. There is nothing I enjoy more than pissing off my business partner.

"Devin Sutton," he says like a mom scolding her child. I know when Luke uses my full name he's angry. "Rochelle just told me you asked her to clear your schedule for the week. These meetings aren't optional. You're selling your company. You *have* to be there." I triumphantly watch as Luke loosens his tie slightly. Apparently the stress I cause is choking him. His thick-rimmed designer glasses might start fogging up soon if I don't do something to calm him down. But what's the fun in that?

"Then move the meetings." I shrug indifferently as I watch Luke swallow back the words he'd like to say. He's a big guy, as tall as I am, and equally strong, but historically he's been a gentle giant, a peacekeeper. It's a

1

hobby of mine to test this theory often to see if he truly has the patience of Job. He always wins, but this stunt I'm pulling may put him over the edge.

"We don't move meetings with eight of the most powerful people on Wall Street. They set the schedule and we show up. Now what's going on with you? Family emergency?"

I roll my eyes, barking back, "You know damn well I don't have any family, Luke."

"Exactly, and I can't think of another single reason why you'd bail on something this important. So unless you tell me you're dying . . ." Luke takes a seat in the leather chair across from me and narrows his eyes, searching for a sign of looming death. "Wait, are you dying?"

"No," I groan, standing to face my enormous office window. We're on the twenty-second floor of my Wall Street office building, and the view of the city doesn't get much better. Though I couldn't care less about that either.

My back is to Luke as I try to limit my explanation. I'm a grown man, and the owner of this company. I don't answer to anyone.

"I'm going back to Clover. I have some business there." I press my hand to the glass. The large window doesn't have any bars on it, but it still feels like a prison to me.

"Like hell you are. You stand to make an enormous amount of money from this sale. We all do. If you blow this off, people will start to lose confidence in you and we'll never get a more lucrative offer. You aren't jumping ship now, leaving us all high and dry because you're feeling nostalgic."

I turn back toward him with force. My back muscles tighten; I fill my chest with air and flex my biceps. Similar to a blowfish, I puff myself up—a way to intimidate anyone in my way. It sounds ridiculous, but it works. I let my eyes flame at the accusation. "First, I won't bail on the deal. Second, it isn't nostalgia driving me."

"Vengeance then? Don't forget I'm one of the very few people who knows who you were before you came to the city. Clover is nothing but a speck in the rearview mirror. You need to leave it that way. The plan has always been that you'll sell the company once we hit a certain threshold. We hit it. This sale will make you wealthier than you ever imagined." Luke pounds the table with his fist and looks at me, his expression showing regret instantly. That isn't who he is; the table-banging guy is who *I* am. It's why Luke spends the majority of his time apologizing for me. It's what makes us work.

"I'm already wealthier than I ever imagined." My voice booms like thunder and Luke looks as though he's face to face with a bear rather than a man. I know it's because he's seen me demolish four guys in a bar fight like I was snapping toothpicks. I've proven I'm fully capable, and nearly always on the brink, of an adrenaline-fueled fury.

"Devin." Luke's voice is quieter now, and that's why I respect him. He has the ability to control himself, temper his emotions. I envy that. "It's almost Christmas. We're trying to close the deal before the holidays. Don't you want to be in New York for Christmas? Ice skating. The tree at Rockefeller?"

"I hate Christmas, you know that too, Luke. It's repulsive . . . the sparkly lights and the delusional fog that falls over people. Everyone acting like all is well in the world just because it's the twenty-fifth of December. Ridiculous."

"What kind of heartless bastard hates Christmas?"

I point my thumbs at my chest. "This kind of heartless bastard." I grin, fully aware I'm aggravating him. "Wait, last Christmas we were at the bar all night drinking until we couldn't see straight. I don't remember you being too fond of the holiday either."

"That's apples and oranges. I might not have had plans that day; it doesn't mean I hate the holiday. Actually I think it just means we're pathetic. Listen, I'm the closest thing you have to a friend, Devin. I don't want you going down there and ending up where they put you last time."

I scoff at the ludicrous suggestion. "That town couldn't touch me now if it wanted to. They should be afraid of me. I'm sure as hell not afraid of them." *Not anymore, anyway.*

"Then why go back? Just use your money to hurt them from here."

"This isn't something you do from afar, it's personal."

I lost nine years of my life because of the corruption in Clover, North Carolina. I fully intend to handle my business with them face to face. The sale here in New York will have to wait. I've finally gotten the mayor of Clover to meet with me. I need this deal to go through under the wire, before the sale documents are signed here in New York. The leadership of the new company will never allow a deal like I'm planning in Clover to go through, so it's now or never.

Luke throws his head back in exasperation. I know this look well. It means I've won. "I've always had your back, Devin."

"Then have it now." I drop into my chair and cross my arms over my chest. "Buy me a week, that's all I need, then I'll be back here signing whatever you want me to sign."

"Fine," Luke agrees reluctantly. "Promise me you won't kill anyone. Just handle your business and come back."

"What's my rule, Luke?"

"I know. You don't make promises. Just nod to let me know you hear me." Luke stands and squares his shoulders to mine. Our relationship has morphed over the two years we've known each other. We've moved from business partners to a type of friendship. Not a clear-cut one, but something I value all the same, even if I don't tell him so.

I nod and grab my coat and briefcase as I head out the door. "One week," Luke shouts behind me and I laugh maniacally, just to screw with him a little more.

* * * * * * * * * * *

Driving to Clover from New York City is a calculated decision for me. I don't want to be at the mercy of a flight schedule if I need to get out of town fast, and I don't want to use the company jet on my personal time. I'm calling this a business deal, but that's far from the truth.

The downside of the drive is the endless time I have to think about where my life has brought me. There's a lot of history for me in Clover, and none of it is good.

Well, almost none of it. My mind rewinds to my childhood, and the long stretch of road in front of me means I have nothing to distract myself from it.

I can attest to the fact that the term *military brat* was coined for a reason. Something about attending half a dozen schools and saying goodbye to every friend you ever managed to make, can be hard. It made me resilient, but if you pair that life with parents like mine, you end up with someone socially stunted.

My father was a commander of a brigade combat team and I spent my childhood following him around the country from post to post. My mother was equally dedicated to the Army as the family readiness leader attached to my father's battalion. She had been responsible for coordinating functions to raise money for the families. She also ensured that all loved ones were up to date on the location of the soldiers while deployed. Two very admirable jobs, but they more-or-less equated to lots of microwave dinners and unsupervised time for me. I'd never understood how two people could be so dedicated to strangers while overlooking their own son.

The move to Clover, my seventh home in seventeen years, had been the worst one. It had been right at the beginning of my senior year of high school. No matter how much I'd begged my parents to let me stay at our last post at Fort Drum in New York until graduation, they hadn't listened. *A family stays together,* my mother had always said. Apparently she'd just meant a family cohabitates, because there had been nothing about us that felt *together.*

The one redeemable thing about Clover is that it's the place where I fell in love for the first time. It's where I met Rebecca, the girl who helped me shake the nagging shadow of loneliness that had followed me around my whole young life. But it's also the place that broke me. It stole a decade from me. Clover robbed me of my life with Rebecca, and I intend to even the score.

Chapter Two

I spent nearly a decade behind bars, a fact few people in my life today know. I was locked up for a crime I didn't commit. Throughout the darkest moments I could count on only one thing, the arrival of Rebecca's letters. They were a source of comfort, especially when my parents died and I was unable to attend the funerals. When the loneliness in prison was so palpable I thought it would suffocate me, her letters were a tangible reminder that someone cared. Over the years she wrote about her life, about what she had become and all the things she was achieving.

Early on, she asked me if it hurt to know she was doing well and, with a completely honest heart, I told her I loved that she was happy. I quickly wrote back that all I ever wanted to hear was that she was taking advantage of all that life had to offer her. Hearing about it gave me peace.

That's not to say there weren't moments when bitterness would overtake me. Jealousy would fill my body like it had been poured into me. I felt the strangest combination of gut-wrenching heartbreak and overwhelming happiness for her. But receiving her letters was still the best part of my day.

She wrote often that she did not believe for a moment I had set the fire that killed Brent Hoyle. She knew I was not capable of something so terrible. Brent was Rebecca's ex-boyfriend and the son of the sheriff of Clover. As much as Rebecca believed I was innocent, a jury of my peers was not as easily convinced. The sheriff spun a story about the fight Brent and I had that afternoon. I was merely protecting Rebecca, but no one seemed interested in the facts. Not the jury and not the town. I was appointed a lawyer who I found out later was the wife of Sherriff Hoyle's best friend. The judge in the case hardly seemed to be awake the majority of the time. The evidence left more questions than answers, and the trial seemed rushed, my defense halfhearted. There were no witnesses called; no one was allowed in the courtroom to watch the trial. A day and a half and it was over. That was the kind of thing that could happen in a small town if no one was there to stop it.

From the moment I was arrested, I was in complete isolation. I wasn't able to see my parents or Rebecca. Everything happened in a flash, and before I knew what had hit me, I heard the words, "life without the possibility of parole."

I was convicted on Christmas Eve, the court making a special concession and working a half-day just to make sure I was dealt with. I spent Christmas Day behind bars with the realization that I would never be a free man again. That is why I hate Christmas, why the sound of jingling bells or the sight of a mall Santa Claus makes me want to pummel someone.

I shake the memories as I pull up to Main Street, Clover, and park my BMW in front of the Winston Hotel. I have some of Rebecca's letters all stacked up on the passenger seat, and they seem to be calling my name. They root me to this plan, a constant reminder of why vengeance is so necessary. People have to pay for the time they stole from me. Written in these letters is the life Rebecca lived without me: Mack, the man she fell in love with and married, her job as a successful artist, and her thriving studio. It's enough to kindle the fire in my belly, to drive me to continue.

I pull a letter out, a Christmas letter, and smile at the stocking-adorned paper she wrote it on. Her swirling script dancing all over the paper reminds me of the feeling I used to get when her letters would arrive.

Devin,

There is no feeling in the world that can compare to spending Christmas morning with your child. Adeline is just a baby, so she doesn't understand the holiday yet, but watching her stare up at the twinkling lights on our Christmas tree makes my heart feel full. I want to give her everything she ever needs and more. Being her mom is like staring into the future, a future that I control.

Mack is over the moon and he's proving to be a wonderful father. I could never do this on my own and I am so blessed to have him. I can't help but wish you were here, able to hold sweet little Adeline in your arms. She would adore you, the way I do.

I dream of all the holidays I will spend watching her grow, every present she will open, every wish she will make. I can't wait to see what my future holds with her. I know now that I am happiest being a mother. It's what I was always meant to do. I only wish she could know you. I wish things were different for us.

Merry Christmas, Devin.
As always, you have all my love and half my heart,

Rebecca

All through the years, no matter how full her life became, she still signed the letters the same way. As she found more and more happiness, she continued to share her heart with me. When it would have been easier to stop writing, to move on, she stayed connected. It was I who eventually cut the ties between us.

I place the letter down and grip my steering wheel tightly, trying to ground myself back to reality as I sit in the parking lot.

Last night, before I left New York to come back to Clover, I told myself I wouldn't look for her. Just as I hadn't looked for her when I was exonerated and released from prison. What was the point? In her letters she left no room for doubt; as time passed, she moved on and was happy. I have my empire in New York, and she lives a couple hours from Clover with her husband and daughter. That's just the way it is.

I don't know why I never wrote her about the Innocence Project that began working on my case. I'm not sure why I didn't let her know they were on the verge of proving my case was handled unjustly and that I was not the killer. I just stopped writing. I was given a settlement, reparations from the state—just over one million dollars. I walked out of prison a rich and free man. It took all my willpower to leave her alone, to not push my way back into her life and try to win her back. I had to put any thoughts of her out of my mind.

That's not to say there weren't plenty of nights spent with various women where I pictured Rebecca in my bed instead. Most people fought to forget the loss of their virginity, the awkwardness of it. For me, I was continually trying to recreate the feeling I had that night with Rebecca. It was only one night, but it left an imprint on my soul. If I close my eyes I can still taste her cherry lip gloss and feel my fingers tangling in her dark luscious hair. The physical pleasure of that night is still enough to warm me to the core, but it was more than that. We were two people completely misunderstood by the world who instantly saw each other the way we were meant to be seen. To me she wasn't just the pretty cheerleader without potential. To her I wasn't the misfit outsider who deserved to be tormented for being different. We connected and then we were torn apart.

These days I have no problem attracting women. I flash a half smile across a crowded room and like fish on a line I reel them in. I raise an eyebrow in a dirty little way, and women swoon. I know putting my hand on the small of a woman's back as we leave a bar helps seal the deal. The flashy cars and expensive suits don't hurt either. But every woman in New York falls miles short. None of them hold a candle to Rebecca. Mack is a lucky son of a bitch, and frankly, I hate him for it.

I did the only thing I could. I threw myself into my work. Invested my settlement money in the business I was starting and busted my ass to make it grow into a fortune. In the process, I hardened my heart against the idea of happiness and began to draw up plans for my revenge against Clover. And now, it is finally time to accomplish that.

Chapter Three

Bellying up for a beer at the Boot Hopper is just about the last thing I hoped to do tonight. The jukebox is playing an endless loop of Christmas music, and someone has made a halfhearted attempt at decorating this place. Strings of tinsel hang from the ceiling and a crooked fake Christmas tree is propped up in the corner. I hate Christmas and I hate Clover, so Christmas *in* Clover is the most despicable combination for me.

I spent the afternoon driving around and surveying the land associated with the deal I'm proposing. When I got back to my room at the hotel, I tried to settle in. Unfortunately, my restless mind and poorly stocked mini-bar kept me from calling it a night. So I went off in search of an escape and ended up here. It's the only place to get a drink in town this time of night, just a sleepy bar room a five-minute walk down the hill from my hotel.

There are a few people who look like regulars, nursing beers and swapping complaints about how this country is going to hell in a handbasket. They throw angry glances my direction as they find a topic they can all agree on: corporate greed. I find it ironic that, in a town full of corruption and cover-ups, these people are concerned with what's happening on Wall Street. And, just because I happen to be wearing a business suit that cost more than their cars, I must be to blame.

I'm about to get the hell out of this dive and go back to prepare for my meeting with the mayor tomorrow, when I feel an intense wave of heat roll over me. It's like a haunting whisper in my ear. I'm compelled to look up, some unknown force willing me. Standing in the dimly lit doorway, passing by the old jukebox, is Rebecca.

I can't breathe, or I've forgotten how. I dip my head slightly, hoping she doesn't see me. I want a chance to watch her, take in every inch of her before this bubble pops and reality floods in. I watch her long hair sway, just the way I remember it, shiny and amazing. She's wearing a tight top and jeans with holes in them. Her eyes seem tired, like she's lived a lifetime already, but she still looks gorgeous. The only unfamiliar part of her is the little girl she has in tow.

The girl's hair is the same espresso shade as Rebecca's, but rather than pin-straight silk, her soft wispy curls are pulled up into pigtails. She looks about three years old, maybe four, and she's in her pajamas—a little red jumper with a picture of Santa across the belly. She's nearly outgrown the clothes, too much of her ankles and wrists are showing. I watch as Rebecca lifts her. The tiny girl responds by tucking her face into her mother's neck. It's a spot I've found comfort in myself, and I miss it more in this moment than I have in years. The child is practically asleep now as they disappear through a door into a back room of the bar.

She doesn't notice me, and if I'm honestly determined not to reconnect with her, then I'll leave. It will be easy to slip out the front door and ignore my desire to know why Rebecca is in Clover, and specifically why she's in the Boot Hopper this time of night.

I came back for a lot of reasons, but seeing her isn't one of them. I can go. I *should* go. But my legs aren't moving, and my curious heart is gluing my ass to this bar stool. Damn that last sliver of humanity I can't rid myself of.

Rebecca emerges from the back room with her arms empty now. She walks toward the bar. Toward me. I can feel my heart thudding against the walls of my chest and I wonder if anyone else can hear the banging. My palms are instantly sweaty and my mouth goes dry. For the first time in a decade, I feel like a nervous kid staring at his crush.

Rebecca flips up the wooden divider and I realize she's a bartender here. The questions swirling in my head can't even be caught and held down long enough to string together. What is she doing in Clover? Where is her husband, Mack? Why is she tending bar in this dive, with her daughter sleeping somewhere in the back room?

Before I can even begin to come up with some hypothetical answers, she's standing in front of me asking *what'll it be?* The sound of her voice strikes my chest and pierces the armor I've layered myself with over the years. She isn't even looking at me; she's tying her small apron around her waist and reaching for a rag to wipe the bar. She looks so empty, like a ghost, and even before I know why she is working here, I feel bereft for her.

I wonder if maybe I'm dreaming, trying to recall if I've drunk myself stupid and just can't remember. Only one way to find out.

"Rebecca," I say, and am surprised that her name catches in my throat, coming out so quiet it seems to spook her. I haven't spoken her name out loud in a very long time. I've thought it almost every day, but I haven't said it.

When her eyes come up to mine, I watch her face light with recognition and then wash with emotion. "Devin?" She says my name like it's a curse word, something she almost can't get out without a struggle. "What are you doing here?" she whispers, examining my face. Her eyes move over my sharp suit, my longer hair, and my grown-up body. I almost forget how young we were the last time she laid eyes on me. We were barely eighteen. Now I'm a regular at the gym, and I've bulked up significantly over the years. Back then, I could barely grow a beard, and now the five o'clock shadow on my face is ever-present, seeming to sprout back up minutes after a shave. I'm a man now, a different man, inside and out.

"I'm here on business," I answer as I consider asking her the same thing. She beats me to the punch with more questions of her own.

"Why didn't you come back after you were exonerated? They kept it so quiet that I didn't hear until almost six months later. I was still sending you letters." She fidgets with the rag in her hand, and I can tell she's trying to figure out if I'm real or a figment of her imagination.

"I needed a fresh start. No looking back." I don't intend those words to cut her, but judging by the way her eyes dart away, I know I hurt her.

"It looks like you've found one." She gestures at my suit and I can see the light leaving her face. The ray of hope she had at the sight of me is dwindling.

She may not like what she's hearing from me, but I want answers of my own. "What are you doing here? You're supposed to be living hours away. Happily ever after with *Mack.*" I say his name with a hiss of hatred I meant to hold back. "Did something happen?" I know it's bad, but I hope he's a cheating bastard. Or maybe he died in some tragic accident. I'm not proud of the thought, but I've spent a long time hating him for getting to spend his life with Rebecca.

"It's complicated." Tears fill her eyes and I immediately feel bad for wanting Mack dead. He's dead, she's widowed and had to move back to Clover, and I'm over here celebrating it like a victory. Luke is right. I am a heartless bastard.

"Did he die?" I ask, trying to look empathetic. In my years as a hardcore businessman, I trained myself to resist empathy.

She shakes her head and searches the ceiling for words that seem to escape her. "There's no Mack. There never was, Devin." I watch a tear spill over as I try to make sense of what she's saying.

"But . . . your letters." I reach in my briefcase and pull out the one I was reading earlier. For nine years while I was in prison she wrote to me about Mack and her life.

"You have them? You carry them with you?" She seems hopeful about this.

Her question infuriates me. Partly because how weak I look for having this letter, like a keepsake, and partly because now I'm getting the impression they are full of lies. I stuff it back in my briefcase and stand to leave. I'm not in Clover for Rebecca, for explanations. I'm here to settle scores.

She leans over the bar and touches my arm, "I have ten minutes before my shift starts. They have a bed made up in the back for Adeline to sleep in while I work. I can ask Carol to keep an ear out for her and we can go outside. I want to explain." She turns and whispers to the other bartender then heads for the door, clearly assuming I'll follow. I want to prove her wrong, have her get out there and feel like an idiot—the way I feel right now as I realize she's not in some mountain town with her

17

wonderful husband living her dream life. But Rebecca's pull is magnetic, so I follow, heading outside to meet her.

"I want to explain," she repeats as we round the corner to the side of the building. The cold air is cutting tonight, but I'm too frustrated to care. I'm seething with anger and I can't speak. She's standing closer to me now than she has in over a decade and I can smell her skin. It is exactly the same scent I remember from all those years ago.

She sits on a crooked wooden bench, but I don't join her. Instead I cross my arms over my chest and lean against the building.

"I can understand if you're upset," Rebecca begins, "I would be, too. But I'd like for you to try to understand about the letters, about me."

"If you're telling me they were lies, then I don't want an explanation. That's not why I'm here in Clover," I say flatly, deepening my voice and making sure not to show the least bit of sympathy for whatever explanation she has. There can be no excuse for lying to a man for all those years.

"Fine," she says, sinking her shoulders in defeat, an emotion I can tell she is no stranger to. "But you're going to listen, anyway." And she's right, I will. "When you were arrested, I spoke out about your innocence. I defended you every step of the way. I knew you didn't start that fire or kill Brent. Hoyle and his men hassled me everywhere I went. I was hoping when college started I'd be out of here, putting it all behind me. But my mother got sick and my father couldn't take care of my brothers by himself. He has a black soul—ugly to the core. I didn't want my brothers to have to deal with that on their own, so I stayed. Then, as they grew up, I tried again to leave, but I made some stupid mistakes that resulted in the best thing that ever happened to me, and she's asleep back there."

Rebecca points toward the bar with one hand and covers her heart with the other. I know she's talking about that sweet little girl she carried in. "I've been working for years to try to get myself out of this place, and now I have something else I'm trying to shake. Adeline's father, Collin. He's a low-life and he's taking every penny I have and using it for drugs. When I try to tell him no, he threatens to take Adeline, and in a place like Clover, I'm afraid that may actually happen. There is no law here for people like me, people who don't support Hoyle."

I suck in a breath as she runs her hands through her hair the same way she did when we were young. I look away, not wanting the familiar gesture to sway me from my position of indifference.

I stand like stone listening to her, reminding myself that I don't care. These were her choices. I was the one locked up. I bite at my lip, nearly to the point of blood. The silence stretches between us, and when it's clear she has nothing else to say, I speak. "What does that have to do with all the letters you sent me? I was in prison and you were out here creating all this nonsense." I don't want to sound hurt, weak. I want to sound angry. "Why make a fool of me?" I pound my hand to my chest and watch her jump at the bark in my voice.

"I wasn't trying to make a fool of you," she counters forcefully, standing to face me. I'm shocked to see her anger brewing now. "You may have been the only one behind bars, but I was in my own prison here. You were the only person who ever looked at me like . . ." she pauses, and points up at my face, "like that."

I avert my eyes, looking instead over her shoulder. I know exactly what she means, how I look at her, but I won't acknowledge that. "So, you thought lying to me was a good distraction from your shitty life? Some fantasy world for you to escape from this pathetic place?"

She reaches up and slaps my face hard. Living in the world of business, I've gotten very good at anticipating things, but, I didn't see that coming. The sting in my cheek, made worse by the cold, is still not enough to distract me from the fact that she is standing so close to me, within reach for the first time in a long time. Not Mack's wife, not happily ever after. Just Rebecca, at my fingertips.

"It wasn't a fantasy, some dream world for me. You were the one who begged me to tell you I was happy. You wanted me to write to you about how wonderful my life was turning out. Would it really have helped you in there to know I cried myself to sleep every night for the first year you were in prison? Would you have been relieved to know I couldn't walk down the street without being harassed here in Clover? When I was pregnant with Adeline, would you have slept better knowing I almost lost her when Collin pulled me down the stairs in a drunken stupor? I don't see how the truth would have served you very well in there."

I don't respond. I watch the fire dance in her eyes, conviction fueling the words she's shouting at me. She means what she's saying, but it still isn't enough. I'm standing in front of a person who made up a fake life and wrote me regularly about it.

She calms slightly and continues. "You were supposed to be in prison for the rest of your life. I thought I was helping you. I didn't mean to hurt you. Maybe, in a way, you're right. Writing to you was like throwing a penny in a wishing well. Every word I put in those letters was what I wanted my life to be. It's how I wanted our lives to be . . . together." The tears gathering in the corners of her eyes hit me like a punch in the gut.

"The letters . . ." My words catch slightly in my throat. I don't like admitting anything, but I hate to see her cry. "They did help me. They probably saved my life some days. So maybe you were right, but . . ." Perhaps she takes my words as an invitation for forgiveness, but that isn't what I intend. As surprised as I was for the slap, I'm even more shocked by what she does next.

She leans in, stepping on her tiptoes to reach my face, and kisses me. Her lips feel exactly the same, and, as if in a time warp, I travel back to the last time I touched her. Every woman I've kissed since paled in comparison to Rebecca. Any mental debate I'm having with myself is temporarily overruled by my body's desire for her. It's been so long. I was convinced I'd never see her again.

My brain underwent a transition over those years apart; in order to become a successful businessman and deal with my past, I built an untouchable heart. The proof of those changes are here in the way I move, in the way I touch her. I pull her in with a forceful tug and then spin her so she is against the wall instead of me. The man I am today is a dominant one. I'm constantly in charge. I kiss her with a hunger that borders on harshness, like I may bruise her lips with my own. I'm angry at her still, and it's coming through in the way I handle her.

21

I can feel her arch as her back scrapes the wall of the building. I'm holding her there with the firm weight of my eager body. This is not like any kiss we shared a decade ago. This is who I am now, not that boy she used to know. As my hand slips under her shirt I feel her recoil and she places her palms on my solid chest.

Her mouth leaves mine. "Stop, Devin," I hear her say, her voice laced with disappointment. Cleary, this is not what she intended with her kiss. Maybe she wants to rekindle a spark the world has snuffed out, or is hoping for a tender reunion. Some kind of absolution for the mistakes she made, maybe. That isn't what I'm here for. If she is hoping to find the boy she missed out on, she's out of luck. He's gone. The only thing left is the man she lied to.

I step back and wipe her lip gloss from my mouth. I straighten my tie and clear my throat, reminding myself I am in Clover for revenge. Not whatever this is.

"I've done well for myself since leaving prison. I'm about to become an even wealthier man once I finish my business here." I reach into my pocket and pull out a large roll of money wrapped in an elastic band. It is payment meant for a construction company I intend to contract with, once the property deal goes through. There is no safe in my hotel and keeping it in my pocket seemed like a better plan than leaving it unattended. I place the roll of money in Rebecca's hand and turn on my heels. I can easily take out more cash for the contractor. She needs this money, and I need to put this all behind me.

I walk away with my hands stuffed in my pockets. "Devin," I hear her call from across the parking lot, but I don't turn around. I plan to slip away into the darkness and walk back to the hotel. That is, until I feel a solid thump on my back. Turning around I see the money lying in the parking lot at my feet. Rebecca stands there with her eyes blazing. "I don't want your money. I'm sorry you think I am some despicable person for lying to you, but I'm not a charity case. Keep your money and get the hell out of Clover. At least now I can stop sitting here wondering what kind of guy you turned out to be. I have my answer." She stomps back into the bar, and again slips out of my life.

Leaning down I pick up the money, putting it back in my pocket. What does she want from me? Forgiveness? Understanding? She needs money. I gave her some. I give money to charities all the time. It's a tax write-off. Nothing more than a business transaction. Why is she making it personal? Does she want us to just pick up where we left off as if we are still kids? Even if I do want her, want us, we're both so different now.

Chapter Four

Thoughts of Rebecca keep me up most of the night. Her perfume has soaked into my skin and it is intoxicating and distracting. I tell myself over and over again that I did nothing wrong, that she is at fault, but still, I can't sleep.

After a shitty night of tossing and turning, followed by an annoying wake-up call from the front desk at the Winston, I start my day. There aren't many places to eat in Clover; so many businesses are boarded up. I settle for breakfast at the diner on the corner of Lexington and Main. A redheaded waitress, without any type of customer service skills, walks up to my table and grunts something about taking my order. She stands with her pad out and a pencil hovering over it.

"I'll take a cup of coffee, black." I watch as she rolls her eyes, as though my order is predictably boring.

I look around the diner at yet another dismal attempt at puking the holiday spirit on its customers. The windows are painted with winter scenes and each table has ornaments hanging over it. Why do people insist on covering every available surface with something sparkly or festive just because Christmas is a couple days away? It's nauseating.

When the waitress returns with my coffee, she's so distracted she nearly spills it on my lap.

"Oh shit," she hollers, shaking her head as she stares out the diner window. "Doug," she yells back to someone in the kitchen. "Collin is out there giving Rebecca hell again. You want me to call the cops on him?"

"Why bother? They won't help her," the booming voice from the kitchen replies.

The waitress mumbles under her breath. "That boy is gonna kill her one of these days."

"Rebecca Farrus?" I ask, craning my neck to see what's going on.

"Yep, you know the girl? I've been working with her for six years, and that girl can't catch a break. She works two jobs and that jackass, Collin, steals her money every chance he gets. Every time she fights back, life knocks her down."

I stand and move toward the door, driven more by the primal desire to protect than by rational thinking. I push it open and stand with my arms across my chest, watching, listening.

"I don't give a shit if it's all the money you have. I need it." Collin's voice is shrill and frantic. He jitters like an antsy child.

"Collin, I have to buy food and pay rent. Adeline and I are about to get evicted. Don't you care about that more than the drugs you're about to put in your arm?"

His hand rises and he swiftly slaps her face. She braces herself on the car behind her. I feel a rage building inside me, but Rebecca doesn't skip a beat.

"I'm already late for my shift," she says defiantly. "If you want money, then let me go make some."

I take two steps forward and ball my hands into fists, anger boiling through me. I watch and realize Rebecca looks like a beaten-down dog, but she has a few growls and nips left in her. It's time for a bigger dog to even up the fight.

Collin continues to speak, not yet noticing me. "I'm going sit in there and watch how many tips you get. Don't try to stiff me." He points his long dirty finger in her face. She straightens herself, her eyes meeting mine.

There is something different about the blue that was once as bright as the sky. I take note how the years of hard living have changed her. She lifts her chin boldly and tries to move past Collin who grabs her arm and snaps her back, pinning her against the car. He presses his body to hers and I realize it is not unlike how I handled her outside the bar last night. I didn't mean my movements to be aggressive in the way Collin does. But this seems like a situation where motivation doesn't matter. I can see why she recoiled from me. Rebecca doesn't need a firm-handed man to direct and control her. She clearly has enough of that in her life.

As I watch Collin lower his mouth to Rebecca's unwilling and retreating neck, I can restrain myself no longer. I cross the parking lot with purpose. I'm behind Collin in a flash. I clear my throat and watch as the scrawny man jumps with fear.

"How about you take those dirty hands off her before I break both of them?" I'm ready to brawl, bracing myself for Collin to lunge, my muscles twitching in anticipation. Once you know how to fight, once you're good at it, you actually look forward to the opportunity to do it occasionally.

"Mind your own business," Collin growls, as he spins to look at me full on. I'm standing about five inches taller than him and I have at least forty pounds on him. He doesn't say much as Rebecca slides out from behind him and steps out of arm's reach. She doesn't tuck herself behind my body. I expected to feel her small arms pressed against me, finding shelter beside me, but instead she brushes by.

"Don't bother, Devin. This isn't your fight," she says flatly. As I follow her toward the diner door, Collin

26

regains the courage to mouth off. "Oh, so you two know each other? That's no surprise. There ain't many men in this town who ain't intimately acquainted with you, huh Beck?"

I spin back on my heels and charge toward the man, who quickly throws his arms up to cover his face.

"Devin!" Rebecca shouts, catching my attention before I can take a swing. She points to a police car lying in wait just around the corner of the building.

I abandon my plan to pound into Collin, and reluctantly follow Rebecca into the diner. Anger still swells deep within me. I'm itching to release it, but can see there would be no point.

Rebecca is dressed in a pink smock and holding a white paper hat that means she really does work here, too. I expect her to be shaking, maybe her eyes wet with tears. Instead, she slips out of her winter coat and hangs it on a hook by the door. She places the paper hat on her head and grabs her apron from behind the counter. "Did you already eat, Devin?" she asks me, as she pours coffee into the mug of a man sitting at the counter.

"That's it? That's all you have to say? Have I eaten?" I ask, as I slide back into my booth. "That didn't shake you up?"

"Just a day in my life, Devin. Now, you want eggs or something? And just so you know, regardless of what Collin was flapping his gums about, I don't make it a habit to lie on my back for every man in town." She lifts an aluminum napkin dispenser and holds it up to her face, checking to see if Collin's slap has left a mark. She rubs it lightly, sighs at the tender redness, and moves on to one of her other duties.

I can't take it. I stand and walk behind the counter to get between her and whatever menial task she's going to do next. How can this be her life? How can she not take my money and go start over somewhere?

"I understand I insulted you by offering you money the way I did. I can see how you would feel that way."

"Is that your idea of an apology?"

"I have two rules in life. I never apologize and I never promise. That philosophy has earned me plenty of success and made me a lot of money."

"And how many friends has it made you?" She raises an eyebrow at me, and I huff at her attitude.

"Why won't you take my money and get out of here with your daughter? I'm offering you a way out; don't be so stubborn."

She perches her hands on her hips. "I am not some problem you can solve with money. The rumors are flying like crazy this morning about why you're here. Everyone is talking about your meeting with the mayor. I have you figured out."

"Oh you do?" I know this small town well enough to realize people are talking. Rumors are always flying. The fact that I have a meeting with the mayor just stirs shit up more. "And what exactly did you hear?"

"You're turning this place into a dump. You're going to buy a bunch of land and have the garbage from all the rich towns around us shipped in. Probably poison our water, make the place smell to high heaven. And don't act for a second like you're doing it for any other reason than revenge. You may think everyone in town is as dumb as a bag of hammers, but people can figure this out."

"Why do you care what happens to Clover? This town has done nothing but treat you like shit. That cop sitting out in the parking lot doesn't seem to care that you are getting slapped around."

"They don't care. But there are people in this town who do. My whole life has happened here, Devin. It's where Adeline was born, it's where my mother is buried." She hesitates as her eyes storm over. "It's where I met you."

"Yet every word you wrote me was about a life somewhere else. Escaping. Now you have your chance and you're too scared."

She points her finger up at me as she blazes with anger. "I am a lot of things, Devin, but scared isn't one of them. I am loyal. There are people I still care about here. The town is made up of some good folks, and run by some bad ones. If you plan to come in here and destroy it all with your money, you can stay the hell away from me while you do it. I don't need you to fight my battles. You used to be different, now you're no better than the rest of them."

I should be furiously insulted but all I can think of is kissing her again. This time I won't be overbearing and rough. I'll kiss her like I did when we were kids. But her face is like stone and I know a kiss won't fix anything right now.

"We are very different people now, Devin. You're driven by anger and revenge. You're not the man I was hoping you still were. You're coming here right before Christmas preparing to cripple the town. What kind of man does that?" She brushes past me and I feel the knot in my gut tighten.

"You are infuriatingly stubborn," I call to her as she walks away to the kitchen. I move back to my booth and grab my briefcase. I have a meeting with the mayor to get to. I have a plan to execute and she is not a part of that.

Chapter Five

The letters are all lies, but I still can't stop myself from looking down into my briefcase and staring at the few I brought with me to Clover. I imagine the tears she cried while writing, the life she was trying to build in her dreams.

I close my briefcase and extend my hand to the pudgy, bald-headed man who is calling my name.

"Mr. Sutton, I'm Mayor Kilroy Trenton. It's a pleasure to meet you. I'm looking forward to going over your proposal. It's mighty interesting." The mayor hooks his two thumbs behind his suspenders and speaks with such a drawl it's almost hard to decipher his words.

"Thank you, Mayor Trenton. I appreciate your time. I'm anxious to get this deal moving. I have an important meeting pending in New York, and I'd like to finalize this first."

"Please, call me Kilroy." He gestures for me to take a seat in the dusty upholstered chair across from his desk. "I'm going to cut right through the bullshit here, Devin, if you don't mind." I nod my head, indicating that is appreciated. "I know your history with this town and the unfortunate circumstances of your incarceration. On behalf of Clover, please accept my apology. However, I'm leery about making a deal with a man whose sole purpose is to fulfill a vendetta. My job is to make decisions in the best interest of this town and its people. Now, if I have your word that you don't intend harm for the town and its *law-abiding* residents, I'll feel much better. Do you see what I'm saying, son?"

I can tell he's emphasizing the word law-abiding for a reason. That term excludes Sherriff Hoyle. He's giving me an out to still seek some retribution and offer my word at the same time. But I don't bite.

"I don't make promises, Kilroy. It's bad business in my opinion. I proposed a deal and you had a chance to review it. Now, whatever my motivation may be or what I'm trying to accomplish does not change the numbers in the paperwork. Clover is nearly bankrupt. I see this as a pretty straightforward deal. I'm going to buy plots of land in Clover for a very fair price that folks will be crazy to refuse. Then I'm going to build a facility that will employ many people here, pumping life into your economy. Because my company has concerns about the current law enforcement here, and we want to protect our business interests, along with this deal comes a private security company that will be funded by me. It will supersede the current sheriff's office and report directly to the U.S. Marshals. More and more towns are doing this with their municipalities and showing very positive results.

"Yes they are, but not necessarily with their police force, more like their water and highway departments. I don't know of any precedent for replacing a whole police force."

"You'd be surprised what companies are doing today to protect their investments. Coal companies, worried about protestors and sabotage, have been doing this for a few years. As long as security rolls to the marshals to keep things on the up and up, it works perfectly. Frankly, Kilroy, considering how Clover is crumbling so quickly, this deal is your only option for keeping this place from going belly up."

I have more to say, but I'm interrupted by the mayor's door banging open. In walks Sheriff Hoyle— older, but still looking as arrogant as ever. He moves with a swagger that grates on me. It's the kind of stride that makes me want to kick his legs out from under him as he passes by, just to show him he isn't quite as untouchable as he thinks.

Kilroy stands, his hand moving to his waist as though he's ready to draw a weapon. "Harold, what in the hell are you doing bursting into my office? You know damn well I have this meeting today, and you aren't welcome."

Sheriff Hoyle flops himself down onto the chair next to me, grinning condescendingly. I want to hurt him, physically destroy him, but I compose myself and listen to his gravelly voice as he starts to speak. His words are slow and drawn out as if he has nowhere to be other than right here, all day.

"Oh come on, Kilroy, you know this meeting has everything to do with me. This boy here is trying to teach me a lesson."

I fix my gaze on the mayor, not sparing an ounce of my attention on the sheriff. "First, I'm not a boy anymore. Second, if I were going to dole out lessons here I'd start with oral hygiene; I can smell the sheriff's onion breath from here. Now, Mayor, if you want to continue this meeting I suggest you get your subordinates under control. Otherwise, I'll be on my way." I lean back and cross my legs casually. This man doesn't know who he's dealing with, what I'm capable of.

"You can't honestly be entertaining this deal, Kilroy?" The sheriff swallows hard and bangs his fist on the desk. "You're considering letting him buy up all the houses in the Chesnutt neighborhood just to tear 'em down and build a landfill? People here are so desperate they'll do it, they'll sell."

"I don't intend to buy *all* the houses," I say, finally turning my head slightly in the sheriff's direction. "There's one house on Merrymount Lane I have no interest in. I'll build around it."

The sheriff lets out a carnal growl as he jumps to his feet. "You son of a bitch, you plan to leave my house in the middle of a dump?"

"Gentlemen," the mayor cuts in, "this is what I intended to avoid. I'll not have it. Mr. Sutton's proposal will put this town back to work again. You and your cronies ran out most of the businesses, and I won't allow you to ruin this deal. He plans to pay people handsomely for their homes and employ a private security department to oversee the operation, as well as offer protection to our residents, all on his dime. Clover is nearly bankrupt; this will save the town."

"This dump will implode the value of my home, the only one left standing in the area. The private security will eliminate my job. My father was the mayor here before you, and his father was the sheriff. The Hoyle family led Clover for decades." The sheriff's voice is booming now as spit sprays from his mouth.

I watch the mayor fighting to keep his cool. "Well, luckily, this ain't no dynasty. And I can't recall you ever having anyone's best interest in mind but your own. So, don't come banging around my office expecting me to scrap an entire deal because it doesn't favor you. That ain't how it works." The mayor narrows his eyes, flashing all the authority he has.

The sheriff's face turns from animated to eerily placid. Any emotion he is wrestling is beaten back, and is replaced with an unnerving look. "The funny thing is, Kilroy, that is *exactly* how it works. You're sitting in that seat because you are meant to toe the line— my line." He bangs his hand into his own chest. "If you're telling me that ain't the case anymore, then you can get ready to lose your job." He stands and taps the front of his tan cowboy hat as he moves toward the door. "You'll be lucky if that is all you lose. And you," he glares over in my direction, "it'll be a shame for anything to happen to that sweet Rebecca. Rumor has it you're playing hero for her again."

My hands tighten around the arms of the chair at the sound of Rebecca's name. Of course he threatens to hurt her. He is above nothing.

The mayor remains quiet for a minute after the sheriff shuts the door. I pull some documents out of my briefcase. "Things in this town need to change. This deal is your best chance." I slide the papers across the desk.

"We're on the brink here, Devin. People are starving, there are no jobs, they're scared of the sheriff's department. Something is going to combust soon. I've been waiting for the right opportunity, and I think this could be it." He lifts the papers and straightens them, as he looks the stack over.

"I'll give you the same candidness you've given me. I could give a shit about Clover. If the whole place falls off the map tomorrow I won't lose a night's sleep over it. But I'm a businessman, a wealthy one. What I'm proposing will financially help Clover. If I can crush a man who robbed me of almost a decade of my life in the process, it's a win-win."

"Some folks here are concerned this will be a landfill. A lot of our neighboring towns are devastated environmentally by fracking and other mining issues.

35

Some are worried about you coming in and wrecking things. What do you say about that?"

"I don't say much. Trash needs to go somewhere and none of the more affluent towns want it in their backyard. A town like Clover is the only place that will take it most times. There's risk in that. I won't try to sugarcoat it." I don't say it, but I know full-well what bringing a landfill to a town can do. Maybe that's why I picked it. The environmental repercussions can be significant, but that worry is far secondary to my desire to hurt the sheriff.

"Frankly, I don't have other options, Devin. I'm going to have the lawyers go over this paperwork, and I've almost got enough votes on the town board. I've been looking at this deal for a week, since the minute you sent it to me, and I may not love it, but it'll work. People understand the urgency on your end and they want change. I do worry about the threats on these people and their families. Normally I'd put all this aside until after Christmas, but I feel like the sooner we can get the vote and you can get your security people down here, the better. Is it a problem for you to be contacted around the holiday?"

"I don't celebrate it. I was convicted of murder on Christmas Eve—that's enough to ruin holiday cheer for the rest of my life." I stand and extend my hand, gripping the mayor's tightly. "I'm going back to New York soon. You need to act on this quickly."

"I like what I'm hearing, Devin. I think we can make this deal happen. If I can get everyone on board, you should be hearing from me on Christmas Eve. I hope you have someone here watching your six. You backed the sheriff into a corner and he's gonna react like a mad dog.

I know I'll be watching over my shoulder." The mayor stands and pats the gun strapped to his hip.

"I'll be fine. I'm not the same kid he messed with years ago. I'll show him what true power looks like."

Chapter Six

Later that afternoon, I sit in the hotel lobby, if you can even call it that, and try to tune out the Christmas music playing over the speakers behind me. I haven't worked the protection of Rebecca into my plan. She isn't supposed to be in Clover. But now, I need to make sure none of this blows back on her.

My phone rings and I look at the screen, disappointed to see it's Luke rather than the mayor's office. "What is it, Luke?" I ask, skipping the formalities.

"Hello to you, too," Luke replies sarcastically. "I'm just checking in. I told everyone you had the plague and were too sick to even video-conference. They've agreed that we'll meet next week, after Christmas. You'll be back by then, right?"

"Yes," I huff. "I'm confident the deal I'm working down here will go through and I can get things hammered out by then. I want to be here to get the security team in place. That needs to go off without a hitch. The rest I can do remotely."

"I looked at this deal you're working. It's a dud. You know that, right? You're going to lose money; it'll never turn a profit. The contractors will make out well, but your end of this doesn't look very good. I can see why you're trying to get it in under the wire. The new owners wouldn't even entertain something like this."

"Not every deal is about money. Trust me, I'll benefit from this more than any acquisition or merger I've done in the past. The wheels are in motion."

"I'm guessing you're making some waves down there. I hope you don't mind, but I sent a friend to keep an eye on you."

I look around the room, and a man I didn't notice before tips the front of his baseball hat, greeting me, as our eyes connect. "Ah, yes, I see. And who is this?"

"He's an ex-Marine sniper and he lends his expertise to those who need it, for a fee of course. He'll stay out of the way; he's just watching your back."

"There is no such thing as an ex-Marine, once a Marine always a Marine." I think back for a moment to how close I came to enlisting, how different my life would have been. "You know I'm no lightweight myself. I can hold my own—I even know my way around a sidearm."

"Just be nice to the kid, he's worth keeping around."

I grunt an acknowledgement and disconnect with Luke as I wave the kid over, willing to humor them both.

"I'm Click." He pulls his baseball hat off and tucks it under his arm, extending his hand to me. His jaw is wide and he has a prominent scar across his cheek. I would know he's a Marine even if Luke hadn't told me. His hair is a high and tight brush cut, so short you can barely tell if it is brown or black. The chain around his neck is clearly holding dog tags, tucked below his plain green T-shirt. He doesn't get any points for originality, or style, in my book. When he releases my hand I watch him stand as rigid as a board, and I sarcastically quip, "At ease, Marine."

"This is at ease," he replies, looking at me skeptically.

As I look him over I realize this is who I would be if things had gone differently. I would have enlisted, served, married Rebecca, and started my life. I'd be in jeans and a T-shirt rather than this suit.

"I'm guessing Luke told you what my job is here? Keeping you from getting killed, or, maybe more importantly, keeping you from killing anyone." He sits down across from me and waits for a response.

"What kind of name is Click?"

"That's what my platoon called me. It was the only noise you heard right before I fired my weapon; otherwise you didn't know I was there."

"And what do you plan to do here?"

"I plan to blend into the scenery and have your back when you need it. You won't hear anything but a click, if that's how you want it."

Clever. If nothing else this Click character seems to have good judgment. "I don't want you watching me, I want you protecting Rebecca. She's my . . . an old friend, I guess. I think the sheriff could target her to get to me. I can take care of myself."

"I have my orders, and I can't deviate from them. I'm getting paid to watch out for you."

"I'll pay you double."

"Luke warned me you might say that. He assumed the offer would be paying me double to leave you alone, not to watch someone else, but I'm guessing the direction he gave me applies. He said he'd outbid anything you propose; so don't waste your breath. Not that I mind you driving up my price." Click's back is straight in his chair, and he looks like he's made of wood. "Now, I have some buddies you can contract for her. They can be here by morning."

"She doesn't have until morning. The mayor plans to act fast, which means they will too. So if you're here to follow me, then I'll follow her." I stand and pull my keys from my pocket. "Get one of your guys here for tomorrow. I have a private security company coming to town by the end of the week if the deal is voted in. You'll be off the hook by then."

"Yes sir," Click shoots to a standing position and steps out in front of me to clear the parking lot before I can step out.

"All clear, Marine?" I ask mockingly.

"If it wasn't I'd have tackled you by now and would've had at least ten rounds off." He straightens his back another notch. "It's all clear."

Chapter Seven

I watch Rebecca's lips turn down as she starts to argue with me. "Devin, I thought I made myself clear. If you plan to go through with this landfill nonsense, I don't want you around." She's behind the bar at the Boot Hopper now and I wonder how many hours she puts in each week at her two jobs. All to have her money stolen by a dirt bag.

"Things are a little more complicated now. I fully expected the sheriff to try to threaten or hurt me when I started this, but I didn't factor you in. I thought you were off in the mountains somewhere, painting and being happy." I can't help but travel down this path, even though I see it cuts at her. "Anyway, I have a man hired by one of my associates to protect me, but he refuses to leave me in order to protect you. So I'm contracting someone for you and he'll be here tomorrow. Until then, I'm staying with you."

"I can take care of myself, Devin. I've been doing it for years."

"So tonight when you get back to your place and there's a man with a gun there, you're telling me you have a plan?"

"Well, they'll have a hard time finding me since I was evicted today. Collin took my rent money and my landlord won't cover me anymore."

"I'll get you a room at the Winston. You and Adeline will be safe for the night. Once this deal goes through, the sheriff won't have any power here, and I'll have someone assigned to protect you full-time if needed."

"Power isn't in a badge, Devin. I'm sure you'll head back to New York and I'll be on my own again anyway.

I'm not staying at that hotel tonight. I'll figure something out on my own. I'm not depending on you; I don't depend on anyone." She walks away from me to serve another customer, and comes back a minute later with a beer for me.

"You need to drop this pigheadedness and take the help I'm offering. I don't see why this isn't good enough for you. You don't want my money—which can get you the hell out of this place—you don't want my protection. What do you want?"

"Devin," she says, shaking her head sorrowfully, "how thick can you be? Do you think it's easy for me to come to terms with the fact that I've been sitting here like an idiot holding a candle for you, wondering if I'll ever see you again, only to find out you're a completely different person now? It's sad and disappointing, and having you around just reminds me of that."

The shock of her statement seems to clear the air out of the room for a moment. "Are you really saying you still have feelings for me? After all these years, you what, still love me?" I ask, not knowing if I'm more afraid she'll say yes, or that she'll say no.

"I loved the man you were. Not this person." She gestures at my suit and slicked back hair. "You have money and power now, and I'm happy for you. You're here for vengeance—to destroy—and I would rather live this terrible existence and have love in my heart than the blackness you have. If I take your money, your protection, what does that make me?"

I want to take her in my arms and kiss her, show her my heart may be damaged but it's salvageable. But my brain, the one that helped me survive and build an empire, won't back down. "Your idealism is idiotic," I lash at her.

"That's great, Devin. Real nice. Listen, you're a paying customer and I can't have you tossed out of here. But tonight when I get in my car, I don't want you following me. I don't need your help." She spins around and goes back to work as I mentally kick myself for being a jackass.

Chapter Eight

I sink into the desk chair in my solitary hotel room. Just like Rebecca said, she got in her car after her shift and drove off. I went back to the hotel and hardly slept a wink, worried about Rebecca and Adeline. I won't be able to live with myself if they are hurt because of me.

The sun is up now and my mind, the one I worked so hard to form and control, is faltering. Every time I try to clear it out, all I see is her face. I think about the fact that for nine years she put pen to paper a few times a month, just to stay connected to me. And I poured my energy into becoming a man who can crush my enemies, rather than staying the man she already loved. I'm starting to feel like a fool.

There's a light knock on my door and I hop up, praying it's Rebecca. I swing it open and deflate like a balloon at the sight of Click standing straight-backed and stone-faced at my door.

"Shit, Click, I thought you are supposed to fade into the shadows and stay out of my way."

"I'm sorry, sir,"

"Don't call me that."

"Sorry," Click nods his apology. "I'm here to confess something, sir—I'm sorry, Mr. Sutton." He's stuttering slightly and I huff my annoyance.

"Call me Devin. And I'm not your mom or your priest. You don't have to come in here and declare all your sins." I'm still disappointed it isn't Rebecca at my door, but I welcome the distraction. I wave Click in and offer him the chair in the corner of the room while I sit on the edge of the bed.

45

"I deployed four times," Click says, hanging his head slightly. "In all my years of service I never disobeyed an order, nor did I stick my nose where it didn't belong. It's just . . . Rebecca . . . she reminds me of one of my sisters. Her daughter is the same age as my niece and—"

At the sound of her name I go from being mildly attentive to fully interested. "What about Rebecca?"

"My orders are to watch your back and keep you safe. I understand leaving my post last night and following her goes against what I'm paid to do and as a result I offer you my resignation, as soon as someone arrives to relieve me. I'll send my payment back to Mr. Miller as well."

"You followed her last night? What happened?" I probe, relieved she wasn't alone.

"I parked somewhere out of her line of sight and kept an eye on her through the night."

"Where did she go?"

"She pulled into the driveway of an address I confirmed to be her father's house, but she never got out of the car. She stayed there all night." Click clears his throat nervously. "She seemed to be doing quite a bit of . . . crying."

I sit silently, feeling Click's words like a punch to my stomach.

"I completely understand what a dereliction of duty this is. There is no excuse and, more so, I have no business coming back and reporting this to you. I just know if it were me, I'd want to know."

"Did she eventually go inside?"

"Yes, when the sun came up, a man—I'm assuming her father—came out on the porch. They exchanged some words." Click's head droops even lower and I can read the conflict raging in him.

"What kind of words?" I ask, assuming the worst.

"She didn't do much talking, but he did. Right there in front of the little girl. He was raging on about how much trouble she is, how much he wished she'd just . . ." Click hesitates on the words, "die, like her mother had."

I shoot up and forcefully pound my fist into the wall. "That son of a bitch."

"I nearly took her out of there myself." Click's voice is steady again, the tone of a Marine. He stands and moves toward the door. "Like I said, I'll stay on until someone else can come and relieve me."

"Why is she taking so much shit from people?"

"I'm guessing she's out of options. Maybe she doesn't have any fight left in her? I'm sorry, again, and I'll let myself out."

"No," I insist, pointing toward the chair Click abandoned. "Do you know why I never respected my father?" I ask, clearly bewildering the poor kid. "Because in a moment like last night, he'd have followed orders. He would have stood outside the door of a fully grown man who was carrying a weapon and would have ignored the woman and child who had no way to protect themselves. He'd have done it because those were his instructions. I don't respect that. I respect men who do the right things, the hard things, in the face of what everyone is insisting they should do." I extend my hand to Click, who shakes it firmly. "You're not fired, Click, you're promoted. Now I have a more unconventional job for you. I need to find a cabin in the mountains that's available for tonight. I know it's Christmas Eve and that may be tough, but if we start making phone calls we should get a place."

"What about the mayor? You haven't heard about the status of your deal yet, have you?"

"I haven't. I'm guessing he came up against some opposition or something, or hit a snag. I'm thinking maybe it's a bust. So I'm going to take care of something else in the meantime. Once I have everything lined up for tonight you can give me some space. I'll be going to get Rebecca, and I don't need an audience for that. Once I pick her up, we're leaving town. Understand?" Click nods that he does, like a good Marine, happy for new orders. "You say you have a niece Adeline's age? What do you know about kids?"

Chapter Nine

The rest of my morning is full of errands. I think Click begrudges the unique orders I give him, but he is right, he knows a lot about kids.

As I drive down the old familiar roads that lead to the house Rebecca grew up in, I consider scrapping this entire idea. Do I really want to try again to save someone who thinks I'm scum? *Am I scum?* Trying to save Rebecca the first time cost me nine years in prison. Am I really going to let it cost me my revenge? But all it takes is me picturing her swallowing her pride and taking crap from her father to remind me why I'm coming for her.

I see her red shit-box car in the driveway, and I know she's here. I pull in and commit myself to this ridiculous plan.

As I walk up the creaky steps, I see the front door is propped open and I hear voices inside. I put my hand up to knock but then, as I hear Rebecca speaking, I pause. I can still bail on this. I don't have to walk through this door. I tune out my own head and instead listen to the conversation taking place inside.

"You made your point, Daddy. I ruined my life and yours. All that time I spent here raising your boys, getting them out of this hellhole town, all the meals I made for you, all the cooking and cleaning I did, what a traitorous little disappointment I am. But I have Adeline to think of, and we have nowhere to go. So stop this nonsense. I don't want Adeline hearing you."

"It's Christmas Eve, why don't you give me a present: leave her here and be on your way. You're just gonna wreck the girl anyhow. You and her idiot father."

The man's voice is so gravely and mad that I almost can't believe this is a father speaking to his daughter.

"I'm not going to leave her, Daddy. She's my daughter. I'll never leave her, and especially not with you."

"Then just finish hauling your garbage in and fix me something to eat. Don't try to make me care about you, it ain't never gonna happen."

"Whatever." Rebecca's low voice shoots through my heart like an arrow. I can't take it anymore, the world just shitting all over her. This girl was, at one point in my life, the only thing that kept me going—the person who cared for me in my darkest hour. She deserves better than this. Where does everyone get off pushing her around like some disobedient dog?

I step inside the house and pass Adeline who is curled up on the couch. I wave to her playfully, trying not to scare the life out of the poor thing. I march into the kitchen where the voices are coming from.

"Devin?" Rebecca stutters, covering her heart with her hands. "What are you—?" I cut off her words with a kiss, the kiss I was thinking about every minute since the last one. My hand caresses her cheek and trails down her jaw. I'm not pawing at her, or dominating her, just gently touching my lips to hers. I can kiss her all day, but I pull away reluctantly, turning my attention to the old man sitting at the kitchen table.

"You are a miserly old son of a bitch, and you are never going to speak to her like that again."

"Boy," he shouts, but as I step toward him, he quiets.

"I'm no boy, and she's no piece of garbage." I put one arm over her shoulder and lead her out of the room. The shock on her face hasn't lessened as the seconds tick by. I lean down to lift Adeline from the couch and I walk them both out of the house.

"Do you have anything in that house you need tonight?" I ask, shuffling her toward my car.

"I want a painting that's in my car trunk. If I leave it here, I'm worried he may do something to it. He always hated it," she says, doing a quick inventory of all her belongings.

"Then grab it and let's go."

Rebecca pulls a painting from her trunk and shakes her head as though trying to wake from a dream. "Devin, Adeline's going to need her car seat. The buckle sticks, I can't get it out by myself."

"I have one."

"You have one what?"

"A car seat. Top of the line, as safe as it gets. No sticking buckles."

"When did you get that?"

"This morning. I picked up a few things."

I watch her search my face, that mental lie detector she's so good at using. "You know how I feel about your plans for Clover. You know how I feel about who you are now. What changed?"

I know I should tell her the truth—I really don't know where the deal stands. I should have heard from the mayor by now. Something went wrong. There is a fifty-fifty chance it's off the table anyway. I'm standing here, looking at her, thinking of what it used to feel like to hold her, remembering who I used to be all those years ago, and I just want to feel that way again. "The deal is dead," I say as I lower Adeline into her new car seat.

"Why are you doing this? You feel bad for me?"

I taught myself over the years not to show weakness, to block questions like this with my bravado. But I'm afraid to lose her, to scare her off like a skittish deer. So, I consider breaking my own rules. I want to promise her the world and apologize for every minute she's suffered. Why am I doing this? How do I answer that question, when I don't even know myself.

Do I feel bad for her? I feel bad that she was stomped on by the world. I feel bad for how much she gave to me, and how little I gave back. "No, it's not because I feel bad for you. I didn't expect to see you here in Clover. I didn't expect to ever have a chance to be with you again. I'm not willing to drive out of this town without knowing if there is still anything between us."

"And what does this mean for us? What are you saying?"

I wish she'd stop asking me questions. I have no answers. A day ago I was completely focused on ridding Clover of Sheriff Hoyle. It's all I thought about for years. I convinced myself that Rebecca was a completely unattainable dream.

Like a car careening in one direction, it's not easy to hit the brakes and start heading the other way. It doesn't mean I don't want her, it just means I need time to shift gears. "I have no idea," I admit. "The people we became are strangers to each other. Even if I want to, I can't be that boy you fell in love with, but maybe there's something here."

I watch as she slides the painting into the back seat of my car. I lean in and skillfully buckle the safety straps on Adeline's seat, grinning over at her astonished face.

"I practiced with a teddy bear for nearly an hour this morning." I reach into a bag by Adeline's feet and pull out a large stuffed bear. "Speaking of which," I hand it over to her and brush her curls back affectionately. When she hugs it so tight it looks like the head may pop off, I laugh.

"Are you the painted man?" Adeline scrunches up her nose and scrutinizes the features of my face.

"Am I?" I ask, reaching across to flip the painting over. The sight of it startles me. A captivating and sensual oil painting sends me back to the night Rebecca and I made love. The night before it all went wrong. I see myself—half boy, half man—holding Rebecca in my arms. It's not gratuitous or offensive. It's sweet. It's real. She captured me perfectly, my face full of awe and bewilderment, excitement and passion. The strokes of color, splattering and streaking in all directions, embody how I felt that night.

"I started painting it the moment I got home. I didn't want to forget a single thing about that night. I didn't sleep a wink, and I finished it just an hour before I heard Brent was dead and you were arrested. I take it with me every time I move. I look at it and sometimes I hate what it represents, everything I lost. And, other times I look at it and love it because I had one night, a night I'll never forget, and I know some people live a lifetime and never experience what we did."

I stare at it another moment, astonished by her talent and the emotion the painting evokes in me. It's like looking at two strangers, naïve children about to be demolished by an oncoming crash of life speeding toward them. I want to warn them. Tell them to watch out for what's coming when the passion is over. I want to tell them not to let go of each other, because the moment they do, life will never be the same. My only hope is she never paints a picture of this moment. My face must be twisted with sadness for the beautiful girl who lost so much, for the boy who never saw it coming. I'm positive if she captures the remorse and anger filling me right now, it will be the most dismal piece she ever creates.

But if she can see under all the sorrow on my face right now, she'll understand. I agree the night we spent together surpassed everything I imagined, and I've chased it ever since. The problem is, I've been looking in all the wrong places. All my efforts and attention have been focused on taking charge of my heart, my life. I don't want anyone to ever be in a position to control me again. Yet, right now, I feel about as out of control as I ever have.

Rebecca speaks over the roof of my car as we both hesitate to get in. "Am I just supposed to get in the car with you and run off, with no idea where we stand?"

"Rebecca, for the first time in a long time, I don't have the answers. I can't tell you I know what that means for us, but tonight is Christmas Eve, and I want to get in the car and get the hell out of here with you. I hate this holiday. Everything about it makes me think of the worst time in my life. But then, I think about Christmas with you. All the ones we never had. I can be angry about everything I don't have, or I can try to find a way to not lose any more. Things can change, if we let them. I'm trying to let them."

"Okay," she whispers, and we both settle into the car. "I can live with that for right now." Rebecca laughs a bit. "But we don't have clothes. We left all our things. Maybe we should go back and get some."

"We can buy new clothes when we get where we're going," I say, as I caress her cheek and she leans into my touch.

As I pull onto the road, I focus on the trip ahead of me and try not to think about anything past tonight. That's all I planned so far. I'm going to give her Christmas. I'm going to ignore my disdain for all things festive and get lost in the joy of seeing Christmas through a child's eyes. The rest will have to be sorted out later.

Chapter Ten

The two-hour drive seems to fly by as we listen to endless versions of different Christmas music. At Adeline's request, of course. I realize it's a damn good thing there are no children in the corporate world. They are impossible to say no to. I listen, begrudgingly at first, to the cartoon characters, crooners, and country singers, all making the holidays their own. It's been so long since I felt the excitement of Christmas, but slowly, it's all coming back to me, as I hear Adeline sing her own version of Rudolf, the Red-Nosed Reindeer.

We stop and split up to do some shopping at the mall. I load up on more presents for the two of them, spending almost forty-five minutes getting them all wrapped with festive bows. When the girl behind the counter asks me if the wrapping is cheerful enough, I tell her to add more bows. I want them to be perfect.

After loading the boxes in the car, I go back in, searching for the girls. Rebecca has picked out some discounted clothes. She has one outfit for her and one for Adeline as well as a set of pajamas. It takes nearly an hour to convince her that money is no object. I tell her I'm not leaving until the bill hits at least a thousand dollars.

She reluctantly agrees, finally seeing I'm clearly not going to budge. I walk out, my arms loaded with bags and boxes, smiling, company in tow. Finally, we are back on course and head up the mountain to our destination.

I pull the car up a long dirt driveway and park. Before I can step out, Rebecca catches my arm. "Thank you so much for the clothes and for bringing us up here. It's been so long since I celebrated Christmas. I try to do what I can for Adeline, but she never really has anything special."

"She has you, that's special." I cover her hand with mine, and though I know I'm sounding like a sap, I don't care. I'm treating this night like an escape, not just from Clover but from myself. This person I became—I'm trying to get away from that guy.

We're sitting outside a house tucked in the woods. I'm relieved to see it's exactly what I was hoping for. With any luck, the property manager came through with the rest of my requests. We pile out of the car and walk up the cobblestoned path, past the barn toward the house. So far, so good. The outside of the house is decorated for Christmas. It's trimmed with beautiful evergreen wreaths and small candlestick lights at every window. The recently fallen snow is cleared from the steps and gives the place an even more romantic feel. I didn't order the snow; that is just a nice coincidence.

At the store, Rebecca and Adeline changed into matching outfits. As she stands now in front of this house wearing a stunning red peacoat and tan woolen trousers, I ache to touch her. "You two look beautiful," I say sheepishly. Compliments are like a foreign language to me now. I still don't know what I'm trying to accomplish here.

I had vengeance in my heart for so long, I'm not sure I left room for anything else. I dance between the idea of wanting her and wanting to run.

When we step through front door, I hear Adeline squeal with excitement and Rebecca coo with joy. "The house is gorgeous, Devin. It's like a winter wonderland in here."

I watch with a victorious smile as Rebecca runs her fingertips across the beautifully beveled chair rail that lines the room. She peeks inside the windows of the miniature winter town set up on a bed of fake snow. She flicks the handles of the nutcrackers, making their mouths open and shut, again and again.

The fire burning in the fireplace adds a quintessential feel to this house. The wood crackles, filling the room with the earthy scent of burnt cedar. Mistletoe hangs in the doorway; stuffed snowmen are tucked in the corner of the room. Twinkling lights and garland wrap around the banister of the long curved staircase. A nauseous wave of disgust should be rolling over me right now, but all I can do is stare at Rebecca and Adeline as they take it all in.

The tree is exactly what I requested. It's taller than I am, and there isn't a single flaw. It's full of life, and the scent of the pine brings me back to simpler times in my life. It has bright white lights strung all the way around, perfectly symmetrical as they weave through the branches. Red and gold ornaments are nestled artfully among the greens, shining against the glistening lights. At the top is a star that's so big it looks like it was plucked from the sky and propped on top. Under the tree is a lush red blanket, ready and waiting for presents. This is what Christmas looks like in a magazine. It's better than I imagined, and judging by Rebecca's expression, I hit the mark.

"You outdid yourself, Devin." She is still searching the room, finding more things that make her smile grow.

"I thought it would probably take a lot to make me enjoy Christmas, so I pulled out all the stops."

"Is it working?" Rebecca asks, searching my face for a sign that I'm happy.

"I'm glad I did all this, but I'm seeing it's probably unnecessary. I don't need all this stuff to help me remember why Christmas is magical, I just need to watch her."

Rebecca's attention turns to her daughter, who takes up residence under one of the end tables by the couch. Her teddy bear, a nutcracker, and a stuffed snowman huddle together listening to her sing Jingle Bells, or really, Jiggle Bells. Close enough.

I scoop her up, settle her down on the plush couch, and she wiggles into it happily. I still can't believe how willingly she allows me to hold her. I don't think I give off a very warm and fuzzy feeling, but apparently she sees something in me that I can't see in myself. Rebecca changes her into her new, perfect-fitting pajamas, and I wait for my next surprise to arrive.

With a thumping clatter above us, I know it's time.

"Devin, I think something's on the roof." Rebecca steps closer to me and her fingers on my bicep send shivers up my body. "Do you think it's an animal? There are bears out here, you know."

"Adeline," I say, as I crouch down in front of her, "who do you think is up on our roof making all that clattering noise on Christmas Eve?" Before she can answer, the jingling of bells comes alive outside the window.

"Santa?" Adeline whispers, and the angelic wonder-filled look on her face forces me to swallow back a lump in my throat, tears nearly forming in my eyes.

"It must be," I say, scooping her up into my arms and heading for the door. I pull it open, and standing before us is the most convincing Santa Claus I've ever seen.

Hell, he *should* be convincing considering how much I paid to get him here on such short notice.

"Mommy," Adeline squeals as she wraps her arms around my neck and buries her face. She looks torn between excitement and nerves, and squeezing me tighter seems to help ground her in this moment.

Santa, with his rosy red cheeks and small round wire-rim glasses, pats Adeline on her back. "Excuse me young lady, I'm looking for Adeline."

She turns to look at him; her eyes go wide then blink quickly, focusing on the sheer awesomeness of this moment. "Dat's me," she whispers, pointing her tiny finger at herself.

"Come on in, Santa," I say, stepping aside so he can join us in the living room. "What brings you here on such a busy night?" I hope to make this special. I want this to be perfect for her. Flawless. It reminds me of Rebecca and myself before we were torn apart. Ignorance and bliss go hand in hand, making me yearn for my younger years and reminding me how precious this time is. Her innocence, looking up at this jolly miracle, is all I can hope for.

Rebecca is in the corner with tears streaming down her face, trying desperately to wipe them away before Adeline can notice.

"Well, I do have a very busy night tonight delivering presents to all the good girls and boys around the world, but I had to stop here first. Adeline, I hear you have been so very good this year, and I want to give you something special."

"A pwesent?" She lights up and claps her hands together.

"Yes, a very special present." He pulls a book with glittery binding and scrawling gold letters from under his arm. "I'd like to read you this very special story. It's called *'Twas the Night Before Christmas*. Will you sit here with me and read it?"

"Yes," she exclaims, shimmying out of my arms and hopping onto his lap before he even has a chance to settle himself.

I sidle up to Rebecca and lean into her slightly. I'm watching her watch her daughter. Her face shows a mixture of awe and sadness, yet also, there seems to be hope. This is better than I ever imagined.

"You didn't have to do all this," she whispers through her tears.

"I know. But do you think she likes it?"

"I think she'll remember this her entire life. Two days ago, I wasn't sure how I was going to explain that Santa couldn't bring us any presents this year. Now, here he is, delivering in person."

When Santa closes the book, Adeline is tucked so tightly beneath his arm it looks like she'll never let go. "Adeline, honey, I have one more thing for you," Santa says, affectionately tapping her nose. She slides off his lap and jitters with excitement, her little curls bouncing with each shake of her head.

Santa pulls a small locket from his pocket and dangles the shiny silver in front of Adeline. Rebecca looks at me and smiles even wider.

Santa reaches into his other pocket and takes out a second locket. "This one is for your mommy. Will you give it to her?" Adeline nods eagerly, snatches the locket, and runs as fast as her little legs will take her, straight into Rebecca's arms.

"Wead it to me, Mommy." Adeline points to the inscription on the back of each locket and I feel a wave of heat rush over me. This seemed like such a good idea when I planned it, but now I'm second-guessing myself.

Rebecca holds Adeline's locket in her hands and hiccups a little cry as she reads it. "This says *all my love,*" Rebecca lifts the other locket to her face, but I can tell she already knows what it will say, "and mine says, *half my heart.*" She can't fight her tears any longer and pulls Adeline into a tight hug.

The last line of every single letter Rebecca wrote to me was always signed the same way: *You have all my love and half my heart.* I want her to know how much that meant to me, how it saved my life many times.

"Mommy, you cwying?" Adeline asks, scrunching her nose and furrowing her brows.

"Yes, baby. I'm crying, but they are happy tears. Now, go say thank you to Santa and give him a hug." She releases her daughter and wipes her face, trying to compose herself.

She leans to me, hanging the locket between us, and asks in a low voice, "How exactly am I supposed to interpret a gift like this?"

"Your letters were a gift to me all those years. I just want you to know how special they were."

"You don't need to get us any gifts. This night is gift enough."

I step behind her and drape the locket around her neck, lingering a moment after I clasp it. The soft bare skin just above the collar of her shirt is so enticing. "I wish you would have told me that earlier. I have a trunkful of presents for both of you."

62

"Debin," Adeline calls, and I spin quickly to catch her as she runs into my arms. "Debin, Santa is coming back when I'm sleeping to bring more pwesents."

"Well then, we better say goodbye and get you in bed."

Santa lets out a hardy, "Ho, Ho, Ho," as he slips out the door, jingling his bells again. The man is good. There was a moment I forgot he really is a guy named Smitty, who accepts credit cards.

It takes only fifteen minutes of being curled in front of the fire before Adeline is fast asleep. I scoop her up in my arms and carry her to the bedroom at the top of the stairs. Rebecca skillfully tucks her in and kisses her forehead, sweeping her hair to the side, out of her eyes.

"She never saw anything like this in her life, Devin." Rebecca says as we slip out of the room. "This is going to be such a wonderful Christmas for her."

We're doing this weird thing, where we can't decide if we should be touching each other. If this is only one night—a holiday celebration—a break from reality—do we belong in each other's arms? I won't push her; I didn't bring her here just to sleep with her.

"Devin," she whispers, curling her index finger and gesturing for me to follow her down the hall. I obey, not for a second able to ignore those blue eyes that seem to have a sultry flare in them right now. "Can we check out the rest of this place? I'm guessing there are more bedrooms?"

"There are," I answer, trying not to look too hopeful, attempting to ignore the feelings of lust and desire surging through me. It seems only Rebecca is capable of getting a visceral reaction from me. I miss it.

As she takes my hand, and leads me down the hall, I am instantly hard, feeling like a horny teenager again.

"This looks like a nice room," she says, peeking her head in and tugging me playfully behind her.

She leans in to kiss me and my hand immediately goes to her hair, touching it and remembering how incredible it feels between my fingers. I'm compelled to give her one more warning. "Rebecca," I whisper, our lips still touching, "I'm not sure I'm any better for you than anything else you have in your life. I want to be here, right now, with you. I want to celebrate Christmas and enjoy this time, but . . ."

"I hear you," she answers, but doesn't pull away from me. "I spent so much time waiting, planning, and scraping to get by. All I want, right now, tonight, is to enjoy this place and you. I'm not asking you for forever. I know time has changed you. It changed us both. But I need to hear you say you want to try, you want to find out. I need to know there is more to you than just the need to destroy something."

I push my forehead into hers and search her face; contemplating if I'll tell her the urge to destroy is still within me. The question in my head is instantly quieted as her hand slides up my neck and runs seductively through my hair.

My eyes roll back and I moan as she slips out of my arms and starts to undress. I instantly miss the feel of every one of her curves. I want her back, pressed against me.

A layer of her clothes comes off and I can barely believe this is about to happen. She sheds her silk panties and slinks into the bed, pulling the end of the blanket up over her body. The glimpse of her perfect figure is not enough for me. I want more.

This time, unlike our first time together, I don't need any encouragement. I strip down, and join her beneath the sheets.

I try to pull the blanket off her, but she tugs it tighter. "I'm not that same girl, Devin. I'm not as skinny, and I have more imperfections, some scars—"

I caress her soft cheek, as I try to ease the blanket away from her chin.

"We're both different people, Rebecca, but I still think you're the most beautiful woman in the world. I always have."

She grows misty-eyed at my words, and rolls toward me, melting into my body. I hear a husky moan escaping through her lips as I draw her into my embrace. Snaring my warm hand, she gently guides it to her bare breast. She may claim her body changed, but this is a sensation that feels exactly the same to me. On our last encounter, all those years ago, I needed the courage and the encouragement to touch her. This time is very different, but still I smile, savoring the nostalgia. I plan to cover her with kisses, I don't want to miss an inch of her. I want to wash away years of suffering with a night of long-awaited pleasure.

She eases me onto my back, and I love the strength she has in this moment. Since finding her again, all I've seen is a woman being told what to do, struggling to keep her life together. Asserting herself in this moment makes me feel oddly proud of her.

I spent so much time trying to own everything, understand everything, and control everything. Giving that up to be clay in her hands feels like a weight off my shoulders, a completely welcomed relief.

I suck in an anxious breath as she hovers over me, straddling my body. As I slide inside her, a jolt of pleasure surges through my whole body. For a moment, it's as though time ceases to exist. We are eighteen again, our lives together not yet lived.

Letting her nails graze my chest, she rocks forward then back, her long silky hair cascading around her. Grasping her luscious hips tightly, I surge into her hot, tight body. Heaven.

Our bodies move together rhythmically, as if we did this a thousand times before. Some things don't change at all. Seeing her body still leaves me breathless. I have to look away as she arches her back and drops her head so low that her hair dances on my thighs. I've had many years to increase my staying power, but here with Rebecca, I quickly find myself at the brink. I let go of her hips, my hands draw back to her breasts, bringing us both pleasure with gentle caressing. I want a chance to touch all of her before this is over.

My fingers explore her and quickly find the spot that has her whole body tensing above me. Rebecca moans again, her voice gravelly with desire. She's moving faster and faster on top of me, and I struggle to hold back, as I continue using my fingers to heighten her ecstasy.

She shivers, her body quivering, as she reaches a shuddering orgasm. Whispering endearments, she collapses on top of me, my name on her lips.

I kiss her face, a cloud of her heavenly hair half-covering her satisfied smile. I feel her weight on me and yet I'm lighter than I've been for a long time. I'm breathless as I speak, but I want her to know what I have to say. "I've been looking everywhere for this. Searching for anything that comes close to feeling this good." I'm not talking about the sex. I haven't even climaxed yet. But clearly, by the softness in her smile, she knows what I mean.

"It is worth the wait, Devin. You're worth the wait." Rolling off of me, she kisses me all the way down my torso, before slipping to my side, her hands still caressing my chest. A sultry, seductive look flashes across her face. "There's nothing stopping us tonight. Nowhere we have to be, we have all night."

The thought of doing this until the sun comes up sends a thrill through my body. I quake as her warm hand slides down and caresses me. I'm still hard as a rock as she wraps her slender fingers tightly around me in a possessive grip. My body tightens in electric anticipation as the stormy need within me builds. She pulls me on top of her, guiding me back inside her warm wet core. I'm leaning down, my face close to hers. Our eyes lock on each other.

"I want this all night, every night," I manage to say just before I lose control, erupting in a surge of carnal pleasure.

When the shockwave subsides, my vision and other senses return to me, and I realize what I just said. I expect her to be looking at me puzzled or hopeful, but instead her eyes are closed, contentment filling her face. What scares me is I mean exactly what I said. I just didn't mean to say it out loud. Is she going to let that comment go unquestioned? She stays quiet and I'm torn between disappointment and relief.

We use every second of our night together to thrill each other, trying to make up for all that was shattered so many years ago. Just before I drift off to slumber, with Rebecca already asleep in my arms, I realize this is the night my entire life guided me toward. Even if we don't know what tomorrow will bring us.

Chapter Eleven

The sun rises and we wake to the sound of Adeline's sweet voice. "Mommy, Mommy!" I hear, as the door to the bedroom flies open and Adeline comes barreling in. We both shift quickly to make sure the blanket is adequately covering us. "It's Cwistmas!" she sings and claps wildly. "There are pwesents downstairs."

Adeline runs out of the room and I hear the thudding of her feet down each step. "Don't open any until we get there," Rebecca calls, looking at me like I'd just preformed a magic trick. "How did you manage that? You were up here all night."

"It must have been Santa," I grin as I pull on my clothes. "Or I may have snuck away after your snoring woke me up. I sure wish you'd mentioned the fact that you were half grizzly bear in your letters."

Rebecca slips her clothes on and throws a punch into my stomach. "I do not snore." She folds her arms across her chest.

"I'm just hoping Santa really did come, and he left me a pair of ear plugs." With that, Rebecca tackles me backward onto the bed. She sprawls on top of me and tickles my sides.

Stopping to let me catch my breath, she whispers to me, "I really enjoyed last night." She rests her hands on my face. "I'm so afraid I'll wake up and find out this is a dream."

I grab the skin behind her arm and pinch it firmly. "Ouch," she shouts, holding her arm. In one move I roll her off me, and sprint for the door. "See, it's not a dream. Last one downstairs has to do the dishes."

She jumps to her feet and bolts for the door, "I hate the dishes," she exclaims as she rounds the corner. I'm standing there, waiting for her and she jumps at the sight of me, assuming I'd already taken off downstairs.

"I don't want this to be just a holiday escape," I say, looking away from her nervously. I hear my phone ring and it breaks both of us from this moment.

"You should answer that," she says as she touches my arm gently. She's letting me off the hook. A hook I can't decide if I want to be on or off. At the sound of wrapping paper being torn open her eyes grow wide. "A-DEL-INE! I told you to wait for us." She bolts down the stairs and I put my phone to my ear.

"Devin Sutton," I say, hoping by some off chance this is just a wrong number and I can return to my idyllic day.

"Devin, sorry to bother you on Christmas morning. I wanted to get in touch with you before the holiday, but a couple of the board members got cold feet after some threats. It took a little more convincing on my part, but I've got all the votes lined up. You have yourself a deal. We'll be casting the vote tomorrow and we'll need you here."

These are the words I've waited to hear for so long. I am about to destroy the town of Clover and in the process take down everyone who hurt me. "I'll be in touch later today. You can expect me there in the morning," I say as I hang up my phone and lean my head on the wall.

As I meet them both in the living room, the stack of presents toppled over and half opened, I try to find a way to tell her I'm leaving.

"Debin," Adeline calls as she scurries up to me.

"Yes?" I ask, kneeling down in front of her.

"Can I keep these pwesents all day?" I look down at her and realize she is wearing both of the sweaters I bought for her, the slippers, and two pairs of socks while she clutches a baby doll tightly in her arms. Her hair is holding all the clips from her stocking and in her other hand she's got two candy canes and a box of crayons.

"You can keep those presents forever, they're for you."

Rebecca smirks down at her daughter and in maternal fashion reminds her of the importance of manners. "What do you say to Devin?"

She drops what she's holding and loops her arms around my neck so hard I have to brace myself not to fall backward. "I lub Cwistmas. I lub you, Debin."

That probably wasn't what Rebecca had meant, I'm sure she was thinking a simple thank you would be sufficient. I wrap my arms around the warm, curly-haired little girl and squeeze her tightly. For a moment I close my eyes and imagine what will happen if I just stay right here with both of them forever. I let myself sink into how that would look, how it would feel, and I drift away in the thought of it.

I realize the man I am can't be enough for them. That will only come when I bring closure to all I've been through. I'm not enough yet, but if I can settle my past, there is a chance I can have a future.

I release Adeline and she runs toward the pile of presents, wrapping paper and bows flying everywhere.

"Rebecca, that was the mayor on the phone. I've got to head back there tonight for a meeting in the morning." I'm hanging my head so low that if she weren't sure what my words meant she'd realize by my body language exactly what I'm saying.

71

"Back to Clover?" she asks, shaking her head and narrowing her eyes. "Why?" There is a nip in her voice, a rising anger.

"The deal, I have to go get the deal settled. The mayor called, they are voting to approve it tomorrow."

"You told me the deal was off." She hands a gift to Adeline and steps toward me, lowering her voice so her daughter can't hear.

"I know I did. You and Adeline can stay here as long as you want. The fridge is loaded with food, there should be everything you need."

"Clover is my home, Devin. You can't demolish and poison it and expect me to be all right with that. People will vote this in and support it for now because they are desperate. You're taking advantage of that." She puts her hand to her forehead, completely exasperated. "Please tell me you didn't know about this before we came. Please tell me you didn't lie."

"Rebecca I just need you to stay here and let me settle things. It's going to be dangerous, and I don't want anything to happen to you. Last night was amazing and I don't want it to end."

"Then apologize to me and promise you won't destroy Clover."

I huff out a snarky laugh. "You know those are the two things I don't do."

"It's why I asked. Do that for me and I'll stay here. I'll wait for you."

I hesitate on the words. I've lived a long time with this philosophy, am I really ready to walk away from it? Is it even a promise I can make?

"I'm sorry I wasn't more forthcoming about where the deal stood. I really did think the odds were against it."

"And?" she crosses her arms over her chest and bores into me with her eyes.

"And, I promise I won't hurt the town. I'll figure something out." I take a step toward her, and pull her into my arms. Resting my chin on the top of her head I pull in a deep breath. "You need to stay here. It won't be safe for you there."

"It won't be safe for you either. We finally found our way back to each other, Devin. Are you really going to let the same people pull us apart again before we even know what sort of future we can make with each other?"

"That isn't going to happen this time. I'll be back here before you know it and we'll have time to figure our future out. I came here to give you and Adeline a nice Christmas. It's not over yet." I pull Rebecca into my arms and run my thumb across her cheek. She's trying to be mad, to avert her eyes from me, but eventually she gives in.

"I'm trusting you, Devin. That isn't easy for me to do. Please don't break my heart." She's fiddling with the locket I gave her and the way she tugs at it, tugs at my heart. She rests her head warily on my chest and I feel the weight of the world come down on me. I've made a lot of mistakes in my life, but I've never had so much on the line.

"How about some pancakes?" I call out to Adeline who is tearing a toy tea set out of the box. "Can we use dese pwates?" she begs, flashing the tiny pink saucers at me.

"Why not?" I throw my arms in the air and head off into the kitchen to pretend I know how to make pancakes, hoping Rebecca will realize I don't and come save me.

73

* * * * * * * * * * *

The presents are all opened and stacked high, the fire crackling, warming the room perfectly. I stare out the window and watch the sun fall behind the tree line. Rebecca has Adeline upstairs, giving her a bath before bed and I can hear them talking about her visit from Santa last night.

I've already said goodbye. It's time for me to leave and it feels like I'm waking up from my favorite dream. I step out the front door, into the biting cold mountain air. I'm only on the top step of the porch, and I regret leaving already. At my fingertips are the two things I dreamed about for years: Rebecca and Revenge. The problem is, I can't have both.

End of Half My Heart

Change My Heart
Book Two of The Clover Series

You really can't have it all, or so Devin Sutton is finding out fast. Returning to Clover was all part of his plan to exact revenge on the town that robbed him of nearly a decade of his life. Unfortunately, things quickly begin to crumble when he's forced to choose between rekindling an old love or destroying the town. Walking the fine line between both might just end up leaving him with nothing.

With his heart full of vengeance is there any room for love?

Chapter One

Rebecca

How long is too long to wait for a man? I sit in this beautifully decorated, peaceful cabin and find myself trying to work out the answer like it's an equation. Do I take how much I used to love him and multiple it by the amazing way he made me feel last night? Add in how obscenely sexy he is and come up with some kind of number telling how long I should sit here?

It doesn't help that I'm surrounded by every possible holiday decoration. Things that are all meant to bring cheer and promote charity of the heart. The twinkling white lights on the tree are clouding my mind. It's like the tiny little village on the table is calling out to me to be patient, to be understanding. It's almost impossible to sit in this charming festive room and be angry. Almost.

Devin Sutton was the first person to look at me and actually see who I really am. During my senior year of high school he swept in and magically popped the bubble that was trapping me in the suffocating small town of Clover. I gave him my heart, my virginity, and now I realize I gave him the last eleven years of my life, even though he wasn't in them. If I'm honest with myself, staying in Clover was about trying to stay connected to Devin, even while he was in prison. I didn't leave because I was afraid I'd forget what it felt like to love him.

I close my eyes and sink away into the memory of last night. All I can think of is making love to the one man who has always owned my body: heart and soul. No one else has ever evoked such pleasure from me. No one has ever looked right into my soul the way that man does. He's done something to me—to my heart—that is impossible to articulate. I've spent more than a decade searching to feel the same way again. After a night with him like last night, I think he is the only person in the world who can make me feel that way, and I might not be able to have him. It's terrifying.

The piercing green of Devin's eyes hasn't dimmed at all over the years. If anything they are even brighter. As he stared into my face, they shimmered in the dim moonlight that poured in the windows, sparkling with flecks of gold and bronze.

It's strange, he's changed so much—his arms stronger, his hands larger—but still I saw flashes of that young man I used to love. But the hints of the past evaporated when the stubble on his broad chin brushed against me, the beard reminding me he was all man now. I felt his muscular thigh graze against my legs and there was no mistaking him for a boy anymore.

In spite of all this, I have a decision to make. How many more days, weeks, months, or years am I willing to wait to have him? When he left this cabin I told him I'd give him a chance, that I would trust him. But every minute that ticks by, my faith grows weaker. I begged him not to go, but I realized the boy I loved really is gone, replaced by a man so stuck in the past that he's willing to walk away from me in order to stay attached to it. I asked him to look forward instead of back. To preserve the town I love and, more importantly, to protect his heart from the hate it takes to do what he is planning. I wonder what he'll do at his meeting with the mayor tomorrow. I wonder if he'll sleep tonight, or like me, if he'll restlessly search for the answers that will save us. I'm so afraid of what happens if he doesn't change his mind. What am I supposed to do then?

Chapter Two

<u>Devin 2013</u>

The trail of dust billowing up from behind my car as I pull onto the dirt road reminds me why people don't bring BMW's to the country. I can hear the rocks pinging up under the body and I know I'm doing some damage. That seems to be a pattern for me lately, leaving destruction in my wake. Just like my car, I'm on my way to wrecking Rebecca.

I whisked her away with the promise of a nice holiday and told her my business deal in Clover was dead. I was wrong, or I lied, I'm not even sure anymore who I'm trying to convince or why.

I'm frustrated that I still don't have any idea what I'm going to do at this meeting. I barely slept, tossing and turning in that stupid hotel last night. I've got a choice in front of me. Do I seek the revenge I've been planning for years or hang on to the girl I've been dreaming about? The girl who last night reminded me what it felt like to be part of something, to be seen, *really* seen. I can't do both; seeking vengeance, in Rebecca's eyes, makes me a monster. She wants me to be the person she used to know, and part of me wants that too.

As I look out over the stretch of road ahead of me, I try to remember why Rebecca is worth more than destroying Clover. I try to remember who we used to be all those years ago.

* * * * * * * * * * *

Devin 2002

The Clover Bulldogs are undefeated and all I can think is, who gives a shit? I've been coming to this school for two months now and the only thing people talk about is football.

So that means I'm stuck here in Clover, North Carolina, counting the minutes until my senior year is over and forcing myself to watch these football players like someone might watch a car accident. I'm disgusted by the whole thing but too fascinated to look away. The team, wearing their letterman jackets like armor, walk around the school like they're kings. Charging through the halls, wide intimidating shoulders locked together, they plow down anyone in their path. They think they're invincible, completely infallible in the eyes of Clover residents. As far as I can tell, they're just dicks.

As a military brat, I've traveled through enough schools to realize they all have their cliques and hierarchies, but down here in Clover the jocks don't just rule the school, they reign over the town. Football is a way of life. Living in Clover and not liking football is like sitting in church and not believing in God. Well, call me an atheist.

When I got here I intended to stay out of the way and mind my own business. I have plans of joining the Marines, another dig at my father. Sure I'd be serving my country, but everyone knows there's an unspoken division and pride that still separates the different branches of the military. My father is an Army man and he wants me to be the same, but I'm not planning on giving him that satisfaction.

Oddly enough, throughout my whole life I swore I'd never enlist. Growing up, I saw all the downsides: the constant moving, the long periods of separation, and the way sense of duty overshadows every other priority. But when the towers fell last year I changed my mind. I stared at the news for two days and all I could think was, why did this happen? There's a war now and maybe some guys will take that as a reason not to enlist. For me, it makes me want to go. No one wants me here anyway. At least over there I can be fighting *for* something rather than fighting *against* everything.

I just need to keep my head down and count the minutes. Or at least that's what I was planning—before I saw her.

Rebecca Farrus is sheer perfection. Her dark hair shines like it's spun from silk. Her blue eyes and perfectly unblemished skin belong on the cover of a magazine rather than in a high school yearbook. There are days you'd swear she's been airbrushed. It's been six weeks, two days, and seven hours since we had our first conversation. She asked me if I had a pen she could borrow. The way I reacted you'd think she wanted to know if I'd take her to prom. I made a few jokes about the principal's unconvincing toupee, and her giggle turned into my drug.

Rebecca looks like someone specifically put on this earth to be head cheerleader and girlfriend to Brent Hoyle, the quarterback of the football team. That's what I thought before I started talking to her. It's actually her perfect smile and shapely body that holds her back from being seen for the person she really is. I love that she finds a reason to catch up with me in the hallway, and I throw crooked smiles at her in gym class. The majority of my day is filled with thoughts of her, my nights with dreams of us.

We're lab partners in chemistry and it's easy to see she's smart. It's just as easy to see how everyone overlooks that fact. For me, sitting next to her is the best part of my day, the best part of my life really. When I make a smart-ass comment about one of the Neanderthal jocks, she doesn't defend them. In fact, she looks relieved that someone finally might be able to see through the bullshit of this town. She gets me, which is saying a lot since no one else seems to. Every minute of my day that isn't spent with her seems like wasted time.

Today's chemistry class is particularly boring. We're ignoring the lecture completely, and I watch her spin a ribbon of her hair around her finger as she whispers to me. Her peppermint gum snapping between her rose-colored lips is so enticing that I have to keep telling myself not to kiss her. As if leaning over in the middle of class and making out with her were even an option.

"I wish I'd been to as many schools and towns as you have, Devin. Everyone here looks at me like the most I should aspire to be is a waitress pouring coffee for the regulars at the diner. They tell me if I were smart I'd marry Brent."

Don't marry that idiot. Marry me, I think, though I'm not sure where that ridiculous idea came from. "You should get out of Clover. This place is screwed up. Where else could a guy named *Ox,* who doesn't have the mental capacity to tie his shoes, be one of the kings of the school?"

"I think he has Velcro sneakers," she responds with a smirk at my joke, and, like every time this happens, I feel like I just won the lottery. "But I don't think I'll ever get out of this town. It's like a trap. Girls like me, we get stuck." As much as I hate the truth in what she's saying, I love listening to the twang in her voice. It's like the melancholy hum of a country song.

"You'll get out of here. You just have to make a plan. Like me, I'm joining the Marines."

"I thought your daddy was Army?"

"He is." The devilish grin that takes over my face is impossible to hide. I really do get a kick out of sticking it to my father.

"Oh Devin, you like to stir the pot, don't you?"

"A little," I shrug, hoping to look dangerous and edgy, probably looking more like a kid with a twitch.

"Well if I do get out of this town, I'm going to be an artist. I paint." Her cheeks blush a bit. It's the first time I hear about her painting. This doesn't seem like something she talks about often. I must be special. I hope I'm special.

"That's cool. Do you take any classes?"

"No. I'd never hear the end of it from all my friends. It's bad enough that if I get a good grade they hassle me for being a nerd. No one in Clover really gets art. It's like they think it's a waste of time."

I feel like she's tentatively testing the water, dipping a toe in to see how deep it is, how cold. She's laid her dream out between us and she's wondering if, like everyone else, I'll push it back toward her. "I'd like to see something you've painted. When we lived in the city I used to skip school and head into some of the museums, acting like I was on a field trip so no one would bust me. I actually kind of liked some of the stuff there."

"Really? You want to see my paintings?" The sparkle in her eye is enough to send my heart thudding into my throat.

"Yeah." I pretend to scratch down an important note about the experiment we're supposed to be working on.

"How about today?" Her excitement takes me by surprise, and I consider pinching myself to wake from this dream. For two months I've watched her, fantasized about her, and now she's here asking me to come to her house.

"I've got cheer practice after school, but if you wait for me we can walk to my house together."

Wait . . . don't answer too quickly. Don't look too anxious. I count out three Mississippis and then shrug my shoulders again. She's definitely going to think I have a twitch. "Yeah, that's cool."

"I'll meet you out front at four." She is aglow with anticipation as the bell rings and we head out to the hallway. I want to say more, keep this connection with her going for as long as I can. But a gaggle of her friends and a swarm of football players sweep her up in their wake and she's gone.

I sit through the rest of my classes, staring at the clock like it is a villain, someone to hate. Its round face and painfully slow moving hands leave me silently cursing it.

When the day finally does end, cheerleading practice over, I watch Rebecca jog over to me. Her backpack hangs over one shoulder, her pleated cheer skirt bouncing up and down. She's wearing a large down coat pulled tight around her, and a fluffy white wool hat holds down her dark locks. The reaction I always have to Rebecca returns. My palms are soaked with sweat and my mouth is so dry I'm not sure I'll be able to speak.

"Hey Devin," she calls as she waves in my direction. It scares me to think about what I might be willing to do to hear her say my name every day.

"You sure you still want to see my paintings? I've been thinking that maybe you were just being nice."

"No." It's the only word I can muster as the sweet smell of her vanilla perfume fills my nose.

"No you don't want to see them, or no you weren't being nice?"

Like a true idiot, I don't understand the question. I understand that I want to see that cheer skirt from every angle. I understand, if given the chance, I'd kiss her and never stop. But apparently I've ceased to understand the English language and simple questions. It's like standing at the blackboard in front of the whole class and screwing up the equation, except this feels worse: more to lose. We start heading to her house as I try to get a hold of myself.

"No, I wasn't being nice. I mean, I'm nice but I wasn't *being* nice."

She wrinkles her brows together and tilts her head, trying to get a better look at me, analyzing my face. "Are you okay? You're acting weird."

I am acting weird. A girl like Rebecca, so beautiful, is probably very experienced. Or at least in my fantasies she is. She's every seventeen-year-old's wet dream, and maybe this is how mine is going to come true. Would she take me into her room, show me some paintings, and then kiss me? Do a strip tease? How far will we go?

I'm not *completely* inexperienced myself. I've rounded a couple bases. As long as a dark basement party with a girl whose name I can't even remember counts.

I've been up a girl's shirt, over the bra—I'm not clueless. Being with Rebecca though, that would be something special. Who cares if she's dating Brent? That's his problem, not mine.

"I'm fine." I nervously clear my throat and add that to the list of things that make me look like I have some kind of disorder.

"I'm really excited for you to see this. You'll be the first one. Every time I tell anyone I paint they act like I'm talking about finger painting something for my mama's fridge. *Oh that's nice, dear.*" I laugh at her impression of every old lady at her church, but then realize she isn't done with her explanation. "It's so annoying living here. They just put me in this box, and every time I try to show people I'm different than what they think, I get nowhere. Even Brent." Rebecca kicks at a rock with her thick-soled winter boot.

At the sound of her uttering my competition's name I snap back to reality. Maybe she isn't speaking in a secret sexy code after all. Perhaps Rebecca isn't bringing me to her house so she can seduce and pleasure me. As disappointing as that realization is, I'm a little relieved. I want her, but do I want all the trouble that comes with having her?

She turns her key in the front door and slides out of her wet boots. I pull off my combat boots and follow her upstairs. We are going *upstairs*. I bet her bedroom is up here.

I try, unsuccessfully, not to gawk at the amazing view I'm getting from behind her. That cheerleading skirt is like a magnet, pulling my eyes toward it. I may have characterized cheerleaders as vapid, mindless wastes of space in the past, but Rebecca is breaking that mold. And if nothing else, cheerleaders certainly know how to dress.

When we reach the top of the stairs I can feel my heart jolt when she says the words I'm hoping to hear.

"This is my room." It's spoken so casually that she might as well be showing me the garage or the backyard. The house is empty. We're about to be next to her bed, maybe on her bed. My mind begins to wander again, meandering through the sensual opportunities that might be quite literally at my fingertips.

As I walk into her room I see them, her paintings, and they're like nothing I've ever seen before. Gone are the thoughts of her slipping out of her cheerleading outfit. And that's when I know she is talented. Anything that can distract me, even for a second, from the raging desire I have to touch her is something powerful.

I look at her paintings and I'm spellbound, running my fingers over the canvas and studying every inch of them. I move from one to the next. Propped up on her dresser, leaning against the closet, they are everywhere. Every splotch, every drip, seems to speak to me, call my name. The depth they hold and the emotion they capture surprises me. Some are heartbreaking. Some are joyful. I see one that looks very much like me. Green eyes, a crew cut, standing in the corner alone. "Is that me?" I ask, stepping toward it and examining the camo clothes and boots, just like the ones I left by her door.

"Yeah, you have great eyes, they're perfect for painting. So many little colors floating around in them."

Her voice is kind of quiet, timid as if she's afraid I'll be angry. I am the opposite of angry. The fact that I was on her mind for at least the length of time it took to paint this, sends my gut into my throat. "I look kind of sad." I sit crouching down in front of it.

"Aren't you?"

I let the question bleed into my pores and take over my whole body. People have called me disgruntled, a loner, angry, selfish, trouble, but no one has ever called me sad before. No one has ever really noticed. I don't think I am any of the things I've been labeled. Being quiet and alone usually makes people think you're that way by choice. I can't imagine anyone choosing the life I live. "Not when I'm with you," I answer, and I know I'd never have the courage to say this if my back wasn't turned toward her. The thought of having to look her in the eye any time in the next week, after admitting that, is terrifying to me.

"I'm not sad when I'm with you either." Her voice quakes a little and I wonder what is going to break this moment. How will I ever turn around and face her?

Something catches my eye, another painting in the corner, half covered by a sheet, and I know I have to see it. I step toward it, so intrigued by just the exposed corner.

"No," she whispers unconvincingly as I pull the sheet down. It's her, completely naked. Her head is hanging in a way that isn't trying to be seductive, but disheartened. I look at every inch, every curve and color and I'm mesmerized. You'd think I'd just settle on the taboo parts, her bare chest and the magnetic area between her legs, but I don't. It clearly isn't painted for that reason. This isn't meant to be a picture filled with lust, but instead insecurity, doubt, and vulnerability. A lack of comfort in one's own skin. Yes, I am standing before a painting of a naked body. The naked body of a girl I've fantasized about, but somewhere, mixed in with my intense arousal, is sorrow for how she sees herself. "Now you're the one who looks sad," I say, still unable to turn and look at her.

I have more to say but can't muster the courage. I want to tell her while everyone else looks right past me, through me, she seems to see inside me. She gets my jokes, and she can hold up her end of any conversation. However, as much as I've spent my life waiting for it, the sensation of connecting with someone still scares the shit out of me. I can picture myself with her years from now, far from Clover. I love the way she challenges me, I love the way she expects more from me than other people do. I love her. Even if I don't plan to say it right now.

I can hear her crying and I'm completely baffled. "I'm sorry," I say, having no idea what exactly I'm apologizing for. As she starts to speak, I hold my breath.

"Do you know you're the first boy I've ever known who can see a purpose for me other than his own pleasure?" I finally turn and she bows her head slightly, oddly similar to that portrait of her naked self. She steps toward me and I finally have the strength to meet her stare. She laces her fingers with mine, and I feel a heat overtake me. "Since I was twelve years old, I've been slapping away pawing hands." The lump in my throat grows as she speaks.

I assume she may be implying she's long since lost her virginity.

"Brent is a persistent bastard, thinking just because we're dating I'm his to have. That's what he is used to, getting whatever he wants. But I won't give that to him. I never have. I never gave him the one thing he wanted. I've never given it to anyone."

She uses her free hand to tuck her long dark hair behind her ear, and looks up at me from under her lashes. "You're the first person who's ever looked at me like I can be more than just the quarterback's girlfriend and a waitress at the diner. You're the only person I've ever shown my paintings to. I feel like you might be the only one who actually sees who I really am."

I know I should say something: agree with her, tell her she is more than just a *thing* to possess. But my voice is failing me. Apparently when all the blood rages toward your pants, your brain gets slightly deprived. I'm still processing the fact that Rebecca has just declared herself a virgin. Relief rushes through me, knowing that the playing field is level and the pressure to impress might be lowered if anything happens.

My silence and the bewilderment she must see in my eyes are met with the soft touch of Rebecca's lips on mine. I lean into the kiss, lose myself in it. Blinding light takes over my closed eyes and I feel like I've just touched the sun. Her mouth opens and I find myself greedy for her, exploring with my tongue and never wanting to stop. My hand finds its way into her hair and I let myself get tangled up in it, the same way I feel tangled in her.

She pushes away from me for a moment but keeps her lips close to mine, her breath the only air I can breathe. "I want to do this today, Devin. I want you."

A surge of blood shoots through my body and my ears are ringing. The hard-on I've been fighting off since the moment I first laid eyes on her is now unavoidable. Has she really offered herself to me?

Before I can run the words though the filter in my brain, the one in charge of managing how cool I am, I speak some truth. "I-I haven't either, Rebecca," I admit, embarrassment showing on my reddened cheeks. The heat of my skin cools instantly as her hands reach up to cup my face. She aligns my averted eyes with hers. At first she seems to be trying to give me a mental lie detector test, and then, when I pass, she smiles widely. "Good." She drops her hands from my face to my shoulders and stands on her toes to kiss me again. This time it is an even hungrier kiss and her body presses tightly against mine, rubbing rhythmically. The sensation, the simple brushing of her body against mine, brings me to the brink, and I quickly realize I need to pace myself.

Rebecca steps back and I instantly feel emptiness, not only in my arms but also in my heart. Even though she's just steps away, it feels too far.

She bites at her lip lightly and looks nervously down at herself. I watch as she pulls her shirt over her head and slips out of her cheer skirt. Unlike any other encounter in my life that involved undressing or groping, this time I'm not clouded by the buzz of a few beers. This isn't a stranger I'll likely never see again. This is Rebecca. This is my moment with my angel.

My body is humming with energy. It takes a conscious effort to not race across the room and maul her. I don't feel prepared for this moment, but at the same time I feel like it's the only thing I've ever wanted. Ever needed. I take slow steps toward her, cutting the space between us to inches. I watch as a nervous shiver moves up Rebecca's arms.

"Are you cold?" I ask, running my hand from her shoulder down past her elbow and finally to her wrist. Her skin is as soft as cashmere. I could touch its smooth magnificence all day. I fight not to stare at her chest, the lace of her bra. I want her to know she is beautiful all over and that I can appreciate every inch of her. I don't want her to feel like the girl in that painting. Not with me.

"I think I'd be better if we were under the covers," she whispers seductively as she slinks away and slips between her pink sheets.

She pats the spot next to her and I hold my breath as I slide between the sheets. In a good way, the bed feels so small with the two of us in it. It feels warm and, for the first time in my life, that sense of isolation and solitude melts away. Every meal I've eaten alone in front of the television, every first day of school I've spent sitting by myself, they all drift away.

I face her, mirroring how she is lying, trying to remind myself to breath. I'm not sure where my arm should be: under her, touching her? I'm not sure about anything right now.

I watch, still in disbelief, as she leans in to me and our lips meet again. This time it feels different, because I know it isn't going to stop here. My limbs seem to respond with some primitive knowledge of what to do. And I am thankful for that small gift.

The space between our bodies disappears. Every inch of us is touching and evoking more frenzy with each movement. She's cold to the touch and I love the way my heat is drawing her in, like a moth to a flame. She slides her freezing-cold, yet delicate, foot between my calves and all I want to do is encompass it and hold it there until it's warm.

I fight the urge to give in to what my body is begging for, completion. I wish I could be lost in the passion of the moment, but there is far too much buzzing in my head. I'm currently pumping myself up for the task of the one-handed bra removal. A skill often spoken about in the locker room, a badge of honor, but not a technique you could really practice alone to get good at.

My hand moves toward the clasp of her bra for the fourth time and then trails away in another direction. Finally I make my move. After three fumbling tries Rebecca reaches around and quickly unhooks the devilish contraption. That's not really fair, she uses one every day. She'd have to be good at it.

I hold my breath again as I watch her slip it off and toss it to the side of the bed. Her arms come up to cover herself and I wonder if she's changing her mind. Regretting this.

"Do you want to stop?" I ask, fully prepared to if she says she does, but praying she doesn't. I'm trying not to look down at her bare chest and make her more uncomfortable.

"No," she whispers, "I'm just nervous for you to see me."

"You have nothing to worry about, you're perfect." I hope the sincerity comes through, and it must because slowly she moves her arms away.

"Wow," I beam as I looked down. "They are . . ." I stammer, "you are so beautiful." I want to touch them, take them in my hands and see if they evoke as much pleasure for her as I know they will for me. But I don't, I wait.

"I love the way you look at me, Devin." She reaches for my hand and places it on her bare breast. I let out a puff of air, as she sucks one in, both of us momentarily immobilized by the sensation. I roll the flesh in my hand and feel as it changes under my touch. It gathers and tightens as she moans, making me feel like maybe I'm doing something wrong, or something *very* right.

Leaning in she kisses my neck, shocking me. I've never considered the amount of pleasure that could come from the mere running of a tongue on a seemingly innocuous spot on my body. But apparently I underestimated how sensitive the area just below my ear is. I hear moans escaping my own mouth and I can hardly believe this is really happening. If I wake up and this is all a dream, I'm jumping out my window.

I want to be inside her, that's all I keep thinking. There is a beautiful body here in front of me, ready and waiting to be touched and all I can think about is plunging into her.

Fighting that off, I nervously begin to explore the rest of her. I don't want my hand to leave her chest, it's so full and fleshy, so pliable, and right now it's mine. If I let it go, can I touch it again? But I finally release it, my hand moving to places I never even considered touching. I'm amazed as her body comes alive in my hands. Her hips seem to be made for my hands to grip and rock. Caressing the small of her back has her arching and grinding into me. I grab a handful of her ass and feel her kisses on my neck grow more passionate. She moves her mouth up to my ear and speaks a breathy secret into my ear. "I think you might be wearing too many clothes."

Like a lightning bolt, I rush to my feet and yank my shirt over my head and wiggle awkwardly out of my pants. I want to be cool in this moment. I want to be everything she has hoped for, but the only thing I can hear in my head is the loud chant, *This is it. It's really happening.*

Rebecca rolls onto her back and tentatively slips out of her silk panties. The same self-consciousness that washed over her when she shed her bra seems to be back.

All I want to do is ease that, make her see how flawless she really is. I join her in bed again, now naked myself, and I run my finger from her cheek to her chin, down the front of her body until I find the spot that makes her throw her head back and moan loudly. I've watched enough movies, sat through enough health classes, to understand the science of all this, but it isn't until my hand is evoking an intense pleasure that I realize the power of it all. Everything I've done since meeting Rebecca has been about making her happy. Now I've found another way to accomplish that and I never want to stop.

I feel her hand come down hard and grip my shoulder tightly as ripples of pleasure course through her and she tries to stifle her panting. My name escapes her lips and I feel like I've conquered the world. Her arms are pulling at me, begging me to come closer to her. I inch my way up and move my body over hers, looking down into her face. Tousled hair, sweat beading on her chest, I have never seen anything more beautiful in my life.

"Are you okay?" I ask, sounding like an idiot.

She grins up at me and tries to settle her breath. "That was amazing." She reaches her arms up and wraps them around my waist, pulling me down slightly, and opening her legs to me. I can feel myself on the verge of losing my composure, the nervousness of finishing too quickly threatening to overtake me. The only thing that calms me is the equally anxious and uneasy look on her face.

"I'm afraid it's going to hurt," she admits, her thighs tensing under the gentle grip of my hands.

I flash her an awkward smile. "I'm afraid it's not going to last as long as you'd like." Averting my eyes, I try to escape my truth, but she won't let me. With her delicate fingers she guides my chin back toward her.

"Well that's good, because if it hurts I don't want it to last too long." We laugh, and I'm so glad she is the kind of person who lets humor take over when things feel too intense.

"If it hurts, I'll stop," I promise her, and I mean it. She nods at me and bites her lip in preparation for any pain.

She brushes her delicate fingers across my cheek and stares into my eyes in a way that makes me want to hide. I'm not sure why, but it scares me for her to look this deep into me. Like at any moment she'll see how empty I feel and realize I have next to nothing to offer.

Her legs loosen again and I gulp back my nerves. Shit, I almost forget the one thing that's been drilled into me since I started middle school. I lean over to pull out my wallet, fumble with the one and only condom I have—the one I've held on to since they were passed out in health class three years ago. The damn wrapper won't budge and I swear if Rebecca has to help me, I might just crawl under the bed and die. If they're so insistent on us using these, why lock them up like Fort Knox? After way too much work, it comes free.

As I position myself back over her I see Rebecca pull in the kind of breath you'd take before going underwater, and I pray I don't hurt her. I guide myself inside her, slowly, only partially and I feel her recoil, her legs snapping shut on my waist.

"I'm sorry." I pull back and feel like shit for hurting her.

"No." She loops her arms around my neck and pulls me back, her eyes granting me permission to try again. She only tenses slightly, then relaxes. The sensation shoots through my body from my curled toes to the hair standing up on the back of my neck.

Warm, all encompassing, like nothing I've experienced before. My pleasure is stilted slightly as I watch her wince. I mutter something about stopping and she quiets me with a slight shake of her head. As I dive farther into her she sinks her fingernails into the flesh of my arm. Under any other circumstances it might hurt, but right now it heightens my pleasure. Afraid that I'm hurting her again, I back away slowly but her legs wrap around me, snaring me like a spider web.

"It's okay, I'm okay," she reassures me. "Just go slow." I move hesitantly, trying to balance my yearning with my desire to make this moment last forever. How could you wish something was complete and hope it never ended all at the same time?

I move a little faster, relishing the heat that surrounds me. Each time I move out it is as if her body draws me back in. As she begins to moan a rhythmic chant of my name, I feel her nails dig into my lower back. She seems to be begging me to move faster now. Our bodies begin to move at a frantic pace, clumsily at first then matching each other perfectly. My hands ball into fists, the sheet bunched between my fingers as I fall over the edge of pleasure.

I can't hold back the dam any longer. My arms buckle and my weight comes down on her as I drop to my elbows. Burying my face in her neck, I nestle in her vanilla-scented hair. She holds me tight while my body rocks and shivers. I go limp on top of her and she caresses me, running her hand over the short bristly hair of my nearly shaved head.

For a moment I lie in her arms and know the ache; all the time I've spent being an outsider in this world is gone. This was where I belong.

We lay there for what feels like the best hour of my life. Everything is perfect until the rumble of a truck engine shakes me from my trance.

"Oh shit," Rebecca hollers as she shoots up and starts sliding back into her clothes. "Brent is here. You have to go out the window. If he knows you are up here, he'll kill you. He's never even been up here." She uses all her might to pry open the old heavy window and gestures for me to go. I don't think to help her, because, frankly, I don't want to go.

I hastily pull my clothes on until I realize the one thing I don't have. "My boots." I remember, as I look down at my socked feet.

"He'll kill you," she repeats pointing out the window again. I slip one leg out and fight to get my footing on the slippery eaves below.

"Rebecca," I call, not ready for this moment to be over. I catch her arm before she can head for the door. "Your paintings are amazing. You shouldn't spend one second of your life sad; if it were up to me, I wouldn't let you."

I watch, my heart crumbling as her eyes glass over with the shadow of tears and she manages a half smile. "Thank you, Devin." She leans in and kisses my cheek, squeezes at my bicep, sending shock waves through me. She disappears out her bedroom door and I reluctantly slide to the ground below me. All I want to do is crawl back inside, let her warm me, and watch her while she paints. Instead the cold air is nipping at my cheeks and I have to hang my head and leave her. Every step farther I get from her house, I feel lonelier, emptier. I walk in just my socks, but I don't care. I don't care how my body feels right now. I can only feel my heart.

Chapter Three

<u>Devin 2013</u>

I slam my hand down on my steering wheel, mad at myself for diving back into the pool of memories. I stop short of reminiscing about the fight Brent and I had the next day when he brought my boots to school, furious and ready to beat the hell out of me. I don't travel down the path of the night my bedroom door was kicked down by three police officers who were there to arrest me for Brent's murder. It makes my head spin and distracts me. It makes me weak. Those are the two things that made me vulnerable the first time I was in Clover.

Rebecca branded me all those years ago. She seared herself like a hot iron onto my soul. I've tried to cover up that mark, hide it, ignore it, forget it, but it's always there. Making love to her in that cabin, surrounded by warm holiday cheer, was like a fresh burn, and it's making me question everything. *I hate that.*

I pull up in front of the address Mayor Kilroy has given me. There stands about a dozen people, all bundled up, puffs of warm breath making clouds around them as they speak. Click's been given the same information and I see him walking the perimeter of the building, an old meetinghouse.

Stepping out of my car, I still have no idea what I plan to do. I had set my heart on destroying the people who put me in prison for nearly a decade. The town of Clover was going to be collateral damage. No love lost for me there.

Simple. Until Rebecca turns up in Clover, complicating everything. She stayed connected to me all the years I was in prison. She knew I didn't kill Brent, and while she couldn't get me out of prison, she tried to help me the only way she knew how. She wrote letters gushing about the life she'd built far away from this hellhole. But it was all a lie, just her attempt to bring me some peace. She never expected me to be exonerated, and she never left Clover.

The problem is, my desire for vengeance is still powerful. I was completely railroaded and left to rot in prison. Who wouldn't want to make people pay for that? But in the back corners of my mind I can't ignore that nagging feeling that if I do I'll lose Rebecca again. I had already resigned myself to life without her. Now that we have a chance to be together, I have to decide if I should walk away from this plan I've constructed.

Turning Clover into a landfill will make her think I'm just a merciless man with no soul. I'll crush the town where all her memories reside. If I go through with this, can she love me? If I walk away from this, can I live with myself? I can't believe I'm actually considering dropping the deal that will take Hoyle's job, his house, his power. It's the only thing I wanted, until I started wanting Rebecca again.

"Devin," Kilroy says as the group around him falls quiet. He gives me a firm handshake and slaps me hard across the shoulder. "This here is the town council. They're the appointed people who have the authority to vote in your proposal. They've been residents of Clover all their lives, and they're anxious to bring jobs back to our town." His speech is heartwarming, but my proclamation that I might have changed my mind will certainly knock the wind out of his sails.

Danielle Stewart

"Kilroy, about the deal," I begin as I keep tabs on Click who is scanning the perimeter of the parking lot now. He's watching out for anything that might cause a problem for us. Little does he know the problem might be this mob of townsfolk when they hear I'm considering backing out. He's a good kid and a good Marine; I'm banking that he'll think on his feet if they turn on me.

"Yes," a small woman says in a nasal voice as she steps forward. "Let's talk about this deal. We're all here, risking our necks to vote this in. I think it's only fair that we get some assurance from you that you don't intend to desert us. I'm sure you know damn well none of us want a landfill here, but we do want to get rid of Sherriff Hoyle. I personally feel we're trading one devil for another. But I'm not sure what other options we have. Hoyle is on a rampage. He and his men are extorting money from every business, some to the point they've had to close their doors. They are breaking dozens of laws every day to line their pockets with more money. They take what they want and leave the rest of us hungry and poor. Anyone who tries to stop them ends up ruined in one way or another. This is the first time we have some money behind us, a deal that says in black and white he'd be out of a job. So that makes you and your trash heap the lesser of two evils."

"Now, Margaret. I told you I'd handle that with Devin," Kilroy says, speaking over the rest of the group's clamoring. "Now, son, you know better than almost anyone what Harold is capable of. These folks are looking to hear from you that you'll hold up your end of the bargain with protection and construction if they pass this deal. We just need you to shake on it."

He extends his hand out in front of me and I scan the group for a sign this might be a joke. Clearly it isn't. If I planned on walking up here and telling these people the deal is off, that just got a lot harder. I wasn't expecting this make-or-break moment. "Kilroy, you have my contract. It's in black and white." I'm stalling but no better answer is coming to me.

"That ain't how it works here, Devin. I don't care what you write down or how your lawyers draft something up. I want you to look me in the eye, shake my hand, and give me your word that you are committed to this deal, committed to Clover."

I hesitate, my mouth agape as I search for the words, trying to decide if I'm bailing out or not. A man from the back of the small group speaks up.

"I've got two girls in high school. I can't be with them every second of the day. If I vote it through and you bail on this deal down the road, who's going to keep them safe when Sherriff Hoyle comes looking to teach some lessons? I want to hear you say you're in this for Clover, because it's our necks on the line. We're willing to swallow the fact that we're talking about a landfill here, but we aren't willing to do it without your word. We need Hoyle and his men gone, Mr. Sutton. It's now or never." The rest of the crowd agrees with nodding heads.

I lived with these people, before I went to prison. Innocent, helpless, and at the mercy of that bastard Hoyle. Their words are pulling me back to that, reminding me what he did to me, what he's been doing to them all along. "This *is* just revenge for me," I admit. If I actually did walk away right now, get in my car, and drive back to Rebecca, how long would it be before I was swept away again by the undertow of revenge. I can't give Rebecca all of myself if my mind is constantly drawn back to this place and everything I left undone. I truly believe if I can settle some scores down here, I can move on with my life, and hopefully Rebecca will still be here when I'm finished.

Everyone looks like they've written me off as a lost cause. I shock them all as I continue. "But even though that's the case, you all still stand to benefit from what we're doing here today." I reach my hand out and grip Kilroy's firmly. "You have my word that I'll hold up my end of the bargain."

"We vote now," Kilroy announces as he shuffles everyone toward the door of the building.

"I've only got one man here." I gesture over to Click who looks as uneasy about this idea as I do. "Isn't there anyone else you can call in for protection? Getting the security team here is a process: red tape and all the terms associated with the deal. You vote then the contracted company comes in; they bring security with them. That's how it works. You need a plan in place for the lag time. Maybe now isn't the time to vote. You call in some temporary muscle or something."

Kilroy is shaking his large round head at me in disagreement. "If we wait Hoyle will have caught wind of this. The whole reason we're here the day after Christmas is because we know the grapevine will be slower passing information around today. We need to get this vote done, notarized, and sent off to the powers that be so it's officially on the books. If we hesitate or call anyone in we might not get our chance. It's better if we get this done and then brace ourselves for any blowback. I've got one trick up my sleeve. You'll see soon."

As I watch this whole scene in front of me I start to think maybe there is a way for me to make this work. Maybe I can still take down Hoyle, and have Rebecca. I'll just need to change the terms of the deal. There has to be something other than a landfill that could come to Clover.

"We've got a vehicle pulling in, Devin," Click calls, pointing up at the hill. He pulls his weapon from its holster in one fluid motion and takes a few tentative steps forward.

"Don't worry, boys, that's the marshal I called in." Kilroy announces, gesturing for Click to holster his gun.

"*The* marshal? You've only got one coming?" Click asks, shaking his head, clearly wondering what he's gotten himself into.

"This was the best I can do. He's the only one I know we can trust. He grew up here. He lives right outside town. He agreed to come here today and help us out."

I watch as an old familiar face steps out of a banged up suburban. "Nicky?" I ask, looking skeptically over at Kilroy.

"That's right. Though I think he goes by Nick now. Nick Topley. You two would have gone to school together, right?"

I don't answer his questions, reluctant to trust anyone I know from my history in Clover. The group of town council members funnel into the small hall used for their meetings, and I force a smile at the approaching marshal.

"Devin Sutton, it's been a long time." He tips his cowboy hat at me and shakes Kilroy's hand.

"It sure has, Nick. You're a marshal now, huh? I never pegged you for a lawman. I remember you putting cherry bombs in the girls' bathroom."

He chuckles and folds his arms over his chest. "I never thought I'd be a marshal either. Sherriff Hoyle and my daddy had some real bad blood between them. My daddy put himself in an early grave by way of the bottle when the sheriff ruined his practice. He was a doctor in Clover for twenty-one years before that bastard broke up everything he'd worked for. I took my wife and we moved outside the town lines. I've got two boys of my own now, and I busted my ass to make sure I worked for a place that had some real law behind it. This town's been waiting a long time for a way out. Sounds like you're offering it."

"Don't paint me as a martyr just yet."

"I know, I also heard it was a dump you're looking to build here. That ain't gonna go over too well. Clover is desperate, they'll go for it now, but at some point you know they'll regret it."

"I'm thinking that over. I don't have a solution just yet, but I am going to try to find an alternative to the landfill."

"That's good to hear. So tell me, fellas, what's our plan here?"

Kilroy clears his throat and heads for the door of the building where the vote will take place. "I'm going to go get this vote underway. Y'all just make sure we're able to get it done without any problems." He disappears into the building and leaves Nick and me standing in the cold. Click still looks like he's on high alert as he stares out into the woods.

"This is Click." The two men exchange a nod of the head as Click goes on surveying the surroundings.

"Click, huh?" Nick makes his fingers into the shape of a gun accompanied by a clicking noise. "That kind of click?" he asks, looking us both over.

I smirk. "Yes, that kind of click. He's a Marine, just back from Afghanistan. Special Forces."

"Sharp Shooter?" Nick calls over to him.

"Yes sir." He nods his head and grins.

Nick's a big guy with a crooked kind of smile. He reminds me of an old-school cowboy, gritty but easy to spot as one of the good guys. He's got the hat and boots but more than that, he's got that air about him. His voice is low and gravely as he continues. "I know we're all sizing each other up, trying to figure out where loyalties lie and if we can trust what's being said. You should know, I hate the sheriff and all he stands for. I want him out of a job and out of Clover. All his men, too. He's a slippery son of a bitch and anything that's ever been pinned on him he's gotten out of. I doubt you know this but I lost my little brother, Sam, over in Iraq three years ago. You know what that means, Click?"

"No sir." Click straightens his back slightly and steps forward to listen intently.

"It means I don't intend for my mother to have to bury her last living son over this shit. I ain't looking for a war or to be a hero. Part of me still thinks the best thing you could have done, Devin, was stay the hell out of Clover. But a bigger part of me wants all this to end, and I think you're our best shot at that. The sheriff's reach is deep. I don't even know which guys in my own department answer to him. Some money and a plan like yours is the only way to run him out of here." Nick

107

squints as he points to a dense acre of trees neighboring the meeting hall. "There's a small ledge up in those woods. It's the best vantage point for keeping eyes on anyone coming as well as getting a good line of sight through a scope at us down here. You a good shot, Click?"

"It doesn't get any better than me." Click asserts confidently, heading to his car to get a more appropriate weapon for the task.

"Devin and I will stay out here. If we get any company you'll have eyes on us from up there."

"Yes sir."

"And, Click, if the sheriff draws down on me, you shoot the son of a bitch right between the eyes, understand?"

Click nods and heads up into the woods.

"I hated what happened to you, Devin. My daddy fought a long time to try to get you some justice. He took a liking to you, felt like you got a raw deal. I think you were a breaking point for him."

"He saved my life." I kick a stone and stare down at my feet. I swore if I came back to Clover I'd never let it drag me into those memories, but here I am dredging it all up.

"He did?" Nick asks, leaning against the side of my car—my very expensive car that isn't made for asses in cheap jeans to be pressed against.

"Brent and I got in a fight the day he was killed. He was planning to attack Rebecca. I broke his arm and the sheriff came on us and put his gun to my head. I ruined Brent's chances at playing college ball. I think Hoyle was going to kill me. Your dad pulled up and yanked him off me."

"He never told me that. So many damn secrets in this town," Nick mutters, shaking his head mournfully. "Who do you think really killed Brent?"

That question had circled my mind for years like a hungry shark searching for chum. "I really have no idea. I do intend to find out. You're the marshal; you're in a better position to know than I am."

"I tried. When I first became a marshal a few years ago I started digging into the case. Strange shit started happening to my kin and me: cut brake lines, weird phone calls. So, I backed off. I was just starting a new job and getting settled in a new town. I couldn't afford the ghosts of Clover surfacing and ruining what I was building."

"I can understand that." I pace around a bit, wanting to ask him what he was able to find, if anything. But I bite my tongue. Settling this vote first is what matters.

"I did make one call before I backed off. During my training I met a man who taught a criminal justice class over at the university in the city. I told him about your case and asked him what he thought. He was blown away by the details, specifically how you could have been convicted so quickly with so little evidence. He was working with some program—I forget what it was called. He said they'd dig around. They didn't seem scared of Clover."

"The Innocence Program?" I ask, stunned that Nick doesn't seem to realize his phone call may have gotten the ball rolling toward my freedom.

"I think so. I dropped it after that, so I'm not really sure. I heard a while later that you were exonerated and making a name for yourself in New York City."

"Nick," I raise my eyebrows and look at him in astonishment, "that call probably made the difference in me getting out of prison."

Nick puffs out a burst of air and shrugs. "Well then, you can pay me back by not getting us killed out here today."

My phone starts to vibrate in my pocket and I fish it out. "What is it, Click?"

"Pickup truck pulling over the ridge. It's the sheriff. Looks like he's got three men with him and they're hauling ass."

"We've got company," I say as I tuck my phone back into my pocket. I jog back to the door of the building to give Kilroy the heads up, but he's already on his way out.

"The vote passed. Already notarized and faxed over to my contact. It's on the books. The town council has agreed to sell the land required and agreed to the rest of the terms. Hoyle is no longer the law here."

"Great timing. The sheriff is pulling in and he seems to be in a hurry to get here." I watch as the old beat-up red pickup skids to a stop just feet from me. Out steps the smug, pudgy-faced Hoyle and three of his men emerge from the bed of the truck. Nick seems to recognize them all.

"Ain't this a motley crew? Roy, Mick, Pete, and Harold. Glad you could join us out here. You'll be saving me the trip." Nick smirks, resting his hand on his hip, just above his holstered gun.

"Nicky Topley, I thought you were too good for Clover," Hoyle hisses, stepping in close to him.

"You can address me as Marshal Topley, and I'm not too good for Clover, I'm just too good for you. Now let's get down to business."

"Well *Nicky,* I don't have no business here with you. Why don't you run back to that fancy Fed office of yours and leave us loyal residents to talk. I hear they're trying to get a sneaky vote passed today."

"Harold, the vote's been passed. It's done and on the books already. There ain't nothing you can do here today to change that. Y'all need to hand over your badges and guns to the marshal and be on your way." Kilroy wasn't looking cocky or trying to rub salt in the wound, but it didn't matter.

"You'd be more likely to pull it out of my cold, dead hand." Hoyle says as he moves in closer until he was nose to nose with Kilroy.

"I wish I'd thought of that earlier. I'da written it into the proposal and I bet it woulda been unanimously passed. But since I didn't, why don't you just turn it over and be on your way." The two men take in deep breaths, their eyes shooting daggers at each other.

Hoyle reaches for his gun and Nick instinctually brings his hand down on his own weapon, ready to draw. "Why don't you just drop them down over there and toss your badges down in the dirt, too." Nick says with a steady tone.

Hoyle is seething as he continues to speak into the mayor's face. "You really are a snake, Kilroy. Acting like you're all on our side so we'll help you get voted in, then turning on us the second you get a chance. It don't even make sense. How do you think you can pass something that says I lose my job? That can't be legal."

"It is," Kilroy asserts as he folds his arms over his chest. "It's in the contract. In lieu of the fact that a large enterprise will be creating a business here in Clover it has been determined that in order to protect their assets and interests the security and law enforcement should henceforth be privatized. The new force will answer directly to the Federal Marshals, with Marshal Topley here as the liaison. The companies coming to Clover are bringing lots of valuable equipment and resources with them that require additional security. Your lawyer buddies are welcome to read the ironclad contract, which lists dozens of examples of precedence all across the country. I can go get you a copy if you like."

Every word the mayor says makes Hoyle's face turn a brighter shade of red. "I've had this badge on my chest for twenty-seven years. I ain't tossing it down into the dirt." He takes his hand off his weapon and walks toward me with his eyes narrowed. "You smug son of a bitch, you're being awful quiet." He bumps his chest against mine as he grinds his teeth together.

"I'm here to broker a deal," I say coolly, my face indifferent to his attempt at intimidation.

"Right, and you really think this town is gonna support a landfill in their backyard? When push comes to shove, you'll have a revolt on your hands."

"I'm not sure it's going to be a landfill anymore. I might put some other options in play. Though I do find it interesting that when the people of Clover had to choose between a steaming pile of hot garbage and you, they didn't hesitate."

"You're starting a war here, boy. Every drop of blood that spills in this town from here on out is going to be on your hands. And what, you squirreled away that little sweetheart of yours and her kid? You think I can't find her? I know every inch of this town and the mountains around it. I'll overturn every rock and check every cabin to find her. That's the mistake you made, boy. If you'da come down here without anything to lose, there wouldn't have been much I could do besides kill you. But now, you've got yourself an Achilles heel, and I intend to slice it open."

I'm trying to hold back the heat that's rolling through my body. I want to break this man's neck in one fluid motion. "If you lay a finger on her, I'll destroy you," I snarl through my gritted teeth.

"You need to hand your service weapon over and be on your way. And that goes for your three deputies here, too. I'll round up the rest of them from your men today," Nick says, as he rests his hand on my shoulder, trying to keep me from killing Hoyle.

One of the goons standing against Hoyle's truck finally decides to speak up. "You boys are gonna be in for it," he grunts as he spits a mouthful of tobacco on the ground inches from Nick.

"Pete, if you spit your dip by my boot again I'm gonna signal my sharpshooter up there to blow that tobacco right out of your lip." Nick strides confidently over to the three men, takes their weapons and badges, forcefully stripping them of their authority.

They twist their faces, seeming to hold back urges to strike like coiled snakes.

"This ain't over," Hoyle sneers as he steps back to his men. "You've all kicked the hornet's nest here. If you think taking my badge is going to get rid of me, you're dead wrong."

Nick moves back toward Hoyle and pulls the sheriff's gun from his holster, then plucks the badge from his shirt. Neither says a word. The sudden silence surprises me as they all pile back into his truck and peel out, kicking dirt and rocks in our direction.

"We've started something here, boys. Let's make sure we can finish it," Kilroy quips, and he slaps my shoulder as he walks back toward the building. Calling back to me, "I plan to sleep with one eye open."

Chapter Four

Devin

As the town council members disperse, I ask Nick to stay behind.

"Devin, you sure know how to stir shit up," he groans as he again leans against my BMW, arms crossed over his chest.

"I try," I say, pulling my coat closed as a burst of cold wind blows through. "Listen, I know you mentioned you looked into Brent's murder and dropped it when you started having trouble. I'm wondering if you stumbled upon anything. Something that might be useful in figuring out who really killed Brent?"

"You thinking of pursuing it? You seem to have enough going on right now. Why dig this up too?" He raises a skeptical eyebrow at me.

"I came here to settle my past, this is part of it. I was exonerated because of the way my case was handled, not because they figured out who really killed Brent. That means there's a murderer out there still, and I served nine years of his sentence. I need to know who really killed him."

"I didn't get any leads when I was digging into your case years ago. Like I said, I got stonewalled every step of the way. But there is one thing to consider." Nick runs his hand over the stubble on his cheek as though he doesn't want to tell me this. He's wrestling with himself.

"What?" I ask, afraid if I don't prod him he'll change his mind.

"When you were released, when they determined you hadn't killed him, I watched how Hoyle reacted. All those years ago he was vehement about making sure you were convicted, about seeking justice for his son. He seemed to call in every favor he had to get you locked up. But when you were free, he did nothing. I would have expected him to leave no stone unturned, seek out the real killer or chase you down. Unless . . ." his word hangs there, and I struggle to piece together the puzzle he seems to have already assembled.

"Unless what?"

"I see only two reasons. Either he killed his son or he already knows who did. You were the diversion, the cover-up. I don't have any concrete evidence. I'm going on what I saw in the wake of your release."

I appreciate how astutely Nick put this together, and I realize I'm talking to the right man. "If I were going to start somewhere, do you have a recommendation?"

"Yes, I recommend you try to stay alive while you get rid of Hoyle and turn this place into a landfill. Then go back to New York."

"I told you. I'm going to work on the deal, try to take the landfill off the table. And I'm not walking away from finding out who really killed Brent. I'd like your help, but if not, I still intend to pursue this."

Nick stares down at his boots, one crossed over the other as he lounges against my car. "I'm sending my kids and my wife upstate to stay with some friends of ours. With them safe, I'm more apt to get involved with all of this. My boss knows my ties to this place and he wants me to take the lead. My daddy loved this town and our family has lived here for generations. Moving out was the hardest choice I ever made. I want this place back to its glory. So with that in mind I have one tip for you. The medical examiner in the case is dead. He was in Hoyle's pocket and he would have written up anything he was told to about Brent's cause of death. But he was a good man and it wouldn't surprise me if he left a trail of clues. I couldn't get my hands on his report, but I think you should try to. There might be something there that could lead to more."

"And where do you think these records are?"

"Rumor has it Alvin Macready, the late medical examiner, kept a copy of all his records locked up in the shed at his house. His wife would be tending to them now I suppose."

"You're suggesting I rob her or go knock on the door and ask nicely?"

"Neither of those things will work. She's a good shot and she hates strangers. But . . ."

"What?" I ask, gesturing for him to get on with it.

"She was always mighty fond of Rebecca. Their families go way back. She and Rebecca's mama were dear friends. I know she respects the fact that Rebecca stayed around to raise her brothers."

"I don't want to bring her into this. It's not safe."

"It isn't," he agrees, "but without sufficient evidence you can't exhume Brent's body, and, in my opinion, that's going to be the only thing that really solves his murder. Most the evidence and reports have been buried away or destroyed. If you can find something in Macready's report that shows discrepancies or a cover-up, I think I can get a court order to dig him up. Maybe even enough to incriminate Hoyle."

I extend my hand to Nick and we shake goodbye. He knows there is nothing more to say on the matter. It's on me now to decide if I want to bring Rebecca into all of this or not. "Thanks for your help, Nick."

"I'm mighty anxious to hear if you can bring something to Clover besides that landfill."

Nodding my head and mentally kicking myself, I hop back in my car and wave Click over to join me. He slides into the passenger seat just as my phone begins to ring.

I used to like when my phone rang. It was either a woman I was going to hook up with or a business deal that would make me money. Now the ringing nuisance just makes the knot in my stomach tighter. This time it's Luke, and I can only imagine how angry he is, considering I've been sending him to voicemail.

"Devin, where the hell have you been?" He sounds half relieved and half furious. "I've called you a dozen times."

"Sorry," I say mindlessly as I crank up the heat in my car.

"What?" he asks, as I realize for the first time in our entire working relationship I've just apologized to him.

"I mean I'm sorry you're so damn needy. You're like a chick."

"Oh," he replies, but I can tell he knows something is up with me. Luckily he changes the subject. "Did the deal get voted in?"

"Yes, just this morning."

"The day after Christmas? Boy these folks are desperate huh?"

"They are. Hey I need you to check something out for me. Krylon, the waste management company we've contracted for this deal, do they do anything besides landfills?"

"It runs the gamut. They have a truck and hauling division and recycling I think. Why?"

118

"I'd like to explore something other than the landfill."

"Having a change of heart about destroying the place? I don't believe it."

"I just want to know my options. What would I need to do?"

"Well you'd need to convince the project manager that whatever alternative you are pitching is worth it to him. Then he'd need to get it approved by the powers that be at their company." I can hear the rustling of papers as Luke digs through the file. "Oh shit."

"What?"

"There is no *he*. The project manager on this deal is Jordan Garcia. *She* won't budge. She's a shark, and if she thinks you're looking for a last minute change she'll make your life hell."

"So we'll throw more money at it."

"Short-term money won't make a difference with Jordan. She'll be looking at the deal's profitability over the long haul. She's sharp. You'll need to find another way to convince her that going with a smaller line of their business is worth it. I wish you luck. How is everything going? Any problems?"

"Well, you read over the deal so you know it was my intention to strip Hoyle and his guys of power here in Clover. They lost their badges and guns this morning. The marshal here is going to round up the rest of them."

"That makes for another snag in your plan. If you have to change Jordan Garcia's mind, it means you're holding up security getting to Clover. It's in the way you've written up this deal. Security is theirs to handle and she'll need the final go ahead from her boss before any team is dispatched. They're no strangers to this new style of business, protecting their company and its assets. The security team will be theirs, and until Jordan gives this deal the final green light, you're on your own. I can't for the life of me figure out why you wrote it up that way."

"Because I didn't give a shit what happened here once Hoyle was out a job and a trash heap was being dumped in his backyard. I thought I'd be gone by now."

"And now you do give a shit?"

"Not everything is black and white, Luke."

"I have literally heard you say, *everything is black and white, good or bad, right or wrong*, hundreds of times over the last two years. What the hell is going on down there?"

"I'm going to try to find out who killed Brent. There's still a killer out there, and I want him to serve the time he deserves." I say, trying to throw this in casually.

"What the hell, Devin?" I can almost hear Luke falling out of his office chair. "Anything else I should know about?"

I pause, debating whether or not I should go on. Rebecca ignited a change in me, but the fire hasn't spread completely through my body yet. There is still a large part of me fighting this newfound humanity. But ultimately, I cave to it, wanting Luke to know the truth. I'm hoping he'll talk some sense into me.

"There's Rebecca," I begin, wondering how much of the story he remembers. After a little too much scotch one night I told him all about my past here in Clover, including Rebecca.

"*The* Rebecca?" he asks, and I realize he remembers exactly what I told him. "The girl from the letters? I thought she was living up in the mountains, married with kids. What happened to her husband?"

"He never existed. She made it all up. She thought I was going to be in prison for the rest of my life, and figured I'd be better off believing she was happy. She's not happy. No one in Clover is."

"Holy shit. So she's there? Are you guys . . .?" He trails off and as much as he doesn't know what question to ask, I don't know what answer to give, because I have no idea what Rebecca and I are.

"It's complicated." I rest my head against the back of my seat and stare up at that the roof of my car.

"Let me get all this straight, Devin. You intend to oust a trigger-happy sheriff's department with whom you have a lot of bad blood. You're going to try to alter a deal in the eleventh hour with a ball-busting project manager who loves to see guys squirm. And you're going to try to solve a cold case—a murder you served almost a decade in prison for. All while attempting to rekindle a romance with a woman who lied to you for eleven years? I'm supposed to believe you're going to be back in New York in four days to sign a deal to sell this company?"

With a breathy laugh I say simply, "Yes."

"I should be furious right now," he tempers his voice, "none of this sounds like you."

"One more thing, Luke. I need you to add something else to the sale of the company. I want to retain some part of this Clover deal. I want to oversee it."

"Jordan will be the project manager."

"That's fine, I just want some sort of stake in it. I want to be able to keep things on track. After the sale of my company on Friday I think I'm going to come back here. I don't think the new owners of my company are

Danielle Stewart

going to want anything to do with this place. I'm sure they'll be happy to know I'll deal with it all for them."

"Devin, the day we went into business together we always agreed you'd sell the company after a couple of years if the money was there. The money is here, the offer is here, and it's time. We agreed two years would likely be as long as we could put up with each other. You'll walk away with a lot of money. You can start over anywhere. Remember your plan? You were going to invest in some real estate, travel, look for your next start up. Why do you want to be strapped down with the remnants of this deal?"

I roll my eyes at the plan. The one I told Luke, but never really intended for myself. This, what I am doing in Clover, has always been my plan. "Just do it," I snap, and can feel parts of me returning: the business-minded, revenge-seeking bastard who thinks only of himself. The longer I'm away from Rebecca, the worse it gets. It's like she's a constant reminder to stay softer, kinder, and when she is out of sight, I return to my old ways.

"So you want me to write in a clause about the unprofitable piece-of-crap deal we're sneaking in before the sale? I don't think we should even draw any attention to it."

"The company I built is profitable and efficient with some of the best minds in the industry on staff. The buyers are getting a gold mine of talent and opportunity. Fine print, Luke," I say flatly.

"Invisible ink is more like it." He pauses and I hear him exhaling the way he does before he gives in to me. "I'll figure something out. Listen, Devin, you have a lot riding on this sale. Your employees up here are counting on you to come through. I can see you have your hands full down there, and I know you never promise anything but—"

"I'll be there Luke, you have my word," I say, hardly even believing I'm saying this to someone else without really having it figured out. For the first time in a long time I don't want to let anyone down.

"I'll have the jet there Thursday night. Try to stay out of trouble until then. I don't want to have to give Click a bonus."

We disconnect and I toss my phone down into the center console. I rub at my tired eyes and wonder what the hell I'm going to do. I've now given my word to Rebecca that I will find a way around the landfill. I've promised the town of Clover protection and freedom from Hoyle: all in time to get back to New York to sell my company like I've committed to Luke. What the hell have I done, and more importantly, why have I done it?

Click is so good at being clandestine that I practically forget he's my passenger. "Seems like you've got your hands full," he says, drawing me back to reality. "How can I help?"

"I think you have a very important set of skills that can help turn all this around for me."

"I've led men before—"

I cut him off with the shaking of my head. "That's not what I'm talking about. I make it a point *not* to check out other guys, but I'm pretty sure you're a good-looking kid. You do all right with the ladies?" I hold back my laugh as I watch confusion wash over him.

"I do pretty well," he replies tentatively.

"Then you'll be perfect for this. I'll set a meeting at the mayor's office for you tomorrow. Make sure to wear something that shows off your, um, *assets.*" I'm putting this down on the list of conversations I never thought I'd be having. I can't do all of this alone. It's time to call in reinforcements.

Chapter Five

<u>Devin</u>

These long car rides are killing me. In New York, I'm always fifteen minutes from where I need to be, no time to get inside my own head. Going from Clover back to the cabin where I've left Rebecca means another two hours alone with my thoughts. Two hours to think of a way to convince her to come back with me, to help me.

I've had to be persuasive in my job plenty of times. When building a company you need people to buy into it, you need their support. But nothing I've ever had to accomplish before has required so much emotion. How do I overcome something I'm struggling to understand? She wants me to stop digging up the past. Why? How could she possibly not want to know? How could she not want to strike out, like the slashing paw of a lion, at those who hurt us? She's afraid. She thinks I'm twisted up in this, and I'll cross a line, something I won't be able to come back from.

I slap at the knob on the radio, cutting short the words of an old ballad that reminds me of my youth. I don't want to hear it. I don't want to have to go back. But I think that's the only way I'll be able pull Rebecca along with me.

If I can get her to remember what it felt like to be cut away from each other, she'll have to see my point of view. I need her to not be angry with me, I need her to be angry along side me. To hate who I hate and want to punish just as I do. I need her to feel the injustice of it all again, the helplessness. I need her to remember the way I remember.

2002

I have my head in my locker, searching for an elusive library book, when I hear her voice. "Run, Devin!" Rebecca is hollering as she rushes toward me. I don't understand, so I don't run, which seems to infuriate her. She shoves me and I twist my face in confusion. "Run, Devin," she repeats, and the urgency in her eyes is frightening enough to get my legs moving. Unfortunately it's too late. I feel a hand as big as a bear's claw grab my collar and yank me backward. My back hits the shiny hallway floor with a thud and I groan. Looking up I see the boxy, smiling face of Brent Hoyle, Rebecca's quarterback thug of a boyfriend. "Devin, right?" he snarls, yanking me back up to my feet and slamming me up against a row of lockers.

"What the hell's your problem?" I shove Brent off me, furious and ready to take him down. I'm no pipsqueak myself. I hit six-feet tall last summer and have been working out ever since. I've transitioned from a too tall, skinny kid to a wide-shouldered guy who could pass for older. But Brent is built like a brick shithouse, jock through and through. His body is thick, and so is his skull. Not to mention he's never alone. He travels with at least two teammates at all times. They seem incapable of ever having an individual thought or trying something the others don't agree with. They are the definition of pack mentality. And in walk the rest of the dogs now. I count at least four of them.

Once I see them, I figure out what this is all about. The larger oaf, who had a tooth knocked out last game, is carrying my boots. The pair I left at Rebecca's front door.

"You seem to have left something at *my* girlfriend's house yesterday." Brent takes the boots from the other guy and rams them into the locker right by my head. "You see, she tried to tell me they were her brother's but I ain't no idiot."

"Your grammar suggests otherwise," I shoot back, knowing full well I'm playing with fire. My joke is met with a rolling laughter that moves through the gathering crowd. The commotion infuriates Brent, and his already red face tints a deeper shade. "I looked at these boots, and remembered where I seen 'em. These are Army boy's boots. You think you're some kinda soldier? With your dumbass high and tight haircut? Let's see how tough you are."

I don't wait for Brent to come at me. I don't duck at an incoming punch or shield my body from the boots he is holding. I just cock my fist back and punch him with the full force of my body, sending him flying backward. My father has taught me next to nothing in my life. He hasn't shown me the art of empathy or how to connect with people on any meaningful level. But he did teach me the very useful skills of combat. How to fight, defend, and attack.

I watch as Brent shakes his rattled head in an effort to steady himself. The whole hallway is silent, gaping mouths and saucer-sized eyes all waiting to see what will happen next. Brent quickly rallies and launches the boots at my head. My reflexes are fast and I duck, both boots missing me. "You're dead," he hisses, pointing an accusing finger in my direction. "I won't even bother handling you here. I want to take my time ripping you to pieces." As the rest of the football team blows by me, each shoves his shoulder and elbow into me.

My nostrils flair, fury filling me as Brent sinks his fingers forcefully into Rebecca's arm and yanks her along. Like a narcissistic, destructive parade, the grisly lot makes its way down the still stunned and quiet hallway.

I shake the ache out of my knuckles as I throw my backpack over one of my shoulders. The eyes of the crowd are still on me. Teachers have begun filling the hallways and shuffling people along in a *nothing to see here* fashion. I slip into my next class and count the minutes until chemistry where I can find out if Rebecca is all right. No telling what Brent could do to her.

The hours tick by and it is finally time to take my seat on the high stool behind the row of Bunsen burners in the back of Mr. Tower's class. Every eye is on me again as I slide in next to Rebecca. She stares straight ahead. No reaction. She looks as though she doesn't intend to feed the beast that is this class full of nosy jackasses.

When Mr. Tower finally begins speaking, all eyes on him, I lean in toward Rebecca. "Are you okay?" I whisper, looking her over, wanting to focus on where I had seen Brent's hand gripping her arm. I can't see anything; she is wearing Brent's letterman jacket, an unmistakable symbol of his ownership.

"I'm so sorry, Devin. I shouldn't have had you come over."

"Did you guys break up?" I beg the heavens for her to say yes.

She huffs out a sarcastic laugh that quickly deflates my hope. "That's like a warden kicking out a prisoner for doing something wrong. All you do is serve more time."

"You don't have to stay with him," I whisper, imploring her to know her own worth. "You can break up with him."

"You just got to Clover, Devin. You don't really understand how it works here. Brent's dad is the sheriff. His mom's family owns half the businesses in this town. If I cross him, I cross *them* and my life becomes hell. My parents could get fired from the mill. The only thing I can hope for is that he gets tired of me and moves on to someone else."

"That's bullshit," I say loud enough to draw everyone's attention. When Mr. Tower clears his throat, the room turns back toward him. "Rebecca, you don't deserve this. You are amazing, beautiful, and so talented. You deserve someone better."

"Like you?" she asks, flashing her blue eyes at me. *Yes*, I want to shout but I don't.

"Like whoever you want."

She looks away, flipping her hair out of her eyes and shaking her head. "He's going to kill you, or at least hurt you really bad. You can't be around me anymore. We can't act like we have feelings for each other."

"Do we?" I ask, arching an eyebrow at her. I know the answer to my half of that question; I know it as if it is the only true thing in the world.

She slides her hand over and laces her fingers with mine, hidden behind the large desk. The sensation, the connection, feels like a piece of me being slid into place. I don't ever want to let go. I want to find something in this chemistry class with an unbreakable superglue-like bond and pour it over our hands. But her words temper my hope.

"It doesn't matter if we do." She hangs her head, looking defeated. "It doesn't work that way in Clover. We just need to give it some time. Brent will move on and then we might have a chance."

* * * *

Avoiding an entire football team in a school of only four hundred students is not easy. I've managed to stay mostly out of their way for almost a week. All I need to do is make it four more days and then Christmas break will start. Rebecca has switched her class schedule so that we barely ever run into each other.

If we pass each other in the hall, she ignores me, rounding corners and ripping a piece of my heart out as she goes by. If I felt like a ghost before I moved to Clover, now I'm downright invisible. Not to jocks of course, but to the only person who ever really saw me. I've spent the majority of my life feeling trapped inside myself, isolated. Rebecca's attention, my brief bond to her, has been like a stream of light entering a dark room. But the door has now slammed shut again, all the light gone.

I continue to remind myself that the Marines are going to be my savior. I'll be boarding a bus in less than three months. Rebecca and this ridiculous town will be a distant memory.

Mr. Clevenhold, however, doesn't seem to be up to speed with the plan of me evading my enemies. The stout, whistle-wearing gym teacher told me this morning if I missed another gym class I'd get a detention. The locker room of the gym is the least supervised, most hostile environment in the entire school and I've avoided it as long as I can. It is the lion's den, and Brent won't hesitate to seek his revenge down there. I sneak down early to put my gym clothes on and sit in a stall with my feet tucked up, waiting for the rest of the class to get ready. I'm not afraid of Brent. I'm not even afraid of the two guys he normally has with him. But I'd be stupid not to think eight of the players here in the locker room couldn't do some damage. My father has told me time and again never to back down from a fight, no matter what the circumstances. It's another reason my father is an idiot.

I hear the familiar husky voices of the players and, hell, I can even smell them. Testosterone and sweat fill the rooms as I listen to chests being bumped and towels being snapped. Brent's voice rises up over the noise and then suddenly the group is quiet, intently listening to their leader. "I swear if she doesn't put out by the night of the Christmas dance, I'm not giving her a choice. I've been putting up with her shit for eight months, and I haven't gotten so much as a hand job. If it weren't for all the action I was getting from Cara and Maggie on the side I'd have dumped Becca by now."

"Dude," one of the mindless players chimes in, "seriously, if she hasn't put out by then you should just make her. You know we'll cover for you. Give you an alibi and shit." I listen as the rest of the group chimes in with their support to this barbaric plan.

My fists ball up with rage and it takes all the self-control I have not to step out of the stall and take out as many of them as I can before they whip my ass. But if they kill me, who will warn Rebecca? I grit my teeth and listen as they continue.

"My folks are going to be gone the night of the dance. I told her I'm having a party. But really it'll just be the two of us. I'll show her a hell of a party." They all chuckle at the idea.

"Can the rest of us get a run at her?" one of the deep-voiced jocks asks, and they all hoot and holler. They're barking crude comments about what it would be like to be with Rebecca.

"Hell no," Brent shouts, quieting the group again. For one small moment, I think maybe he has some morals after all. That thought is quickly dashed. "I'll be done with her soon enough, then you guys can all get your shot."

A whistle blows and Mr. Clevenhold's voice echoes through the locker room. "Let's go, men. Class starts now."

"We'll be up in a minute," Brent shoots back, not seeming to appreciate the teacher's authority. I expected the stiff-backed, scowling Mr. Clevenhold to come yank them all up the stairs, or at least have something to say. Instead, all I hear is the sound of the man's footsteps fading away as he leaves the room.

"Hey Brent, whatcha gonna do about Army Boy? I know you're not letting him get away with that sucker punch."

Again I want to jump up and remind everyone a sucker punch is something you don't see coming and is normally unprovoked. My hit was neither of those things.

"He's been ducking me for a week now. Chicken shit. I'll deal with him after Christmas break if I have to. I want to make sure he pays. I'm not talking about a beat down either. I plan to ruin his life. He wants to join the

Marines? I'm going to make sure he can't." I hear a loud thud, likely Brent's fist hitting a locker. The group makes its way toward the gym and I'm left pulsing with anger. Everything about these bastards makes me furious. I'm seething at the thought of what they'd said about Rebecca, what Brent plans to do. The operative word here is *plans*. There is no way in hell I'm going to let that happen.

I race out of the locker room, still in basketball shorts and a cotton shirt, and dart into Rebecca's health class. Up on the board is a poster of a giant penis. Mrs. Duhamel stands with a large pointer, whacking it repeatedly as she indicates the different parts of it.

I freeze and my face goes beet red. "Mr. Sutton," Mrs. Duhamel starts firmly, "are you in desperate need of a penis tutorial, or is there some other emergency?"

The entire class erupts in laughter and Rebecca covers her face, mortified for me. "I need Rebecca," I croak, and the laughter roars once more. "I mean . . . the principal wants to see Rebecca, right away."

Her face glows with hot embers of embarrassment as a low, exaggerated "*ohh*" rings out from the students, assuming she is in some kind of trouble.

"Off you go then," Mrs. Duhamel sings, slapping the pointer against the large penis poster a few more times.

When we are safely in the hallway, out of earshot and away from that mortifying poster, Rebecca turns to scold me. "What the hell are you doing? I told you, we can't see each other at all anymore. It's for your own good." I grab her hand and tug her along behind me out the double doors of the school and into the cold. "Where are you taking me? It's freezing out here," she protests.

I don't say a word until we are nearly at her front door. "Is anyone home at your house?"

"No, my daddy is at the mill and so is my mama. What's going on?"

She puts her key in the door and I fall in behind her. I'm winded, the cold and brisk walk mixing with my adrenaline. Planting my hands firmly on both her shoulders, I hunch down to lock my eyes with hers. "Rebecca, Brent is going to hurt you."

She shakes off my hands and steps back. "We've been over this, Devin. There is a difference between bad and as bad as it gets. It can easily get worse for me if I break up with him. I just need to wait until he's done with me."

"No, Rebecca." I throw my hands up in exasperation. "I just overheard him in the locker room. There's a dance this Friday, right?"

"The Winter Formal. We're going together, then Brent is having a party at his house."

"He just told half the football team that if you didn't—" I search for the right words. Something to get my point across but not make this any more uncomfortable for her than it is. "If you don't give him *what he wants*, he's going to take it. Forcibly."

"What do you—" she gasps. "He said that? To all of them? And what did they say?"

"I'm not telling you anything else. The details aren't important. But you have to end it with him. He's untouchable in this town and he thinks he can do whatever he wants to you and not get in trouble."

"If I break up with him, it'll be worse. He'll never leave me alone."

"We'll figure that out." I step in closer to her and touch her cheek gently, watching the frightened tears form out of thin air. I want to kiss her so badly, find out what that pink lip gloss tastes like. Is it different from the peach one I tasted the last time we were together? But what would that make me? A moment when she feels boxed in and scared, she doesn't need me complicating it.

"I won't let him hurt you," I whisper. "I'll kill him before I let him touch you again."

She nods her head and buries her face in my chest. It feels so good to have her in my arms. I slip my hand behind her hair and touch the silky skin of her neck. I just made a promise, now I have to figure out how I'm going to keep it.

* * * *

An hour before Brent was supposed to pick Rebecca up for the dance, she called him and said she was too sick to go. That did not go over well. I held her hand as the cursing on the other end of the line got so loud she had to hold the phone at a distance just so it wouldn't hurt her ear.

Our bags are packed, my old rusted car gassed up. Now all we have to do is work up the guts to really go. I keep thinking at any moment one of us will realize how crazy this plan is. "We'll stay here at my house until everyone is at the dance. Then we'll get in the car and go."

Rebecca nods in agreement, though her eyes don't look as convincing. "Are you sure we can do this? I mean we only have four hundred dollars between the two of us. We have no place to stay."

"We'll figure it out. Anything is better than staying here just waiting for Brent and his cronies to hurt you. I can get a job. We can sleep in the car for a little while if we really have to. We've got a few of your paintings in the trunk, someone will buy them, I know it."

"Christmas is next week. It'll be the first time I spend it away from my family, my brothers." I hate to see her sad, but I remind myself how sad she'll be if Brent gets his hands on her. "You're such an optimist, Devin. How did you get like that?"

"I don't know. I never used to be before I met you. There are a lot of things that are different now." The honesty fills the room and I think it will create a bubble that will push us apart. Instead she moves toward me and slides her arms around me, tucking herself against me. I want to protect her. I never want anything to ever hurt her. It scares me how much I'd be willing to do to keep her safe.

We sit quietly, her nestled in my arms on my bed. It isn't a lack of overwhelming desire that keeps me from making a move on her, the timing just isn't right. It isn't what she needs in this moment. Though I still can't get our night together out of my head.

When we finally break our tangled bodies apart from one another we head for the door. I'm loading Rebecca's duffle bag into the trunk of my shit-box car when I hear it. It's the squeal of tires and rumble of a pickup truck engine rounding the corner up my street. I turn my head to see, but I already know it's him.

"Get in the house," I call to Rebecca, but she's frozen in fear. Her eyes flutter with terror as she sees Brent's red pickup roar into my driveway and block us in. He's out of his truck. My mind flies through the reality.

We aren't leaving. We aren't getting out of Clover. The only positive thing is Brent's alone, which almost never happens. Apparently the rest of his cronies are at the dance, not looking for a fight tonight.

"Bags packed?" Brent asks, walking up to me and ripping Rebecca's bag out of my hand. "You ain't leaving town now are you?"

"Brent," I try to think on my feet, some explanation or reasoning, but his fist is hitting my face before I can get another word out. I go down. Hard. The ground is freezing cold below my hands as I try to right myself. Brent doesn't give me the chance. His steel-toe cowboy boots are making contact with my ribs again and again. My air is gone, all of it. I'm rolling away but I'm getting nowhere. It isn't until I see the pink trim of Rebecca's jacket flashing by me that I realize I can't quit. I can't just lie here and get my ass beaten. If I do, then Brent will follow through with the plan he's had all along for after the dance. He'll take her.

I watch between blows as Rebecca lunges for Brent and he strikes her down with a hard backhand to her face. That's it. That is all I need to fill my body with the adrenaline and rage that will change this fight. I grab the foot he is about to kick me with and yank it out from under him, taking him to the ground. He's off his feet and the playing field is even. I crawl on top of him, clumsily trying to get the upper hand. I begin pounding my fist down into his face, once, twice, as hard as I can. I pray I can just knock him out long enough to get in the car and go. But it doesn't work. His two monstrous hands shove me off and we both make our way to our feet, stunned and faltering, equally dazed.

Rebecca is on her feet again, too, and I shout for her to go in the house, but she still doesn't listen. My breath is catching in my chest and I'm pretty sure one of my ribs is broken. Brent lunges toward me and I grab his extended arm. With a move my father taught me when I was ten years old, I use his own momentum to spin his arm backward. I throw my weight into the move and I don't stop until I hear a snap, followed closely by an agonizing scream. Brent falls to the ground, clutching his arm and howling like a sick dog.

The flash of blue lights in my peripheral vision shakes my stare from Brent and I turn my body to see a large man charging at me. I'm down again. Tackled.

"What did you do to my boy?" the man is yelling, his hands buried in the collar of my shirt. He's lifting me up and then pounding my back into the ground, again and again.

"My arm, Dad, he broke my arm," Brent croaks as he rolls onto his back and continues to writhe in pain.

I watch a fresh wave of fury flood the man, his tan sheriff uniform contrasting against the burning red of his face. "The scouts are coming this weekend. The scouts are coming to watch him play. This was our last chance." He slams me down again and now uses his forearm across my neck to hold me down. I'm suffocating, and I can hear Rebecca's voice screaming for him to stop. His free hand reaches down to his belt, and before I can even blink there is the barrel of a gun waving in my face.

"Sherriff!" a man shouts as my short, unfulfilled life flashes before my eyes. "Sherriff, what the hell are you doing?" The man's face comes into focus. It's Craig Topley, the father of a kid I go to school with. I've seen him there to pick Nicky up a few times, and I know he's a doctor in Clover.

The sherriff, still choking me with his plump, hairy arm, is shaken from his rage-filled trance as Dr. Topley pulls at his shirt and lifts him off me. "What the hell are you doing? Pointing your damn gun at a kid?"

"Mind your own business, Craig. This ain't your concern."

I roll to my side and bring my hands to my neck. The sensation of still feeling suffocated is freaking me out. Like maybe I'll never breathe again.

"It just became my business," Dr. Topley shouts, dropping down to my side and starting to check me over. My vitals, my ribs, the welt on my eye.

"Forget about him, check my boy's arm. This piece of shit scum broke it. The scouts are coming this weekend. That bastard just ended Brent's last chance at college."

"And you almost just ended this kid's life," Dr. Topley snaps. "You're going to have to answer for that."

I hear a rumble of laughter come from the sheriff's round belly, and I focus on his pudgy face long enough to see the maniacal smile he's flashing. "Answer to who, Craig? I am the law here. You know that." He holsters his weapon and reaches down to lift Brent to his feet. "And you'd be smart to keep this to yourself, Craig. You don't want anything happening to that thriving practice of yours."

I feel Dr. Topley's fingers tighten around my wrist as he checks my pulse to the point where I wince slightly and he lets go.

"And you," the sheriff barks into his son's face. "You idiot, coming here starting trouble over that little skank. You just ruined your life, and you still didn't get the girl. If dumb was dirt, you'd have yourself a damn acre. Waste of space, screw up." He tugs him away and tosses him in the back of his squad car.

"You okay, kid?" Dr. Topley asks as he traces his finger left and right in the air in front of me to see if I can follow.

"I'm fine," I groan, feeling Rebecca's body kneeling beside me. "Are you okay?" I ask her, looking at the scrape on her cheek. She nods at me and the tears she's been fighting back start to spill over. And just like before, no amount of physical pain hurts me more than the sight of her crying.

"That son of a bitch can't keep getting away with this. He's destroying this town and no one is even trying to stop him. He's run out the businesses, he intimidates everyone into doing what he wants." Dr. Topley's face tenses and his lips purse into a scowl.

"We're leaving town," I say as I lift myself cautiously to my feet.

And with a painful blow, worse than any I'd just sustained, Rebecca says the one thing I prayed she wouldn't. "I don't think we should, Devin." Her head hangs low, long brown hair veiling her face. I can see a tremble in her hands. "I'm going home. I'm going to spend Christmas with my family and just stay away from . . ." I hear her voice catch in her throat, ". . . from all of you. I'm not worth this much trouble. No one is." She grabs her bag from the front lawn and starts the walk back to her house. I want to call out to her but I don't know what I want to say. I don't know how to convince her that running away is the right thing to do when I'm not even convinced myself.

"You need to get checked out, Devin," Dr. Topley insists as he looks me over one more time.

"Can you get her home safe?" I ask as I head in to my house, ignoring his suggestion about getting checked out. "Just make sure she gets there, okay?" Dr. Topley quietly steps away from my house and jogs to catch up to Rebecca. I close the door behind me and wish the whole world would disappear.

I crawl into my cold, now empty, bed and force myself to sleep. At least my parents aren't home to question me. My mom is working on yet another project, no doubt, and my father is at a retirement party for one of his buddies.

I push out every thought of her. I ignore the smell of her hair on my pillow. I pray she isn't waiting for me in my dreams.

I don't know how long I've been sleeping, but I wake to the sound of hard thumping on my door. It's followed quickly by the voice of a man I don't recognize. Lost in the fog of my dream I hesitate to answer, and my door swings open. Three officers storm in, and I jolt up to a sitting position.

Their words don't make any sense to me. "Devin Sutton, you are under arrest for arson and the resulting murder of Brent Hoyle. You have the right to remain silent . . ."

Apparently in the wee hours of the morning someone had started a fire in the Hoyle household. The officers tell me I'm lucky Mr. and Mrs. Hoyle had kept their plans to spend the evening at their cabin on the Blue Ridge Mountains. It could have been much worse if I'd have killed them too. When Brent's body was found, a warrant was immediately issued for my arrest. And nothing after that moment made sense in my life.

Chapter Six

Devin 2013

"You scared the hell out of me, Devin. Why didn't you call first?" Rebecca is standing in the doorway of the cabin I left her in with a shotgun in her hand as I step out of my car.

My honest response to the question is that I wasn't sure until thirty seconds ago whether I would pull into the driveway or not. "Sorry, I got caught up and thought I'd better just pop in. Where did you get the gun?"

"This is the mountains in the south, everyone has a gun." She lowers it and relaxes her shoulders. "It's a two-hour drive, you weren't exactly in the neighborhood. Everything all right?"

"So far so good, but I need to talk to you about something. You're going to call me crazy but just hear me out." I step past her into the house and I'm immediately filled with the warmth of it. Not the temperature, but the ambiance. I already miss who I was for that one night I spent with Rebecca and Adeline and I'm wondering if that version of myself is gone.

"Want some coffee?" Rebecca asks, and I'm taken aback by how comfortable she's made herself in the house. It's nice to see her reaching for mugs like she'd put them there herself.

"I'll take a cup, thanks." We didn't kiss on the doorstep or fall back into each other's arms. I'm not sure if I really expected that, but part of me was hoping for it. She's tentative, I can feel it and imagine it's the waiting that's done it. She told me when I left that she'd give me a chance, but I'm sure her patience has grown thin while sitting here alone in this quiet cabin. She's hesitant and guarding herself and I'd be an idiot to blame her for that. "Where's Adeline?" I ask, trying to break the silence.

"She's napping, worn out from playing in the snow and arranging her dolls a million different ways. Thank you again for all the presents. These lockets . . ." she trails off, and I watch as she runs her thumb over the words engraved on the back. I move toward her, standing so close that I can feel the heat coming off her skin. Rather than any of the clothes I bought for her, she's wearing the T-shirt I pulled off before I left. The mixture of my cologne and her perfume reminds me of being in bed with her. I'm immediately desperate for that again. The power she has, the effortless way she gets in my head, makes me a mix of mad and impressed. I take the locket from her hand and look down at it. I read the words again as I run my own thumb over it.

"We really had something, didn't we Rebecca?"

"We did," she agrees, leaning back against the counter, daring me with her eyes to kiss her. "I'm wondering if it was enough? Enough to mean anything today. Are you wondering that?" She asks as she moves her hair away from her face and I rest the locket down on her; the back of my hand brushing across her skin. I lean to her, unable to fight against it another second, and kiss her like it's the first time. Or maybe I'm kissing her like it's the last time. Either way, the kiss is ravenous; we're pulling at each other's clothes, and she's hopping up onto the counter before either of us have a chance to catch our breath.

"Is this what you came back for?" she asks in a breathy whisper, breaking our kiss just long enough to smile. Then it hits me. She's assuming this two-hour drive back was because I couldn't stand to be away from her, because I wanted to have her in my arms again. I did miss her, and I did think about her and this moment, but that isn't truly what brought me back. Remembering that rips at my guts.

When her coy comment isn't met with a devilish smile on my part, I can tell she realizes something's wrong.

"This isn't what you came back for." She shrugs and I don't give her a chance to push me away; I step back giving her space. She hops down from the counter and straightens her clothes, grabbing the coffee pot and acting like nothing has happened.

I settle in a chair at the breakfast nook and watch her pour my coffee, praying she doesn't scald me with it, although, I would deserve it if she did. "I had a conversation with Nick Topley this morning. You remember him?"

"Nicky? Of course. He's a marshal now, isn't he?" She's like ice now, deflated and unrecognizable compared to the woman who was just in my arms.

"He is. The mayor called him in since he felt we could trust him. Luckily, Hoyle went without much trouble, but I'm sure he's still planning something."

"I'm sure. You'd fall out of your chair if I told you stories about what Hoyle has done since you've been gone. I'm glad you came up here to let me know how it went." She says shooting a passive dig at me.

I suck in a breath like I'm about to step onto Mars. "Nick and I talked about Brent. About who might have actually killed him."

I watch the tremble in her hand grow as she slides my coffee toward me. The blood has drained from her face and her lips are pursed together.

"Why on earth would you want to dig that up? You were exonerated, can't you move on?" Rather than taking the seat next to me, she heads back to the counter and leans rigidly against it. She's looking at me like I've blindsided her, and she's pissed.

"It's not enough. I was exonerated because of how my case was handled. There's still a killer out there. Nick said—"

"I don't care what Nick said. If you're here with the intention of telling me you are going on some hunt for a killer, then stop right there."

I consider raising my voice, telling her that she couldn't possibly understand what it feels like to have served another man's sentence. Whoever committed the crime needs to pay. It's part of finding peace for me. It's obvious, though, just by the way she's standing, that an argument like that won't be effective. "I'm working on changing the deal from a landfill to something else. Something that could restore Clover back to the town it once was. I'm doing that for you, but I need this, Rebecca. I need your help to be able to find out who really killed Brent. Nick thinks if I can get my hands on the medical examiner's report and find any type of inconsistency he can have the case reopened on a federal level. The files are all supposedly locked up at the widow's house. Lulu Macready. She knows you and likes you. Maybe you could . . ."

Rebecca snatches two dishes from the counter and tosses them into the suds-filled sink. She comes back to the table and takes my coffee mug, the one I've only had two sips out of and yanks it away, tossing it into the sink as well. "Do you remember how I told you to go to hell when you tried to give me money and when I found out you were going to turn Clover into a dump? I don't want to be around a man with a vendetta and revenge in his heart. I've spent enough time with those kinds of men. It makes you reckless, selfish, and short-sighted. I can't compete with that. So if you're dead set on dredging up history for the purpose of making someone pay, then you're on your own."

"If I don't make the person pay, who will?"

"God. It's His job to judge the guilty, not yours."

"How can you not want to know? This person took so much from us. Think about who we would be right now if I hadn't spent all those years in prison for his murder."

"You might as well go back to prison. All you're setting yourself up for is more wasted years. I can't spare any more time on something so evil. It's behind me. I need it to be behind you. I won't have Adeline around the danger and hate that comes with what you're looking for."

"I need to know," I insist. "That day I was arrested for Brent's murder wrecked my life. Hoyle pulled every string, called in every favor, to get me convicted. I want to know why. I want answers."

"And what if you don't like the answers you find? Then what?" she asks barely above a whisper as she turns to the sink and starts on the dishes.

"What is that supposed to mean? You know something I don't?"

Staring at her back, I feel like she's lying to me as she mutters, "No."

"Rebecca, I'm going to work like a maniac to get Clover back to a thriving town. I'm trying to alter an already agreed upon contract to do away with the landfill. That's no small task. Today, when I was nose to nose with Hoyle, I didn't lay a finger on him. That was for you, all of it. If you knew the man I was when I rolled into Clover last week compared to who I am since finding you again, you might be more forgiving."

"I'm not settling, Devin. I'm tired of it." She sloshes her hands around in the soapy water and stares out the window in front of her. "I know what I want for my daughter and myself, and I'm not taking anything less than we deserve. Not anymore, not since seeing you again. You gave me what I needed. You showed me she and I are worth more than I was giving us credit for. You and I could have a fresh start in front of us. It's up to you if you want to take it or not, but I'm done looking back."

I want to be the one to give all those things to her. I'm glad she is seeing her own worth, and all I can hope is that when all the dust settles she's still there waiting for me. Though it's not looking promising at the moment.

"Lulu won't give me a thing without you."

"She'll likely shoot you before you hit the first step of her place." She drops a dish heavily into the water and spins around, wet hands splashing water to the floor. "I'm not helping you, Devin."

My phone rings and we both groan at the noise. "It's Nick," I tell her before answering.

"Devin, we've got a problem. Where are you?"

"I'm at the cabin with Rebecca."

"Good. I just got word that the couple you rented that place from has a son who hunts with one of the deputies in Clover. I think Hoyle might know where she is."

"I'll get her out of here. Find her somewhere else."

"Why don't you bring her to my place? My wife and kids leave tomorrow to go stay with friends of ours upstate. She's making a big dinner. I'm sure she'd like the company, and it will give us a chance to regroup."

"Shit, I thought we'd have more time than this. Text me the address. We'll be by your house later on." I hang up my phone and slide it into my pocket, immediately moving through the house to find Adeline, wherever she is napping.

"What's going on?" Rebecca asks, walking quickly to catch up to me.

"Hoyle knows where you are. We need to leave. Now. Nick offered us dinner at his place tonight before his family heads to somewhere safe. It will give us a chance to figure out where you and Adeline should go."

"Could you stop talking about us like we're cattle? *I* actually decide where we go."

"I know," I say, lifting Adeline out of the bed she's nestled in. "It's not safe here. If you don't want to come back with me then I'll buy you two tickets to anywhere in the world and make sure you have everything you need. You'd be safe and happy." I'd buy the ticket in a heartbeat, but I'd hate to see her leave. It's a sick game of fate we're playing. I spent years trying to get right with the fact that I can't have her anymore. Then I have my chance and I can't get my shit straight. I'm holding my breath wondering if this roller coaster is about to crest on another hill.

"And you'd stay here, digging up the past?"

"I'd stay here," I admit as Adeline stirs against my shoulder.

"Debin?" she asks in a whisper.

149

"Hey kiddo, we need to pack up our stuff and go for a ride."

"I misted you," she says as she nuzzles into me for a moment.

Rebecca rubs her daughter's back and Adeline falls from my arms to hers.

"Come on, baby," Rebecca whispers as she kisses her daughter's ticklish ear. "We're going back to Clover with Devin."

Chapter Seven

Rebecca

I can't figure out if I'm immensely strong or pathetically weak. Adeline has drifted back to her nap in the back seat of Devin's car and it gives us an excuse to be quiet. It's a blessing because I have nothing productive to say. I've run through a few cutting digs I could throw his way, a few snarky comments. Since the moment I saw him at the bar a few days ago, I keep telling myself to stop falling. I need to stop sinking into this man like he's an old warm coat I'm slipping on. He's quicksand. Maybe he doesn't mean to be, maybe he doesn't want to be, but he is. And just like the real thing, the more I move and fight it, the faster I'm getting sucked into it.

With other men in my life I've known fear. I've worried about what they might do to me. How they might hurt me. With Devin I'm not scared of what he will do, I'm scared of what he can't do. I don't think he'll ever set out to hurt Adeline or me, but I can easily see us being left in his wake.

Even now his damn cologne is filling the car and calling to me. His hand, resting on the center console, keeps begging to have my fingers laced through it. From the corner of my eye I watch the line of his jaw tighten as though he, too, is biting back words he'd like to say. I wonder how much that crisp green designer shirt cost him? Did he buy it off the rack or was it tailored to hug his toned biceps so perfectly?

I pray no one asks me why I decided to come back with him. I believe he was genuine in his offer to fly Adeline and me anywhere in the world and to provide for us. I could go to Paris and paint. I could go to California and walk the beach, Adeline filling her pockets with seashells. The possibilities are endless, but none of that pull seems stronger than the undertow of Devin. It's like he's a train, barreling down the tracks, recklessly speeding with no regard for the people around him. I have this ridiculous notion that I'm strong enough to stop him. It's more likely I'll just get run over with everyone else.

We pull up to Nick Topley's house and I feel a wave of nerves roll through me. I try to avoid any interaction with people from high school. In a small place like Clover you tend to see each other around everywhere, but I always make it a point to keep my conversations quick and not too personal. Hanging out at Jeannie and Nick's house will probably make that impossible. They'll ask how I'm doing, even though the grapevine will have already given them their answer.

I hear Adeline stirring in the backseat as Devin turns off the car engine. "We's home?" she asks, her face full of sleep lines and drool.

I turn and pat her leg gently. "We're going to visit some friends. They have two little boys that you'll be able to play with. Doesn't that sound fun?" She shrugs her shoulder and wipes the sleep out of her eyes.

"I'm glad you two came with me," Devin says as he steps out of the car and works on unbuckling Adeline from the car seat. "I didn't think you were going to."

"I'm not sure why we did. I haven't seen Nick or Jeannie in years. I'm imagining this is going to be pretty awkward. Not to mention I still have no clue what you . . . what we . . . ." I trail off, knowing the timing of this conversation won't work.

"I know," Devin says simply. He lifts Adeline in his arms and heads for the door. We stand in front of it waiting for it to open and I feel his soft yet powerful hand settle on the small of my back. Part of me wants to plead my case for the ticket to Paris; the other part of me looks over at the man holding my daughter in his arms. She's nestled there, his forearm hooked behind her knees and her hand tugging at the collar of his shirt.

His low, gravelly voice sounds apologetic. "I need you here." His half smile is enough to tip the scales and I feel myself forgetting all the warnings I've been giving myself. He's caught me again, and in this moment I'm a willing captive.

Chapter Eight

<u>Click</u>

I don't back down from a challenge. I've served three tours in Iraq and one in Afghanistan as Marine Corp Recon. My men and I acted as elite forward-operating troops who were the "eyes and ears" of our respective battalion. We gathered intelligence and I led clandestine, unconventional attacks against an enemy. Years of that type of work have made me resilient and, at times, recklessly fearless. Yet as I face my latest mission, I feel wholly unprepared.

I shouldn't. On top of my years in the Marines I have other things that helped make me the man I am today. I was raised in a town just like Clover by a large, overbearing Italian family who treated heartbreaks with lasagna and whose normal speaking voices would be considered a yell by the rest of the population. My mother is of Sicilian decent and my father was born in Milan. My parents had the type of marriage that, at first blush, you'd assume would never work, until you realized no one else would put up with either of them.

Every holiday was like a dance, moving between hostile arguments, limoncello-induced affection, and an obscene quantity of food. As the youngest and only boy of five children, I learned early that sometimes you just have to attend a tea party or be your sister's baby doll for the afternoon. I was, and still am, a sucker for the tears of my sisters. As a little boy it meant I did as they said, and as I got older it meant I made the men in their lives stay in line. I became the keeper of four hearts, and it was no easy task.

But all of that dulls in comparison to the undertaking before me. I'm a Marine, not a businessman. I'm a gun, not an olive branch. The town of Clover, North Carolina, has just been thrown a lifeline, and it's now my job to make sure they don't lose their grip on it.

I ask myself again, why did I agree to help? Orders are orders. I've already broken rank once with Devin, and I don't plan to do it again. On top of that, when you spend a long time watching a place get destroyed, like I did when I was deployed, the opportunity to be a part of something like this is tempting. I've seen neighborhoods leveled and schools destroyed. I've seen stunned people wandering around, picking up the pieces. I want to be part of rebuilding something: helping free it from tyranny and watching it thrive. Clover is my best chance at that right now.

Devin has instructed me to schmooze and sway this woman, Jordan Garcia, by any means necessary. Of course I'm assuming that doesn't include the interrogation techniques I've employed overseas. So I'll have to find another way.

I sit nervously across from the mayor and try to keep him on track. I interrupt him as he continues to explain the history of Clover to me. "Mayor, thanks for allowing us to hold the meeting at your office. Jordan, the project manager, should be here any moment."

"And you go by what name, again?"

"Everyone but my mom calls me Click, sir. It's a name I picked up over in Iraq."

"And your Christian name?"

I swallow hard and raise my chin up one more notch. "Vitorino Coglinaese," I choke out, silently cursing my parents.

"Well, okay then. Click it is. We don't have many I-talians here in Clover, but I know you to be a hard-working people. You've got quite a southern twang in that voice, where ya hail from?"

"I'm from Sturbridge, Tennessee, and yes, we stuck out like a sore thumb there. No other Italians in our town. My father's family had some old mob ties and he wasn't interested in living that lifestyle. No chance of that in Tennessee."

"Now, my other question is, do you really feel like you're up for this? I'll level with you—the job you've been given seems a little out of your league. That's a whole lot of responsibility, boy. The task of changing this deal falls on your shoulders. I don't know what Devin is off doing, but you'd think he'd make time for this meeting. What are you, about twenty-two?"

"Twenty-six, sir." I'm very accustomed to being underestimated. It's the baby face and the fact that I don't normally go around talking about where I've been or what I've done. I'm quiet, not because I lack confidence but because I've found it's the best way to know my opponent, to fade into the background and just listen. Being an underdog doesn't usually bother me, but this time, I might actually agree with the mayor.

"To be honest, sir, I wasn't expecting the opportunity. I was on a simple security assignment here and thought I would be on my way. Devin's made it clear, first and foremost, we need to convince Jordan Garcia that a landfill isn't right for this town."

"I've got a bottle of Jack Daniels in my drawer that might convince him." His words are interrupted by a knock on the frame of the open office door.

There stands a woman with the longest legs I have ever seen. She's wearing a tailored white button-up blouse tucked into dark brown pants, looking perfectly polished. Her belt matches her shoes. Her outfit looks like it was built around her, fitting every curve with precision. Her nails are painted with shiny rose polish, the same as the hue on her plump lips. Her hair is a luscious black with a beautiful wave to it, and her skin is bright and smooth. She looks exotic, with her long lashes and deep brown eyes. I realize I'm staring, just waiting to hear if her voice is as angelic as her body.

"Excuse me," she says, taking a step into the office.

Kilroy looks slightly annoyed to be interrupted in the middle of our conversation and before such an important meeting. "Darlin', you must be here to inquire about the coffee girl job. Martha out front can get you an application." He barely spares her a glance as he speaks.

"Oh, son of a bitch, please tell me this town isn't so antediluvian that you still have a job you refer to as *coffee girl*." The woman plants her hands on her high hips and narrows her eyes.

I want to jump in, to warn Kilroy that this is who we are meeting with, realizing now that he had wrongly assumed Jordan would be a man. But he cuts in before I can.

"Well," Kilroy shoots back, now looking fully annoyed, likely because he doesn't know what antediluvian means, "you look like a girl and you'd be pouring coffee."

The grin on her face grows wide and victorious. "If we apply that logic, then you'd be the *office swine*."

"I have to tell you girl, if you are angling for the coffee job, you've burned a bridge here." Kilroy's red face combined with the woman's funny retort makes me nearly burst out laughing until I remember my role here. Schmoozing. This is not schmoozing.

"Whatever will I do with my life now?" She walks the rest of the way into the office and sits in the chair next to me. "I'm Jordan Garcia, Project Manager from Krylon Waste Management. I'm here practically against my will because I drew the short straw. In a matter of three minutes you've proven the point I was trying to make before I left New York. Our company should stay the hell out of these Podunk southern towns. So let me make sure I have this right—you're the old-boys-club mayor I'm going to have to put up with." She turns toward me as I straighten my back slightly, readying for a direct hit. "And you are the ridiculously underqualified soldier with no business background I'm meeting with?"

"You're a woman," Kilroy groans, his mistake clearly hitting him.

"Is that the only prerequisite for becoming the mayor in this town? Being aware of obvious facts? Because I've heard in Boston there's a chimp using sign language that might give you a run for your money next term."

The mayor's jaw falls open. I watch as he lounges back in his chair and starts to laugh. At first it's a low chuckle, but it erupts into a frenzied bark. "Ooo, girlie, I'm gonna like working with you. Garcia right? You're like a Spanish hot tamale." He points at her accusingly. "You're a hoot."

"That's me." Jordan rolls her eyes and turns her attention to me, and I know I can pass for a deer in the headlights at the moment. "What are you, like twelve?" she asks, while looking me up and down.

158

"Twenty-six, ma'am," I reply dutifully for the second time in ten minutes.

"Oh, hell no." She waves her finger in my face and I get a nose full of her flowery perfume. "You can call me a bitch, you can call me a pain in the ass, but if the word ma'am ever crosses your lips in my direction again, I'll castrate you with a dull knife. Call me Jordan." She huffs out a breath of frustration and pulls her long hair into a quick bun, ready to get down to business.

"I feel like maybe we all got off on the wrong foot. Jordan, I'm Click, and I've been appointed by Devin to be your contact here in Clover. As you mentioned, I don't have the most experience, but I'm a hard worker and a fast learner."

"I'm not calling you that," she replies curtly. "Click is not a name."

"You don't want to know his Christian name, it's a mouthful. Click is easier, trust me," the mayor interjects.

"I can assure you I *don't* trust you. But fine, if you insist on being called something so ridiculous I'll concede, but only because I don't want this meeting lasting longer than it needs to." She pulls a large stack of papers from her briefcase and places them forcefully on the desk. "Here's where we start. Click," she hesitates on his name and shakes her head, "I'll see the land, evaluate the town, and report back to my boss. Then I'll bring in the security team. These men have all been vetted thoroughly. They have no ties to this area and no skin in the game. They range from former military to retired police officers. They need to be given a schedule and duties, and then they need to get their boots on the ground. Let the town see them, meet them. If I understand correctly, they are replacing a group of narcissistic, power-hungry bastards. Another pitfall of doing business in the south."

"Yes, m—," I nearly say the word before I'm met with a glare from Jordan that scares the hell out of me. "Yes, Jordan. I agree. There is one thing I'd like to discuss first about the construction and facility."

"Yes, Clink?" She smirks at me.

"First, it's Click. I think a woman who tosses around the word antediluvian can surely get a name right. Second, now that Mr. Sutton has spent some time down here in Clover, he believes a different line of business would be a better fit for the town." I get the words out just as I practiced, but Jordan is already shaking her head.

"No one wants a landfill in their town. But they need to go somewhere. That's the deal we've brokered, and that's what we're putting in Clover." She slips her designer glasses on and begins reading over a document.

I've told myself I'm not trained for this, but maybe I'm not giving myself enough credit. If Jordan were an enemy combatant whom I needed to win over, what would I do? I would learn her weaknesses, what drives her. I'd do recon.

"Mr. Sutton assumed that would be your response. You have a reputation for being inflexible." I've stepped out onto thin ice; now I have to see if it will hold my weight.

"I am certainly not inflexible." She snaps her head in my direction and I know I've gotten her attention. "My job is to make my company money. You've got no coal here; you've got no railroad tracks. That limits your options. That doesn't make me inflexible; it means I have a brain in my head. I'm sure you're not used to that with your womenfolk down here. What I think you are both missing is that I don't need a damn thing from you. I'm here to evaluate the land, get a handle on the town, and meet with contractors who will start the work. The town voted to approve the plan. Once I file these papers with my office, there is no turning back. The majority of the land we're buying is owned by the town and we've already acquired it by the deal getting voted in. Any resident of Clover who doesn't sell can be worked around. You have no cards to play." She winks at the mayor.

"You're right, and I'm not asking you to apply business logic to this, I'm asking you to do me a favor and humor me." I soften my eyes and put on the most pathetic expression I can muster. "You have other lines of business in your company, right? Recycling, hauling? Mr. Sutton believes either of those could be a good fit for Clover."

"Well, little boy, when your daddy gets home and he's ready to talk, why don't you have him give me a call." She stands up and brushes the wrinkles off her blouse as if she's trying to remove the smell of Clover from her designer clothes.

"Jordan." I deepen my voice and it stops her in her tracks. "You're not going to bully your way through this deal. This is the farthest south your company has ventured. I grew up in a town just like this. I'm telling you right now, you won't get anywhere unless you get the buy-in from the people of Clover. You might have your contracts and your documents, but that all stacks up to a heap of hot cow shit in a place like this. Now, the mayor and I can help you there. All we're asking is that you *consider* altering the deal. Come meet people, come see this place, and then you tell me you still want to dump trash here."

I've looked her over, and I've pulled in every ounce of training I have to try to piece together what will work with her. I think about everything I've learned from my sisters, some of the most vocal and judgmental people that ever lived. She's wearing all designer clothes, shoes, and glasses. It's her shield, her status. She admitted she knew she was coming to small town USA, yet she didn't alter her attire to accommodate the conditions. Her three-inch heels tell me she's never walked on a rocky dirt road. She's never been to the South. She doesn't know what people are like down here, the charm of it all. She's working off stereotypes and assumptions. She's used to the fast-paced, cold-hearted hustle and bustle of the city.

The necklace she's wearing has four birthstones. I doubt she has kids because there's nothing maternal about her, but whoever they represent mean something to her. The chain is worn down a bit. She has flashy everything, except this. It tells me she is connected to someone, somewhere.

That's how she looks, but what does how she acts tell me? She's a woman with a man's name in a man's world. She overcompensates and fights back. This isn't the first time someone thought she was *the coffee girl*, and it likely wouldn't be the last. Strong-arming her would only backfire. Threatening wouldn't work either. The only way to get Jordan to see Clover deserves better than trash is to show her why. She's never experienced what the South has to offer, so I can be her guide. I need to make her fall in love with this place. From everything I've heard about Clover so far, I'm sure I'll have my work cut out for me. But, as I saw overseas, even the most desolate and destroyed places usually had something redeeming about them.

"What exactly are you proposing, a meet and greet? Some kind of honky-tonk square dancing party where you bring all your kinfolk?"

"Girl, you don't square dance at a honky-tonk." I look over and, though I wish he isn't, the mayor is dead serious. I stand and half smile at Jordan. I can feel myself doing this, trying to make her swoon with my casual confidence, and I feel like an idiot. I can't be a businessman, but my mom raised me to be a down-home southern gentleman and that might just be what will work on Jordan Garcia.

"Let me walk you down to your car," I say as I take her briefcase from her hand. She narrows her eyes at me as she tries to snatch it back. "I'm not carrying it because you can't, I'm carrying it because you shouldn't have to." This is my test, telling me if I'm on the right track. She searches my face, hesitates, and then rolls her eyes dramatically. What she doesn't do is take her briefcase back or tell me to go to hell. I might be on to something.

Chapter Nine

Click

"Are you sure you don't want to change your clothes, Jordan? The last few stops were pretty tame, but a lot of the land where the landfill will be is rough fields and woods. If you really want to see it, you'll have a tough time in those high heels." I've pulled open Jordan's car door for her again and she finally looks like she's getting comfortable with it, or at least like she will tolerate it.

After we left the mayor's office, Jordan sat impatiently in my car while I stood outside and made a hasty call to Nick, begging him to tell me where I should take Jordan to show her the gems of Clover. There had to be people here who'd make her realize this place was worth saving. He suggested we stop over to see Miss Trivet at her seamstress store. There we found a small woman with trembling hands and a sunny disposition. With a sweet singsong voice, she told Jordan how she made clothes out of scraps of fabric left from special orders. She pieced them together and donated them to the kids of Clover who couldn't afford new ones. Jordan was cordial but seemed completely unaffected by the selfless woman with the gap-toothed smile. When Jordan excused herself to freshen up in the ladies' room I used the opportunity to get my next lead from Miss Trivet.

She pointed me in the direction of Dr. Charles Blithe, who sets up a free clinic in his office once a week for anyone who didn't have health insurance. His waiting room was overflowing with hacking coughs and groaning patients. He spared a few minutes to meet with us and filled us in about the flu that was making its way through town. He described how living in poverty increases susceptibility to illness. Many of the people of Clover were without the means to buy healthy foods, and with no health insurance, they're less likely to seek out preventative medical care. To make matters worse, it was common for families to cohabitate to share costs of living, but this overcrowding meant illnesses spread like wildfire. He told us about little Katherine Elizabeth, the six-year-old girl he'd recently sent to the hospital in the next town over. Her cough had progressed to pneumonia. Her parents had been reluctant to bring her in, afraid she needed more in-depth care and they'd have no way to pay for it. The ambulance ride alone was enough to put them into bankruptcy.

Again I watched as Jordan politely listened, taking it all in, but never seeming to let it reach her heart. This woman had ice running through her veins. Sick kids, kids who can't buy clothes . . . nothing fazed her.

As we visited these places, driving the quiet roads of Clover, I wondered what was going through her mind. The houses were in need of repair. There were no pristinely landscaped yards or flashy cars in the driveways. Yet, she spent most of her time staring at the screen on her phone, the chirp of incoming emails an incessant reminder of the challenge I had ahead of me.

I mustered up every ounce of chivalry I had all while trying not to look completely transparent. It wasn't that big of a stretch, considering I'm generally a good guy. I'd always treated women with respect. When I was younger it was because I didn't want to catch the flat end of my mother's wooden spoon. The older I became, the more I saw the importance of being a gentleman. It was a habit that turned into a part of my character, probably just as my mother had planned.

I opened her car door each time, though she practically raced me to it. When we headed down the sidewalk toward Dr. Blithe's office, I casually switched spots with her, gently moving her away from the street. I introduced her, I flattered her, and I offered her every accommodation I could. Whenever we entered a building, I pulled the door open and gave her the *after you* gesture. When she stood to excuse herself to freshen up at Miss Trivet's seamstress shop I stood as well, doing the same when she rejoined us at the lopsided table we were chatting around. In reality, this wasn't so different from what I would have done regardless of my need to sway her.

She breaks the silence in the car as we head to our next destination with a huffy accusation. "I see what you're doing here, Click and you're wasting our time. You're not going to charm me into anything. You can stop laying it on so thick."

"Is that what you think I'm doing?"

"I'm plenty capable of opening my own doors and I'm a grown-up, so I think I can walk safely by the side of the road without aimlessly falling into traffic. It's insulting."

"I don't open the door because you're incapable. My mother told me you open the door for a woman because she deserves to make an entrance. I don't walk closest to the traffic because I'm afraid you'll swoon or get so distracted you'll walk into the street. I do it because God forbid a car loses control, I'd want you to be safe. None of this is a reflection on your competence; it's a testament to your worth. I believe women deserve to be treated special, because they are. I can't put into words what the women in my life have done to shape me. I think that alone makes you all worth a little more."

For the first time since I met Jordan, I've rendered her speechless. Her slightly parted lips and raised eyebrows make me realize I'm telling her something she hasn't heard before.

I watch her searching her mind for a rebuttal, but I haven't left her anywhere to go. "It's annoying," she says, reaching into her bag for some lip gloss. She flips down the mirror in the visor and I watch her roll the fruity smelling glaze across her plump lips. "I get it, Click. This really is a nice town, down on its luck, full of people all trying to pull themselves up by their bootstraps." She says all this with a mockingly fake southern accent.

"I'm just trying to show you that Clover is already struggling. They could stand to catch a break, and you could be the one to give it to them."

"That's the thing about business, Click, there can't be any heartstrings to pull at. Especially for a woman. It's what everyone in my office is waiting for. They want me to screw this up, and going back to them telling them about Miss Trivet and Dr. Blithe will prove them right. *Women are too emotional for business. Women don't belong at this level.* I fight against that every day, and you're asking me to play right into it."

"I'm just asking you to think about these people before you run off and start dumping trash here. You know as well as I do that will be the end of Clover. There won't be anything here for these folks to take pride in, nothing to draw people here. Even if it does come with some jobs, it won't be enough. And what happens when the environmental consequences kick in?"

She reaches for the nob on the radio and turns up the country song just loud enough to keep me from pressing her more. "Where are we going now?" she asks, folding her arms across her chest like a defiant prisoner.

"We're going to visit Timlin Smith. And again, I think you're going to need to change your clothes. Those heels aren't going to make it across his yard, let alone the land he's taking us out to see."

"These are my clothes," she says, pulling her coat closed. "I didn't pack any other shoes and this is as *casual* as I get. I can get around just fine, trust me. More importantly, why are we evaluating land as the sun goes down? We're not even going to be able to see anything."

"Afraid of the dark?" I ask, raising an eyebrow at her.

"Shut up," she says rolling her eyes.

We drive the winding roads leading to Timlin's quaint country ranch. On the side of the house is a carriage hooked up to a regal looking horse standing at attention in front of it. I watch Jordan from the corner of my eye, trying to make sure she doesn't see me staring. No matter how hard she seems to be fighting it, the site of the carriage has her face lit like a child's on Christmas morning.

"What is that?" she asks, leaning closer to the dashboard, trying to get a better look.

"I told you we're going to check out some land. Timlin offered us a carriage ride. I thought it might be a nice way to see how peaceful things are here." The one thing about this approach I'm taking with Jordan is that I've had to shed my normal stoic and *man of few words* qualities. It's odd being this chatty, but it's also nice to actually socialize a little.

She groans, trying to be annoyed with me, but she's already out of the car and walking straight for the horse. I have to jog to catch up with her, and I watch as she timidly pats the nose of the beautiful beast. A puff of hot air blows from his nostrils and a grumbling neigh sends her jumping backward into me.

"Nothing to be afraid of." I look into her face and she shakes me off.

"I know." She slowly pats his nose again and I cover her hand with mine, guiding her over his mane and down his neck.

"Don't they have carriage rides in New York City?"

"They do. I've never taken one. I'm always too busy. It's nothing like this. The city is never quiet."

"You're about to hear a kind of peaceful you've never even imagined existed."

"I didn't grow up in the city, Click. I know what peaceful sounds like."

"I assumed you grew up there; where are you from?" The fact that she isn't from the city originally makes me think my plan may not work. My whole angle is to show her what this place has to offer, make her fall in love with its charm.

"Why, are you writing a book?" she snaps, returning to her blustery bravado as Timlin comes out to join us.

"Hi there, folks." His southern drawl is heavier than most and it's perfect for what I have planned tonight. He's dressed in overalls and zips his large winter coat up to his chin. "In the carriage you'll find some apple cider, a warm blanket and some of my wife's delicious Christmas cookies." He pulls a small stepstool down, and extends his hand to help Jordan up. "And under the seat you'll find a nip of Miss Coroline's blueberry moonshine. If you get real cold, that'll warm you up."

"I don't think any of that will be necessary. We're just hoping to get a look at the land and see what we're working with." Jordan settles herself on the cushioned seat so far over that there is no chance we'll even accidently brush up against each other.

"I don't bite," I tell her, pulling the blanket over myself, offering her the other half.

"I'm sure you do, soldier." She reluctantly takes the blanket, likely out of necessity as a chilling wind blows by.

"I let it slide the first time, but I'm a Marine, not a soldier."

"Whatever, all the same. Your bullets still kill people."

"It's not all the same," I cut back more defensively than I intend. "And I don't carry a gun because I enjoy it or because it makes me feel powerful. If I could be sure the other guy didn't have one, I'd be happy to leave mine at home."

"You're armed right now?" She looks me over, wondering where my gun might be.

"Yes."

"Barbaric. I'll never understand what makes a soldier, or Marine, or *whatever* tick. It takes a special kind of messed-up person to be able to go and kill someone just because he's told to."

I've heard plenty of this in my life, or variations of it. I don't engage in political conversations about war. Why we're there, who's right or who's wrong. It's not because I don't have an opinion, it's because it doesn't change my job there. The only thing that makes me engage Jordan on the topic is believing there has to be a reason why she feels this way and that could be the key to connecting with her. That's what I need to do in order to convince her to even consider changing the landfill.

"What is it? You've got some hang up about the war, about the military. Let me guess, your political views have you towing that line? Or did you lose someone over there? A cousin, a brother? Because, trust me, *that* I can understand. I lost people over there, too."

"Don't try to understand me. This is something you'll never get. Just mind your own business and let's get on with this."

"I'm sorry, Jordan. I didn't mean to upset you. It's a beautiful night, let's just try to enjoy it."

"No, let's focus on the reason we came here."

The absolutely picturesque and placid woods make me a little homesick. The rhythmic thumping of the horses' hooves and the warm light of the lanterns, swaying from the sides of the carriage, are mesmerizing. "You can resist my charm, you can even resist the absolutely beautiful surroundings right now, but you cannot resist these cookies." I pass them over and she shoos them away. "A peace offering." I push them back toward her once more and she takes one.

"Do you know how long it's been since I've eaten a carb?" She giggles with her mouth full. She reaches over for another cookie and I pour her some cider to wash it down.

"Not going to try to liquor me up with the moonshine and get me to change my mind or maybe get a little handsy?"

"I'm not that guy." Though I have to admit if the opportunity arose I'd be hard-pressed to not indulge in a woman as good-looking as Jordan. She's the kind of beautiful that you find yourself staring at, examining her features to try to understand how so many perfect things could come together.

"Sure," she huffs as she reaches for a third cookie. "Every guy is *that guy*. But you're smart not to try it with me. You'd lose a limb."

We ride in silence, taking in the surrounding land, spotting deer, and hearing owls hoot. Suddenly the carriage lurches to an abrupt stop and Jordan's cider goes tumbling in to her lap. "Hot," she shouts as she jumps to a standing position. I wipe at the front of her pants, dangerously high on her thigh trying to clean up some of the hot drink.

"What's going on Timlin?" I ask as Jordan slaps my hands away. "Why did we stop?"

"Tracks. Two, maybe three, off-road vehicles. No one comes this far into my property. There's a light up ahead. Someone's out here."

I pull Jordan's arm and yank her back to her seat. "Turn the carriage around and take her back to your house. I'll check it out and catch up with you in a little while"

"We're at least three miles from the house, Click, we can't just leave you here," Jordan protests, still trying to cool her legs.

"I run three miles every morning before your eyes even crack open. I'll be fine."

I jump out of the side of the carriage and draw my gun. "Do you really think that's necessary?" Jordan asks as she jumps down beside me.

172

"What are you doing? Get back in the carriage."

"No, my company is the one building on this land. It's my job to know what's going on out here."

I turn to convince her one more time when I hear the familiar pop of a gunshot. The wood of the carriage splinters behind her head and I instinctually tackle her to the ground. My full weight comes down on her and I hear her yelp in pain under me. "Are you hit?" I ask, wondering if the shot might have gotten her.

"No, but I think you just popped my shoulder out of the damn socket," she says through gritted teeth. "Get off me, I'm in the mud. These pants cost a fortune."

I hear another pop as the carriage moves jerkily back and forth next to us. Timlin crouches near the harness as he calls quietly to us. "The horse is spooked. I'm going to cut him loose so we can take cover behind the carriage before he runs off with it and we're left out in the open." I nod my agreement and pull my weight off Jordan, yanking her behind the carriage.

"What the hell is going on? Did someone just shoot at us?"

"Yes," I say flatly as I hear the hooves of the large horse running off while Timlin joins us behind the now stilled carriage. "Are you armed?" I ask. As I see Timlin cocking his shotgun and peering around the side of carriage, I have my answer.

"I'm retired Army and I live down South, of course I'm armed."

"Stay here with her. I'm going to try to flush them out. If I go down, you two take off into the woods and don't stop until you hit the house."

"Go down? Like get shot?" Jordan is shaking now, and I can feel her nails digging through my jacket into my forearm.

"You're going to be fine. I promise." I pry her hand off my arm and slowly make my way toward where the light had been, but all is dim. I hear the roar of engines and the slamming of car doors. Tires kick up rocks as the trucks pull away. Two more shots sail over my head, and I lift my weapon to fire back. A red pickup truck is barreling away. I steady my hand and, with the precision I've mastered over the years, shoot out the left rear tire followed quickly by the back window. I'm not looking to kill anyone, even though I could take out the driver easily. If I never kill anyone again in my life I'd be just fine with that. All I want to do is have them running scared, in the opposite direction of Jordan. And I've accomplished that.

When the night falls silent around me, the rumble of the engines gone, I head quietly back toward Timlin and Jordan.

"It's me," I say, making sure Timlin isn't too trigger-happy. "It's all clear. You two okay?"

"We're good," Timlin says, getting to his feet and walking toward me. "You get any of the bastards?"

"I shot up their truck as they left. I'm going to scope out the area they were in, see what they were up to." I round the other side of the carriage and kneel next to Jordan who is sitting stone-faced, staring into the woods.

"They're gone," I say, reaching my hand down to help her up, but she doesn't take it. "I know your clothes are ruined. I'm sorry about that."

She shakes her head, and rubs at her shoulder. "I think it might be dislocated," she says through a grunt of pain.

"I'm sorry about that, too. I saw the bullet hit the carriage behind you and I just reacted. We landed pretty hard. I'll take you back to town and get a doctor for you."

"I want to see what they were doing over there," she insists as she stands, shaking off my assistance.

"I'll check it out while you get settled back into the carriage. Timlin can help you. Then he'll track down his horse." My hand is on the small of her back, and it feels so natural to me to be touching her. So comfortable.

"I'm going to see," she insists, cradling one arm with the other. She strides away from me with her head high.

We walk across the rocky earth and I watch her ankles bending and turning, her high heels not made for this. I try to pull back all the branches of the overgrown woods long enough to let Jordan safely pass through them. I pull out my flashlight and point it down at her feet, showing her where the dangerous holes and unexpected rocks are.

"Well aren't you prepared, just like a good little Boy Scout?" She huffs and continues to try to navigate the rocky terrain in her flashy shoes.

"We're coming up on the clearing," I say as I hold a branch high and put my hand on Jordan's head to make sure she passes under it safely.

She takes a few steps forward and then stops abruptly. "Don't move," she demands, throwing her uninjured arm across my stomach as I try to pass her.

"That barrel . . . it's full of dioxin. That's what the plaque on the side means. It's highly toxic and burns the skin if you touch it. Breathing it in isn't much better. Don't go any closer."

"What the hell is that doing out here?" Timlin asks, sidling up to us.

"It was likely Hoyle's men, but why?"

"Even for a dump, the EPA is still heavily involved. I can't imagine how anyone could get ahold of it, but if this poison is all over the place, they won't let us move forward until it's cleaned up. My company would stand to lose a lot of money in the process."

"That bastard," Timlin groans and lets out a whistle attempting to call his horse. "He was real spooked, I might not be able to get him back tonight. We need to start walking."

"You can't walk the whole way back in those shoes. You're hurt. I can carry you," I say quietly to Jordan, not wanting to put her on the spot.

"That'll be a cold day in hell," she snaps, blowing past me.

She is a stubborn, hotheaded woman. And damn if that doesn't turn me on like crazy.

Chapter Ten

Devin

"Jeannie, is there any chance you have room for two more for dinner?"

"Of course, Devin, we always have room for a couple more here. That's why I make so much food. Just in case." She disappears into the kitchen, and I wave Nick over. Rebecca, knowing that last phone call must have meant something was up, comes my way, too.

"I just got word from Click that he and Jordan ran in to some trouble over on Timlin's land. Apparently they were surveying it and saw some trespassers. They exchanged some gunfire and found some toxic chemicals. Looks like Hoyle is trying to poison the land to slow the process. It could be a real nightmare."

"Are they okay?" Rebecca asks, making sure by her tone that I realize that should be the most important thing.

"I think Jordan is shaken up and Click mentioned her shoulder might be hurt. I told him Jeannie is a nurse and could check her out. I hope that's all right."

"No problem. If it's something real bad we'll bring the doctor up here. I'm going to go call this in, let my superiors know what's happening. We've got marshals in the area, but not enough to cover this much ground. That's where your security team was supposed to come in."

"They will, but Jordan needs to give her company the final go ahead before *we* have the go ahead to get them here. Which means she needs to find an alternative to the landfill, and soon."

"I don't get why you haven't met with her? Shouldn't you be trying to force her hand?" Rebecca asks, and I can feel the prickliness in her voice.

"Word has it Jordan isn't the type of person who reacts well to demands. I think a good guy like Click will have a better chance at swaying her."

"You're not a good guy?" Her brows knit together and I can tell she's goading me on. We haven't finished our conversation, she doesn't have any answers, and she's upset. I've brought it on myself, but it doesn't make seeing her hurting any easier.

"Good is such a moving target." I try to busy myself, not wanting to look her in the eye. I look down at my phone instead, scrolling through old messages.

"That's the spirit." She smirks back at me and laughs. Then she turns to watch the kids bounce through the house as Jeannie makes room for Click and Jordan at the table.

The knock on the door is met with a level of tension that speaks volumes about the nerves running through everyone.

"It's me," Click's voice calls through the door, and instantly shoulders all begin to relax.

Nick pulls the door open and Click steps in, followed closely by the knockout Hispanic woman I've heard so much about. I look over at her mud-splattered clothes, the mess of a knot her hair is in, and the way she is hunching to accommodate her sore shoulder. This is not the schmoozing I've instructed Click to do.

"Oh my word," Jeannie shouts, charging toward Jordan, who is visibly uncomfortable with the well-meaning physical contact. "You are a mess, you poor thing. Come on upstairs with me and I'll get you cleaned up and check out that arm. Nick, get me a big glass of moonshine. It looks like I'm going to need to set that shoulder and you'll want a little something to dull the pain."

"Right behind you, hon. Will you guys keep an eye on the kids?" he asks as he retrieves a large mason jar and heads up the stairs.

"I said to charm her, not almost get her killed," I say, shoving Click's shoulder back jokingly. "You okay?"

"Fine, but I think she might be in shock. She hasn't said a word since we started the three mile walk back to Timlin's house."

"Poor thing," Rebecca sighs, walking over to the kids who are trying to carry every toy they own up the stairs at one time.

Click leans in closer to me as he speaks, "I see you have Rebecca back here. I guess that's a good sign. Is she going to help you get the medical examiner's records?"

"No. She said she doesn't want any part of it. She's just back here because Nick got a tip that Hoyle found out where she was. We came here to regroup. How about you? Did you make any progress? I'm pissing Rebecca off for lots of other reasons. I can't let this landfill be another obstacle. I need that win. Not to mention the more time I spend here with Nick the more he keeps pressing me for another option."

"She's dug in pretty deep with not wanting to consider anything else. I felt like I was making a little progress, taking her around town, introducing her to all the people, trying to make her see the charm in all of it. The carriage ride was supposed to help with that, but, needless to say, I'm not sure how she's feeling now."

"Well you have your orders, so find out what she's feeling. Get her to change the deal. We need that security team here."

Headlights flash through the large front window and draw our attention. "You guys expecting more company?" he asks, moving toward the side of the window to stealthily look out.

"No," I say, crossing the room and shuffling Rebecca and the kids aside. "Nick," I call up the stairs, "someone just pulled in."

Click draws his weapon and squints to get a better look at the approaching guest. "It's a man, six foot three maybe, wearing a suit, short blond hair, dorky kind of glasses."

"Luke?" I make my way to the window and shake my head at the sight of him. I pull the door open and wave for Click to lower his weapon. "What the hell are you doing here?" I ask, extending my hand to him.

"I flew in this afternoon. I'm not taking the chance that you aren't coming back on Friday to sell this damn company. Even if I have to help you sort this stuff out myself." He steps in and looks stunned to see Nick storming down the stairs with a shotgun in his hands.

"It's okay, Nick, he's my business partner from New York."

"And how the hell did he know you were at my house?" Nick asks, lowering his weapon but not softening his tone.

"I checked in at the Winston and asked the girl at the front desk. She didn't know, but a guy sitting in the lobby told me I could find you here. He said to let you know he said hello. His name is Pete."

"Son of a bitch." Nick passes in front of the window and peeks outside, surveying the front yard for a sign of another car. "He's one of Hoyle's men, and he was sending us a message. I'm not waiting until morning. I'm driving my wife and kids out of here tonight."

A howling scream comes down from upstairs and echoes against the walls. It is Jordan, likely having her shoulder set, but I can tell the shotguns and screaming are unnerving Luke.

"What the hell is going on here?" he asks, giving me a look like we should run.

"Jordan had an accident earlier today. A run-in with Hoyle's men who were dumping toxic waste on the land for our deal. He's sending us a message. She's upstairs with Nick's wife getting her shoulder set."

"Jordan Garcia? The project manager is upstairs having her shoulder set? Toxic waste? Sending messages? What the fu—" Luke locks eyes with Rebecca who's maternal glare could freeze someone in their tracks. "I mean, what the heck?"

"I know. We're going to take care of it. I'm still selling the company on Friday." Luke slips out of his coat and Rebecca extends a hand to take it from him. "Thank you," he says, surveying the room and nodding his head.

"You can save the lecture," I growl, and then introduce him to everyone in the room. Hands are shaking and greetings are passing between all and the only thing I can think is how strange it is to see Luke out of the city. I'm surprised he came.

"No lecture from me. As a matter of fact, it sounds exciting. I've been sitting behind a desk too long. I could use some action. How can I help?"

181

Nick eyes Luke and warns, "You can start by being more careful who you talk to. I'm going to get Jeannie and the kids packed up. They're leaving after dinner."

Chapter Eleven

Click

When I'm not sure what to say, I tend to find something to do instead. I'm stoking the fire I just built in the pit behind Nick's house. Dinner was one of the best meals I've had since I left home. Jeannie's hospitality is reminiscent of my mother's, and I have to fight off the memories of home.

If I weren't worried that I might have permanently scarred Jordan, I'd be thinking that southern meal might be a good ploy to win her over. She barely touched her food.

When I saw her come down the stairs wearing one of Jeannie's cotton shirts and a pair of jeans, I had to do a double take. I thought the formfitting business clothes were the sexiest thing I'd ever see her in. But somehow she makes the thin fabric of the pale blue T-shirt equally as enticing. Her hair is wet, brushed out straight, and her makeup is all washed away. She looks gorgeous, a natural beauty.

Everyone has stepped out into the backyard now and is discussing the trip Nick has in front of him. It will be a five-hour drive each way, but he insists he'll drive his wife and kids himself.

I listen as Nick pulls Rebecca aside. "I think you and Adeline should come too. You'll be safe there and she'll have a ball with the kids. With any luck it will only be a couple days while we get things settled here. Hoyle is bound to screw up and find himself and his men behind bars."

"I need to stay here. I think Devin needs someone to keep reminding him not to lose himself in all this. If I go, I'm afraid of what may happen to him. "

"I can't argue with you there. When push comes to shove, I imagine you're going to be the only person who can reason with him. What about just Adeline going? Jeannie would be happy to take care of her."

Rebecca runs her hands through her hair. She looks torn and tired, and I feel terrible for her. "I think that will be best," she says, choking back some tears. "Our bags are still in Devin's trunk. I'll get her things together."

They disappear back into the house and I look up to realize Jordan is watching the same scene, and she looks shaken by it all.

"You good?" I ask, sidling up to her and looking down at her stoic face.

"I'm ready to get back to the hotel." She's not looking at me. She's staring into the fire, lost in the crackling, jumping orange flames.

"Everyone's going to hang out here I think. Splitting up isn't usually a good idea when—"

She cuts into my words. "When people are shooting at you?"

"I'm sorry that happened today. I shouldn't have taken you there tonight after the sun had set. I wasn't thinking about the danger."

"I guess that contradicts my *you don't need a gun* theory."

"Like I said, if I was sure the other guy didn't have one, I'd gladly give it up."

"They're sending the kids away? They think that's best?"

184

"Don't you?" I ask as I take a seat on the bench by the fire. She surprises me by sitting down next to me, closer this time than in the carriage. Closer by her choice, and I'm happy for that.

"I think if it's dangerous enough to send your children away, you should leave, too. I wish my father had."

"Your father?" I ask, realizing she wasn't just a spectator watching Rebecca decide to let her daughter go, she was lost in her own memory.

"Never mind. It's the moonshine talking. My shoulder hurts like a bitch and I took a few too many sips I think."

"Tell me," I plead, touching her leg gently. I'm not near as worried about how this could help me connect with her then eventually sway her. I just want to know what can be causing that much hurt on her face.

She pulls in a deep breath and kicks her head back. I watch as she stares up at the stars. "You can't really see them in the city, all the stars. It's like they drift to the quiet places instead. Maybe they don't like all the noise and commotion." She shivers and brings her hands to her mouth, blowing her warm breath on them. I slip out of my coat and, without a word, drape it over her shoulders. She opens her mouth to protest, but seems to change her mind as she pulls my coat closed around her. "And what is this one, giving your coat to a woman? What's the reasoning behind that?"

"Nothing special, you looked cold."

"Do you put everyone else's comfort before yours all the time? That must be exhausting. Fighting everyone's wars, giving the coat off your back. Don't you ever just think of yourself?"

185

"No, I try not to put myself first too often."

"Why not? Aren't you afraid to end up with nothing?"

"If enough people out there act the way I'm acting, then someone will give me a coat when I need it."

"And what if there aren't enough of those people in the world? What if it doesn't come back around?"

"Then at least I got to see you in my coat. You look good in it." I can feel my cheeks heat up as I say this, and I'm nervous for her reaction. Everything I've seen from her so far tells me I should expect an angry outburst. Instead, she looks resigned. She nods her head and starts to open up to me.

"You think I'm Spanish right? I mean my last name is Garcia; I even have that little Columbian accent every now and then when I talk. Dark hair, dark skin, dark eyes. It's what he wanted people to think."

"I assumed you were," I say when she seems lost again, deciding if she'll go any further.

"You asked me if I lost someone over there. If that is why I disagree with the war, with what you did, what you stand for. The answer is, I lost *dozens of people* over there."

"Dozens," I say skeptically, not understanding what she means.

"I was born in the Tolakar Province in Afghanistan, on the banks of the Kunduz River. The village was as close to perfect as any place I've even seen in my life. My father was an activist and moved us there from the city to keep us safe while he spoke out against the government. He believed in equality for all, especially after my sister and I were born. You obviously know enough about my country to understand the danger that comes with that type of opinion. After the fourth attempt on his life, the one that caused my sister to lose her leg, he sent my mother, my sister, and me to the United States. That alone was a difficult journey and getting us out of the country was not an easy task for my father to accomplish. For me however, arriving here was even harder. Up until that point I thought my life was perfect. We were relatively well-off to everyone else in our village, educated, and overall content. I knew there was danger, but I didn't want to leave. I was ten years old. I had to say goodbye to everything I ever knew."

I listen to her speak, the exotic names of her town rolling off her tongue, and it takes me instantly back to my time there. I can't believe I didn't pick up on this sooner. I can't believe I missed this. "That must have been really hard, but it sounds like he thought you'd be safer."

"We didn't just flee our country and abandon our friends and family; he had us turn our backs on our culture and our religion. We dressed according to the current fashions here; we learned Spanish, perfected our English, and changed our name. We had a whole backstory about where we were from. I hated it, and I hated my father. I called him a coward and told my mother she was no better. I swore on my eighteenth birthday I would change my name back, take back the culture and heritage they'd forced me to leave behind. I even considered going back to Afghanistan. Back to see all my friends and extended family. Back to a place I could be myself again."

"Did you?" I wonder if she and I ever walked the same ground over there? Did the places she saw as flourishing slices of heaven turn into the rubble and despair I passed through? Her hair falls forward as she leans toward the fire and it's like a curtain keeping me from being able to see her face. If it weren't so intimate, if it didn't cross the line, I would brush it back for her, tuck it behind her ear.

"Six months before my eighteenth birthday was September eleventh. The towers came down, the world changed. People I knew, people I swore I would reconnect with were being profiled and persecuted just for the headdresses they wore or the place where they prayed. I realized my father was right, or at least his intentions were right. I was safer this way. Nine months later the rebels invaded my village and killed dozens. Right behind them came the Marines, trying to kill the rebels and in turn killing more of the innocent people. Kids I ran the streets with, women who cared for me. Dead. My father, dead."

"I'm sorry," is all I can muster. I had come up with a hundred reasons Jordan may not agree with the war, but this was not one of them. This, I couldn't have imagined any more than I can pretend to understand what it must feel like. Even with no personal tie, I felt myself overwhelmingly sad at times for the destruction of so much over there. If it were my home, it would be shattering to see it fall.

Her voice is stern now, cutting as she shakes her head. "That's why I can't understand what you do. What kind of person can storm into a place as peaceful and idyllic as the one where I grew up and spill innocent blood. That ability has to be born from hate. A hate I'll never see as justified."

"No," I say softly, amazed she doesn't understand this simple truth. "I was in junior high when the towers fell. My oldest sister worked in the city at the time. She walked across the Brooklyn Bridge with droves of other people, covered with ash, terrified. I lost a cousin overseas before enlisting myself. I didn't become a Marine because I hate your country. I didn't go over there because I hate your people. I went because I *love* my country, and I *love* my people. I want to protect them. That's why I signed up. I'm not saying war is perfect. There's nothing in my eyes that justifies collateral damage. I won't defend that. I won't defend the politics of the war either. All I can tell you is what was in my heart when I signed up, and it wasn't hate."

She doesn't say anything. She just leans her head over to my shoulder and rests it there. I want to hold her, wrap my arm around her, and tell her everything is going to work out. But I don't. And I'm not sure why. I'm supposed to be schmoozing her and that would certainly fall into that category. Maybe that's why I don't do it. It feels tainted to me.

"I miss my dad, I'm drunk, I'm scared . . . and my arm hurts," she whispers, still staring into the fire, still leaning against me. "And I'm mad that I'm telling you all this."

"Why?"

"Because I don't tell people things; I don't do this. I'm sitting here in jeans and sneakers about to stare into a fire with a bunch of strangers. I don't share my warm and fuzzy feelings and plot how to save the world. I do paperwork, oversee jobs, and I leave. I always leave and go on to the next one."

I can hear Nick's car engine rumble to life and Jordan jumps beside me then winces, grabbing her tender shoulder. "It's just Nick, the kids are probably heading out now."

Rebecca steps back into the yard and when Devin appears behind her, she melts into his arms, sobbing and sniffling. "I shouldn't have sent her off. She's never been without me before. You need to figure this all out, and fast, because I want my baby back here in Clover with me." She's speaking into Devin's shoulder and I watch him caress her hair. I can't hear his quiet words, but I'm sure he's promising to do what she's asking.

I hear a sniffle escape from Jordan and I realize she's doing a poor job of trying to hold back her own tears. "Can I get you anything?" I ask.

I've spent most of my adult life in the desert with a heavy bag strapped to my back and a weapon in my hand. I've had buddies, people fighting alongside me that I would consider family. I've swapped fears and memories with them, but nothing quite like this. Listening to Jordan tonight feels different. I'm not just hearing the late night ramblings of a fellow Marine; I'm torn up inside wondering how I can help her. How can I make her feel better, even if it's only for a minute? I have this urge to fix her, help her, protect her, and possess her. It's actually scary how much I want to say to her right now. I finally wrap my arm around her, but she shrugs me off and composes herself.

"I'll take some more moonshine."

Chapter Twelve

Rebecca

No mother should have to kiss her baby and send her off. I've never spent a single night away from my child. I've worked two jobs since Adeline was born and I've still managed to tuck her in every night. Where we slept wasn't important, as long as we were together.

I keep telling myself not to blame Devin for this despair, but it's hard. I'm watching him try, or pretend to try, I'm not sure which. Is he trying to pacify me by changing the landfill, as he plows ahead with the rest of his twisted plan? And am I falling for it?

I've told myself I won't kiss him again until I know the answer; I won't let myself get swept up in him until I'm sure he has a handle on himself. He's come here to destroy. People. Land. He came in like a tornado, ready to blindly wipe out anything in his path. As I grasp for straws, desperate to find a way to hang on to hope for him, I take small comfort in the fact that maybe the storm in him isn't quite as strong. But the sun isn't shining yet, either.

There are flashes of this egotistical and self-centered man the more I see him around Luke. He's back to being the boss. I hear him talk to Nick about updates on the town and his whole demeanor seems to change. It's frightening to think how long he's held onto this anger. If it were a seed, something planted and cultivated, I'd imagine by now he'd being overrun by it. The tendrils are twisting around his heart, and tightening every day.

I pull my sweater around me and take a seat on a stump next to the crackling fire. Looking over at Jordan and Click, I feel tears gathering in the corners of my eyes. They're cute. Her head's on his shoulder, and the innocence of it brings memories of Devin and me, when we were young. Breaks my heart and makes me happy, all at once.

Watching Adeline leave makes me think of my own parents. I've never given my father any slack; he's a toxic person. But the older I get, the rougher my road has become, the more I can understand how he became that way. He was never a soft man, always a little cold and indifferent to me. Especially once I hit my teen years. He just seemed uncomfortable around me, like he didn't know how to talk to me. The boys, my brothers, were more his speed. He made it abundantly clear that I was my mother's child. So when she died, I became pretty much parentless. Devin was gone. My mother was gone and my brothers needed me. They became my purpose in life. Creating something for them and making sure they had a way out of this place was my focus.

I don't agree with the vile nature and the hate my father lives with, but I can understand how it came to be. And understanding it is what frightens me. I look at him alone and miserable, stewing in his own unhappiness. I see Devin with his equal number of reasons to be mad at the world. It makes me realize he can justifiably be led down the same path of hate. A man who feels he deserves to be striking out like a mad snake. The only peace my father ever finds is the small light of joy he gets from yanking other people down, cutting their legs out from under them. If he sees that glimmer of suffering in their eyes, it's like points on the scoreboard for him.

Does Devin find that same joy in hurting people? It feels like it. Is he just a few destructive moments away from being as venomous as my father? And if he is, shouldn't I do exactly what I've done with my father: keep my distance as long as I can and see him only when it is completely unavoidable?

A thought strikes me. Had my mother lived, would my father be different? Or if he'd found a new love later in his life, could that have saved him? Can I save Devin? Can anyone really save another person, or do they need to save themselves?

I let the cold air fill my lungs as I stare back into the fire. I want my daughter. I want Devin. I want Clover. I'm so tired of never getting what I want.

Chapter Thirteen

Devin

I'm not a slumber party kind of guy. Prior to Christmas Eve, in recent history, the closest thing would be a hook-up who didn't get the hint to leave in the morning. Needless to say, the five adults crammed into a very small two-bedroom house was not my idea of a good time. Even though Nick was going to be gone most of the night, Rebecca insisted we sleep in the kids' room instead. Maybe she wanted to be surrounded by stuffed animals and crayons, which did absolutely nothing for me.

I crammed myself into a twin bed that was about a foot too short for my legs and she slept in a racecar toddler bed. Besides a comforting hug by the fire, we never touched each other. I can't tell if she's pissed, or hurt, or in love with me. I think there's a good chance she isn't sure either. She keeps begging me to put this all behind me. But when push comes to shove, she stays. Rebecca is loyal, fiercely so, and probably to a fault.

I come down the stairs with a kink in my neck and find everyone already up. Click and Jordan are sitting at the kitchen table with coffee; Rebecca is doing the dishes. Nick is dressed for work, though I can't imagine he's had more than an hour or two of sleep. Luke is on the couch with his laptop open, bitching about the Internet signal.

"Good morning," I grumble as I make my way to the kitchen for my own dose of caffeine. I'm met with a bunch of huffs and sighs that tell me no one here is happy, and I'm pretty sure they are all blaming me for one reason or another. "Okay, shitty morning," I correct.

"I'm heading to work. I want to check in with my captain and see if I can get some more marshals here in the absence of your security team. He's gonna be pissed. He wasn't a fan of your proposal in the first place. Now that you've run off the old sheriff's department and my men have relieved them of their badges and guns, he's going to want to know why you haven't come through with your end of the bargain."

"Jordan just needs to come up with a new proposal, get her boss to sign off on it, and security will be here the same day. Within hours."

"About that," Jordan snaps, "there is no new proposal. I'm done with all of this. If I had known you were coming down here to seek some personal retribution and stir this shit up, I'd never have gotten behind the deal in the first place. And then to try to change something so dramatic in the eleventh hour just because your girlfriend is busting your balls, it doesn't get less professional than that. The deal has been voted in; Clover is getting a landfill."

I bore holes through Click with the laser stare I'm giving him, but when he doesn't speak up, I have to. "After what's happened, including getting shot at, you can't see the need for why I'm here? Why you're here? Clover used to be a proud, self-sufficient city. You can help restore it to that. You can have a hand in ridding it of the narcissistic, crooked people who've been running it all these years. And you won't even try?"

"That's not my job," she retorts, slamming her coffee mug down. "I'm not in the business of rescuing communities from the mess they've gotten themselves into. And don't try to stand there for a second and tell me you came down here with that intention. You came here to destroy it and found a couple reasons not to. Now you're putting that on me to fix. I can't. I can't fix that. If you want Hoyle stopped, then let me put the paperwork through and get you your security. I'm meeting with the construction company we've contracted with today. After that, I'm moving forward." She stands up and slips the sneakers back on. "I need a ride to my hotel to get myself ready."

"I'll take you," Click chimes, and he stands practically at attention.

"Nick, please thank Jeannie for the clothes and for setting my shoulder. I appreciate the hospitality."

"You must not," Rebecca says icily, standing in front of the door. "You must not really appreciate it, because if you did you'd realize what a landfill would do to this very family. To the people who helped you out."

"They only had to help me because of the trouble you guys started. Devin proposed a landfill. It was his idea. He contacted my company, drew up the papers, and put up much of the capital. He wanted this place to suffer. He wanted to complicate everything in Clover. I've been doing this job a long time and no one has ever shot at me before. You've been a mom for a few years now. Did you ever have to send your daughter away before? I'm seeing a common denominator here." I watch Rebecca charge forward and I hook my arm in hers before she can tackle Jordan to the ground.

"Trouble was already here, you snobby bitch. You don't get it because you walk around in your fancy clothes and look down your nose at people like us. But people like us are the ones who, for years before the textile mill went overseas, made those clothes. We're the backbone of this country and people like you are killing us. Devin might not have come down here with good intentions, but the difference is he's now trying to do what's right. You're just trying to do what's easy."

Jordan blows by Click, who's looking stunned by how close we all just came to a catfight. He hesitates, but then follows behind. "You change her mind," Rebecca calls to Click. He nods, though he looks as though he's drowning.

"My mornings used to be pretty quiet before you rolled in, Devin," Nick says as he plants his cowboy hat atop his head and slides into his boots.

"Story of my life," Luke laughs as he tries once more to send an email on the spotty connection.

"I'm heading out." Nick stands, ready to go. "Feel free to come and go as you please from the house. I'll actually feel better knowing there are people here. I'm not much of a cook, but Jeannie wrapped up leftovers for us for dinner tonight. You three planning on staying here for the day?"

"No, I'm going to the medical examiner's house. I need to get a look at those records. I want to be able to find something that you can use to reopen the case and maybe even exhume Brent's body."

"Rebecca, are you going with him? You know Lulu will shoot him dead on her doorstep if he shows up without you."

"I haven't decided."

"The sooner you get me something, the sooner I can try to get Hoyle looked at for the murder. There's no telling how much more damage he can do in this town as long as he's pissed and on the loose."

"You really think he killed Brent?" Rebecca asks, staring down at her feet.

"I don't know, but I know Devin didn't, and there's no one in prison for it right now. So the answer likely lies under the ground with Brent."

"If she says no, we're not pressuring her," Rebecca says as she spins in my direction. "Lulu and my mother go way back. She's not someone you go pushing around. We ask, and if she says no, it's no."

"Absolutely," I lie, fully intending to do everything in my power to obtain those records. Money, threats, blackmail. I won't stop if a simple *please* doesn't work. I realize this is what Rebecca is talking about, what this brings out in me—a blind determination that causes damage in my wake. I hear her, but I'm not stopping.

Luke fist pumps as I hear the chiming of emails pouring into his inbox. "I've got a good connection now. I'll stay here and watch the house. Do I get a gun?"

"Do you have a license to carry?" Nick asks, looking skeptically at the man who could really be summed up as a "suit."

"No, but, come on, this is the most excitement I've had in years. I want to do something cool."

"Cool?" Nick shakes his head and tips his hat to Rebecca and walks out the door without another word.

"Just watch the house and call me if anything comes up," I tell Luke as I put on my coat. I'm dressed in a crisp white button-down shirt and my casual dress pants. I'm hoping these look enough like church clothes to endear Lulu Macready to me.

"Yeah, yeah, I'll hold down the fort," Luke shrugs. "Oh, come on. The Internet just went down again. What am I supposed to do all day if I can't work?"

Rebecca tosses the remote over to him and smiles. "Looks like you have a good old-fashioned day off."

We hop into my car and I think about how this will be the true test of how Rebecca really feels right now. In the past week I've stormed my way back into her life. I've tossed money in her face, which she promptly rejected. I told her I was here to turn her hometown into a trash heap. Then I whisked her away to a winter wonderland for a Christmas she'll never forget and a night of passion I can't get out of my head. All while insisting it didn't mean forever.

Now I tell her I'm going to pursue a killer, a person who robbed us both of so much. She's asked me to move forward with her instead of looking back. I've said no, and instead drag her along with me. Even if we do get the answers I'm hoping for, I'm not sure she and I will have anything to salvage. She's not wrong. What this hunt brings out in me isn't something you'd want to be around. I can't fault her for that. I just can't stop. At the end of the day, justice might be the only thing that I walk away with. Not love, only justice. I used to believe that was enough. That I could patch up the holes in me with the knowledge that others were paying for what they did. I'm not as sure about that any more. Being in Rebecca's arms is a pretty curative medicine, too. I'm starting to think I need both to heal.

"Anything in particular I should know about Mrs. Macready?" I don't really feel like I need the tips, but I can't take the silence filling the car any longer.

"She'll want you to call her Lulu, but let her tell you that. She's tiny, but she's a pit bull. No one messes with her. That's her driveway there."

I pull in and assess the old, dilapidated house. How does the widow of a medical examiner end up living in a place that looks like it could topple over any minute?

"Rough shape." I point up to the house wondering if Rebecca knows something I don't.

"She gives away everything she has. Feeds the hungry, buys school supplies for kids. Some people say she has a giant heart. My mom always said it was penance. She wasn't blind to her husband's ethical decisions at work. The money he got for doing Hoyle's bidding probably feels better to pay forward than spend on herself."

I take that in and process it as an angle I might be able to exploit. Maybe if she's looking for true absolution, handing over those records will be a good start.

We walk up the creaky steps, and before we have a chance to knock, we're face to face with someone who can best be described as a meek old woman. Her curly white hair looks like springs popping off her head. She's feeble, not at all as I imagined her. Her back is hunched slightly; her hands are bony and frail.

"Rebecca Farrus, as I live and breathe." She shuffles out her door a few steps farther onto her porch, and Rebecca bends to gently hug the woman.

"It's been too long, Lulu. I've missed you."

"Likewise, dear. I hear through the grapevine that you've been working as hard as ever. Still holding down those two jobs?"

"I'm lucky to have them in these hard times. Lots of folks would be happy to have the work, so I don't complain."

"You never did any complaining. All those years you spent raising your brothers. Getting them both off to college. I bet you're still sending them money, aren't you?"

"Anything Adeline and I can spare. Cole is in his junior year and working at a restaurant to help pay his way. Nate is set to graduate this year if he can come up with the money to finish. He's been doing construction, but he hurt his ankle so he can't get as much work. I'm hoping to get some money together soon to send to him. I just need to get back on my feet." I didn't know these things and I swallow hard as I think through the worries Rebecca carries around with her every day. I've made her jobs unsafe to go to. Forcing her into a position that will likely get her fired from both. I don't intend to watch her struggle for money ever again, but, if history is any indicator, she's too proud to just take it from me if I'm acting like an arrogant asshole. I'll need to work on that.

"Still having problems with that ugly ol' Collin?"

"He's still around, but I don't hear from him quite as often now."

"I'd imagine, with a big hulking guy like this following you around now. Gonna introduce me?"

"I'm sorry, Lulu, where are my manners? This is Devin Sutton."

I extend my hand, intending to receive a gentle shake, but she shoos me away. "I already know who you are, I just wanted to hear her say it. Everyone knows what you're in Clover for. Taking away what little we have left here, along with our pride." I had opened my mouth to speak, to tell her it's a pleasure to meet her, but I didn't get the chance, and now I'm not sure what to say. She's caught me off guard, which rarely happens to me.

"Devin is working on changing the plans, Lulu. He's just got to convince one more person and then they'll try to figure out something that can help Clover rather than hurt it."

Danielle Stewart

"How kind of him to start something terrible then try to stop it. Does he speak? Or should we just keep standing out here talking about him."

"I do speak, Mrs. Macready, and I'm sorry for the trouble I brought to Clover. I've seen the error of my ways, and I'm looking for a way to fix it. I'm doing my best to correct it." I can tell from Rebecca's body language she is annoyed by this statement. It's the phoniness in my word choice and tone that must be driving her mad. Laying it on thick is my approach, but it doesn't seem to be sitting well with Rebecca.

"Lovely." She plasters the fakest smile possible on her wrinkly face and turns to go back in to her house. "Y'all coming in?"

"Yes, ma'am." Rebecca smiles, tugging me along behind her. I thought for sure that door was about to slam in our face, not swing open for us.

The interior of the house matches the exterior in its condition. It's sparse, nothing has been replaced for what looks like decades. Though it's relatively clean, everything seems to be on its last leg.

"Get out with it. Whatever it is that you came here for, let's hear it. Your mama meant a lot to me, and I respect what you did after we lost her. That's why I let you in, but it won't keep me from kicking you out."

"Mrs. Macready," I start and, just as Rebecca had told me, she asks to be called Lulu. "All right, Lulu, you seem to know a lot about what I'm doing here, do you know why I'm doing it?"

"I'm guessin' you ain't too pleased you sat in prison for near on a decade for something the court came out and said you didn't do."

"You sure know your stuff, Lulu."

"Compliments will get you nowhere. Now if you think I have something here that can help you, my husband's records for instance, I'm sorry to tell you I don't. We had a fire in our shed years back and they were all lost. I hear the copies in Clover's sheriff department were lost as well. The people from the Innocence Program who were trying to spring you out of prison were not too pleased with all that information."

"They came here looking for the records?" I ask, so out of touch with what transpired while the Innocence Program worked on my case. I was informed of almost nothing, just that information was hard to come by here in Clover.

"They did, and I told them the same thing I'm telling you now. They burned up in the shed. And it wouldn't matter anyhow. All they said was whatever Sherriff Hoyle wanted them to."

"Would you be willing to testify to the fact that you knew your husband falsified reports?"

"I'm saying I know he did. But I'd swear under oath that he didn't. For two reasons, he's my husband, and he didn't do it because he wanted to, he did it because he had to. The type of control that monster Hoyle has over people, it's stronger than the devil. My husband, God rest his soul, had no choice.

"He got mixed up with Hoyle and then fell deeper and deeper. All he ever wanted to do was protect his family, and unfortunately that meant breaking the law at times. Now those records are all gone; someone burnt down my shed and made sure of it."

We're playing chess now. Her move, my move, and I don't want to step off my strategy. I need these answers.

Danielle Stewart

So I think about what I would have done if I were this man.

"If all he ever wanted to do was protect you, then he'd have some kind of an insurance policy. Something to make sure Hoyle didn't give you any problems in case he wasn't here to protect you, right?"

Her nostrils flair and the glassiness in her eyes clears for a moment. "Rebecca Lynne Farrus, this man is a wily one. You best keep both eyes on him. He surely knows his stuff. Yes, my husband left me something. One day, after the fire, Hoyle came by to visit and, though he was being cryptic, I could tell he was angling to find out if there was anything else that my husband might have held onto that could incriminate him. I told him there was, and it had been entrusted to someone who would surely go public with it if anything ever happened to me. That was bullshit though; it was just a journal with his personal notes about every case. I never gave it to anyone else, but that lie is the one thing that keeps me from having any trouble with any of Hoyle's men."

"Can I have it?" I ask in a completely deadpan manner, trying to cut through the nonsense.

"Why would I give it to you?"

"There's no better insurance policy than getting rid of the guy altogether. I'm sure that book incriminates him in dozens of crimes, along with most of his men. It could be the key to getting him out of Clover for good."

"And it would drag my husband's name through the mud. My boys both still live in town. One teaches at the high school and the other works at the bank. Dredging this up now, painting their daddy as a lying criminal, I don't see any advantage to that."

"It wouldn't have to be that way," I interject. Business 101: overcome the objection. "I think this town would be very open to the honest truth that your husband wanted no part in this and had no choice. The way Hoyle works, many of them know that type of pressure. They'd understand. Especially with the benevolent way you've lived your life. You've never profited from the wrongdoing, have you? Maybe he asked you to turn these notes over and you were just waiting until it was safe to do so. I call that admirable. You and your husband would be heroic."

"How do you even walk with all that bullshit around you? You must need boots up to your knees. You can stop right there." She uses her hand to cut through the air and keep me quiet. "I've already made up my mind."

"Lulu, I'm—" She cuts me off again with a wave of her hand before I can feign an apology or act innocent in the matter.

"You can have the damn book, but you need to know why I'm giving it to you. It ain't anything to do with you coming in here and convincing me it's the right thing to do. It's the same reason you got this desperate town to sign off on a deal that will likely destroy them. You are the lesser of two evils. Giving you this book is my best shot at getting rid of that man for good—for the town and me. But that don't make you a good man; I want you to know that. I want your word that my husband won't get slandered in all this, even though I doubt your word is worth much." The way this conversation is going I'm not completely surprised by her words but it stings more to hear them while in Rebecca's presence. All I can think is: does she agree?

I assumed Lulu Macready would be a firecracker. I even planned to have to do a little persuading, but I didn't expect her to call me out like this. I hesitate for a moment while I find the words. "You're right." I hang my head slightly. "I'm focused on only one thing, and that is revenge. That book you're going to give me is going to help me move that forward. That's why I'm here and that's all I care about right now." No use trying to bullshit someone who can already see right through you. "But in the process, if you truly believe Hoyle used your husband, threatened and blackmailed him, I'll be getting a little payback for you, too. I can bring to light what kind of a man your husband was to keep that journal, and, if you really believe in penance, this could be a good place to start."

She folds her arms over her chest and narrows her eyes at me. "It's a shame you're gonna have to ruin them nice clothes of yours."

I look down at my crisp white shirt and then back up at the cackling woman shuffling across her living room floor. "I'll get the shovel. My husband buried the book years ago. I can't get it myself. It's in the crawl space under the house by the furnace. There'll barely be enough room for your giant head under there, but you'll make do I'm sure."

I stand and follow behind her, reaching for my cell phone. "I'll call one of my men. They'll come out and dig it up."

"No," she insists. "It's now or never. I don't want anyone having time to find out what you're doing here. You get under that house and dig it up now and get on out of here. I'm sure you're used to paying someone else to do your dirty work, but if you want that book, you're going under there to get it yourself."

"Lulu," Rebecca says meekly, and I wonder if she's going to come to my defense since she's stayed virtually silent while the woman has handed me my ass so far. "I know this isn't easy to part with and there's even some risk to you."

If I didn't know any better, Rebecca's trying to talk Lulu out of this, change her mind. I know Rebecca doesn't stand beside me on this, but I wasn't expecting her to stand in front of me and block my path. I feel the door to our future closing the further I push this. The way she looks at me is changing by the second. As hard as I try to ignore the subtle difference in the distance she stands from me, I can't. The few feet between us, the slightly downturned angle of her lips, all of it is shouting, *you're losing her, Devin.* She's too good for this. Just like someone with a communicable disease, I should be quarantined. Instead I keep bringing Rebecca closer and closer to me, dancing between the idea that she's the cure or that I might just infect her too.

As we walk down the front porch steps and I take the small shovel in my hand, I feel the tightness in my chest grow. Lulu pulls the lattice away from the side of the porch and hands me a flashlight.

I don't do small spaces. Call it claustrophobia or whatever, but spending years cooped up in a prison cell makes wide-open spaces a necessity. I peer under the house and realize I'll need to army crawl the whole way, through mud and under spider-infested exposed pipes. And part of me thinks maybe there is no book. Lulu strikes me as the kind of woman who might just send me under here to scare off a possum that's been causing her problems.

"You don't have to do this," Rebecca whispers, touching my shoulder as I kneel down. I roll up the sleeves of my white shirt as though there is a chance I'll be able to salvage it after this mess.

"I want that book," I say as I suck in a deep breath and crawl forward into the darkness. Lulu has given me instructions: head to the back left corner of the house, find the insulated hot water pipe, and start digging.

It's ten minutes of swapping between digging and brushing crawling shit off me before I feel something hard against the tip of the shovel. It's a metal box, and once I've struck it I can think of nothing else but digging it up. Right here at my fingertips could be the answer to who really killed Brent.

Once I have the box in my hand I have to fight the urge to open it. I can't sit under this house and flip the pages looking for my answers. I shimmy my way out from under the house and watch as Rebecca stares at the box in my hand.

"Is that it? Is it in there?" she asks as she bites at her nails nervously.

I don't bother knocking the mud off me. I'm a complete mess, and I will be until I can get back to Nick's house for a shower, so I might as well get used to it. I take a seat on the rickety porch steps and flip open the latches of the metal box. Lulu is gone now, back in the house I assume, maybe run off by the cold or having second thoughts about handing this book over.

I'm not prepared for what awaits me on the other side of the green lid. Money. Stacks of it. Maybe twenty thousand dollars or more. Rebecca's caught a glimpse of it, too, and takes a few steps forward to get a better look. "I wonder if she knows that's in there?" she asks, but I can barely hear her voice. I'm focused on only one thing. I push the money aside and dig to the bottom of the box until I find the sharp edge of a book and I pull it out anxiously. It's nothing spectacular, just a plain blue covered journal with a very sloppy scrawl across the front. I flip through the pages trying to make sense of the words in front of me, hoping maybe the notes about Brent's case will magically appear. It takes almost a minute for it to register that what I'm looking at is not English. It's not anything. It's a series of numbers and words that don't seem to be words at all. "What the fu . . ." I throw the book back down into the box and step back to the door to talk to Lulu.

"What is this?" I bark, but the little old woman looking at me through the screen door doesn't seem surprised that I am flashing my true colors.

"Code. Don't ask me to break it, I don't know how. You seem smart, I'm sure you can figure it out. Take it with you and go on." She shoos us with her hands and acts like we're no more than a pair of unwanted varmints she can't wait to get rid of.

"Did you know about the money in the box? Was that part of your angle? Get me to dig up the cash for you?"

"The only game I was playing was testing your character. You could have left with both without saying a word. I was just wondering if you'd mention what else you found down there."

"I'm glad I could be of some entertainment here today. Now if you'll excuse us we have to be going. We've got a book of nonsense to try to figure out." I storm down the stairs, blowing by Rebecca and the money, taking only the journal with me.

Rebecca jogs to catch up and slides into the passenger seat. "Devin, you can't storm off like that. Not after what she just gave you."

"Right now she's given me nothing. It's just a book filled with a code I don't know a damn thing about. She probably played me to get that money dug up. I just want to get back to Nick's house and out of these filthy clothes. Ridiculous." I slam my hand down into the steering wheel and let more expletives fly.

Out of the corner of my eye I see Rebecca jump, and lean away from me. "Next time we have the same old argument and you act like you have no idea what I mean when I talk about you losing yourself in all of this, think about this moment. It's getting hard to see past this," she gestures at my dirt-covered clothes, "and you aren't making it any easier. I've seen my father slip down this rabbit hole before. He never came back up."

"I'm nothing like your father, Rebecca. I'd never hurt you. I'd never say those things to you."

"I'm sure there was a point in his life he thought the same thing. No one starts out there Devin, they just end up there."

We drive back to Nick's house in silence, and the only thing I can hope is that Click has had more luck today than I have. Jordan has to change the deal and she needs to do it fast before Clover slides any further into destruction and I lose Rebecca forever.

Chapter Fourteen

Click

"Miss Garcia, I'm going to level with you." I watch Jordan roll her eyes as she listens to the stocky, gray-haired construction foreman we've come to meet with. "My family has lived in Clover for almost four generations. I've heard all the rumors that Devin Sutton is looking for something other than a landfill here, that the town all wants something different. It sounds like you're the only one still pushing a dump. My company can support any type of construction you decide on, and frankly, we're all hoping you go another way."

Jordan straightens her back and folds her hands together, looking like a lawyer ready for cross-examination. "If the town didn't want a landfill why did their appointed officials vote for one?"

"Because we've been under the thumb of thugs for near on twenty years, and Devin's deal promised to rid us of him. Now maybe that looks shortsighted to you, but you can understand we were desperate."

"I can't understand that. You jumped from the frying pan into the fire, and now you're looking for a way out. If you're not comfortable doing the construction needed for the landfill I am happy to contract out with a company with fewer ties to Clover. But then you really do lose, because not only will you get all the trash, you won't get a dime for it."

The man runs his hand over his short bristly hair, looking completely exasperated. "Ma'am, this is my home. My oldest daughter is pregnant, about to give my wife and me our first grandbaby. Now, my girls have had to watch Clover fall apart in front of them, but I was hoping by the time that new baby was old enough to go to school, this place would have some life back in it. Instead they'll have to worry about what kind of run off is in their drinking water. I'll have to explain what they're breathing in every day. Is it wrong to want better for them than that?"

"We're talking a different language here, Mr. Flint. I speak business—dollars and cents. The people I answer to, that's all they care about. I can go back and tell them about you and your daughters or about how Mrs. Trivet makes clothes for all the kids who can't afford them. I can go back and tell them what a proud people you are— explain how, even in the face of terrible hardship, you band together and keep going. You're the backbone of this country; you're the pillars of self-sufficiency and strength, blah, blah, blah. But they'd still just look at me and ask for the bottom line. And the bottom line is the most profitable deal for my company involves trash being trucked in here and dumped. It involves demolishing houses, forests, and businesses. It's loud trucks at all hours of the day and night. It's exhaust fumes and smells. But every word of that was in the deal that Clover representatives signed. No one tricked them. There was no fine print."

"I understand that, but folks were scared. It was getting to be like a warzone here. They thought if you could just get rid of Hoyle and his men, it would be worth the dump. Haven't you ever felt scared Miss Garcia? Haven't you ever needed help?"

"That's a choice they made. Asking me to change that now is like asking me to move a mountain."

"We're right on the edge of coal country ma'am. I've seen mountains move. All it takes is enough people getting behind it, believing in something."

I'm hopeful in this moment, reading Jordan's silence as deep contemplation on her part, but that hope is quickly dashed. "That's not how things work in the business world, Mr. Flint. I am truly sorry." She shakes his hand firmly and leaves the small office trailer we've been standing in.

I follow her out to the car feeling like I want to scream at her. I'm angry at how heartless she is, but I'm finding I'm even angrier with myself. How can I look at her and see anything more than just a cold-hearted selfish woman? Why do I keep dreaming about kissing her, holding her? Why do I keep trying to see her differently than she is?

"You really are something else," I bark as I jump in the car and slam my door closed, not bothering to open hers this time.

"Excuse me?" she asks as she falls into the passenger seat.

"There is no excuse for being such a hypocrite. Drunk or not, you opened up to me about where you are from and what kind of man your father was. He fought and died to help further the cause of equality and promote education for women. I wonder if he knew what you'd be doing with your education."

She lets her seatbelt loose from her hand and it goes snapping back behind her. She slaps my face so hard I grunt at the pain. My hand goes up to my cheek to cool the sting and I look over at her furious expression.

"Don't talk about my father. He accomplished nothing."

"He wanted his girls to be educated. *You're* educated. He wanted you to be free to make a difference, to make whatever choices you wanted. You have that now."

"I'm one girl."

"Sometimes that's all it takes. You don't have control over what happened to your village and all the people you cared about. But you have control here. You can either participate in the destruction of Clover or help bring life back to it."

"You give me way too much credit. I'm a woman in a man's world. The job I have right now is not the one I want forever; but in order to get to that one, I can't go around pitching deals just to feel all warm and fuzzy. I'm supposed to partner with men like Devin, create profitable deals regardless of the collateral damage, and then move on to the next one. If I can do this job long enough, probably twice as long as the men next to me, I can move on to something higher in the company. Screwing this deal up will screw up my entire future. Making waves and proposing nonsense makes me look like a fool. I've spent every minute so far trying to convince them I'm not one."

"You don't give yourself *enough* credit. I believe in you, and I think you could find something here they'd think was genius, but you haven't even tried. I believe you're capable of finding something equally as lucrative. I need you to try."

"Why? Those are your orders? To get me to try?"

"No." I swallow hard, not allowing myself to consider the complications that might come from my words. "I need you to try so that I know you're a good person. Because I can't be falling for someone who isn't.

214

Tell me what I see in you is real, that I'm not just pretending you are a beautiful, strong, intelligent woman who cares about people."

Her eyebrows rise practically to her hairline and she looks as though she must have heard me wrong. The moment of silence feels more like a decade, and I'm squirming in my own skin.

"Click." She brushes back a few tears, making sure to catch them before they even drop from her eyes. I imagine she feels it doesn't count as crying if they never touch her cheeks. "I want to help here. I just don't know how. I don't have the answer."

"I've seen you walk miles at night through the woods in three-inch heels. I've seen you go toe to toe with anyone who crosses you. You are a force, Jordan, a beautiful, determined, admirable force. That combination is terrifying, and, if you get out of your own head long enough, you can come up with something." Revealing my feelings for Jordan isn't something I'm completely comfortable with but it just comes out of me. I've spent a lot of years falling in line, doing my duty, and being alone. Any girlfriend I've had up until this point has never been serious. I didn't have someone in my life before I deployed and didn't have much time to think about it while overseas. Jordan is the first woman I feel that spark with, and I'm finally in a position to act on it. Something about that is making my words come more freely than usual.

She closes her mouth tight and shakes her head, dumbfounded. I try not to take the silence personally. I put the car in reverse and start heading for Nick's house. Maybe she's thinking of some master plan, or maybe she's considering jumping out of my car. Either way, I'm keeping my trap shut for now.

I pull the car into Nick's driveway and see Devin and Rebecca are already there. The girls' fight this morning left an awkward tension that won't help Jordan's shaken confidence. "Do you want to go somewhere else?" I ask, giving her an out.

"No, I want to apologize to Rebecca. I pulled a cheap shot this morning by bringing up her daughter."

That's what I was hoping to hear, and I feel a weight of worry lift off me. We make our way through the front door to find Luke, Rebecca, and Devin all sitting around the dining room table staring at a book.

"Hey," Devin says, lifting his chin to greet us, but keeping his eyes on the book.

"Does it do tricks?" I ask, pointing down at the old dusty cover.

Devin stands and I take notice of his filthy clothes. "What the hell happened to you?"

"Did you get shot at, too? That's pretty much what I looked like when it happened to me," Jordan chimes in, taking a seat at the table as though nothing had ever been said between her and Rebecca.

"I dug this up from under an old lady's house. It's the personal notes of the medical examiner who worked on Brent's case. As far as I can tell it's a complete waste of time and maybe I should have her house surrounded by trash too. It already looks like a dump there."

"Devin," Rebecca calls across the table with scolding eyes. "She didn't have to give you anything. You could have walked out of there empty-handed."

"At least my four hundred dollar pants wouldn't be ruined," Devin retorts, ignoring Rebecca's wide-eyed reaction. I can tell something here has shifted, and the unease in the room is palpable.

"Does it have any answers in it? Enough for Nick to request the case be opened again?"

"Who the hell knows," Luke grumbles as he flips through the pages again. "It's in some kind of code. Half words that make no sense and half numbers."

"Let Jordan look at it, maybe she can come up with something," I say and am met with narrowed eyes from both Jordan and Rebecca.

"Sure," Jordan says, reluctantly taking the book. "But first I have to apologize to you, Rebecca. I was out of line this morning, bringing up your daughter. I know I'm no one's favorite person right now, but that's no excuse for me to be rude."

"I'm sorry, too." Rebecca smiles tentatively and reaches a hand across the table to cover Jordan's.

"Wonderful," Devin's loud voice cuts in. "But can we go back to trying to figure out what's in the damn book?"

I watch Rebecca wince, then roll her eyes. I've known a lot of guys like Devin in my life. I've also seen how hard it is for a woman to love them. I feel bad for Rebecca right now. Not because Devin is some asshole, but because he's trying not to be and it isn't completely working.

Jordan flips through the pages and pulls out her phone, typing in a few things as she quickly works through one of the pages. "It looks like it's a combination of literary references and some kind of alphanumeric code."

"What do you mean literary references? I didn't see that," Luke says defensively, rounding the table to look over her shoulder. I feel instantly protective of her, but I bite my tongue. She's plenty capable.

"Right here. It says Romeo and Balthasar, from *Romeo and Juliet*. Then on this page it says Tranio, that's from *Taming of the Shrew*, another work of Shakespeare."

"Oh, we were thinking Romeo referenced the military alphabet and the rest I assumed was gibberish," Luke says, now nodding his head in agreement.

"Do you think you can break the code?" Devin asks, sliding back in his chair and looking overly anxious.

"Why doesn't someone just shoot the son of a bitch? That would get rid of Hoyle once and for all." Rebecca snaps as she pushes away from the table. An awkward quiet falls over us as looks pass between everyone.

"I'm going to call Adeline. You detectives crack this cold case without me. Let's make sure we destroy everyone we can in the process." She sulks away and Devin runs his hands through his hair and huffs out a tired breath.

"She doesn't want any part of this?" Jordan asks as she flips through more pages of the book.

"She wants me to move on. Leave the past in the past. I can't do it, though. I won't be any kind of man for her if I'm always looking behind me, wondering what really happened."

"And the landfill, she doesn't want you to do that either?" Jordan pushes for more answers.

"No. Same thing, she sees it as destructive, and if I'm capable of that then I'm not the man she wants to be with."

"You're batting a thousand, huh?" Jordan smirks up at Devin and then returns to reading the journal.

"You can certainly help my average here if you take the landfill off the table. Have you given it any thought? Or are you still being a ballbuster?"

With that, Jordan drops the open book on the table and stands abruptly, much like Rebecca did. "It's all Shakespeare and a substitution code. The numbers represent letters, but not in the general sense of one is a, and two is b. It looks like he may have it scrambled a bit. Every entry starts off the same way, with the month written out at the top. This is clearly May, the only three-letter month. So take the numbers here and the corresponding letters M-A-Y and start creating a key. If you use the months for each entry you should be able to create it rather quickly. Then, the Shakespearean stuff you can just research. I doubt it's anything all that cryptic; he probably just enjoyed it. I'm sure you can figure it out." She slides the book back toward Luke and walks up the stairs.

"Where are you going?" I call behind her.

"I'm not all that interested in breaking cold cases either. Not what I'm here for." She disappears up the stairs and I hear a door slam firmly.

I drop my head and turn back toward the table, hearing Devin's gravely voice cutting at me. "Click, I gave you one job, and I don't see any progress."

"Not with you calling her a ballbuster. She's got her own baggage, but I was getting somewhere before you brought it up again."

The rumble of a truck engine draws my attention and I peek my head around the curtains and see it's Nick pulling in. The poor guy's house has been taken over with moody, stressed-out people. He must really be looking forward to coming home.

"Hey y'all," he says as he enters the front door. "Shit, Devin, what happened to you? Lulu chase you out into the woods and give you a beating?"

"Worse. She made me crawl under her house and dig up this stupid book with her husband's notes in it. But it's all in code."

"Yikes," Nick says as he kicks off his boots and moves to the kitchen for a beer. "Can you crack the code?"

"I think so," Luke says, now pouring over the book and scratching things down on some scrap paper.

"I hate to be the bearer of more bad news," Nick starts as he settles on his couch, "but the townsfolk have called a meeting for tomorrow morning. They're all livid about things that have been happening on their property. Obviously Hoyle and his men are behind it. I've got some marshals here, but we can't spare enough to cover this much land. They want to know where the security is that you promised, and, for that matter, my boss is wondering the same thing. The mayor wants you at town hall at nine a.m. You think you'll have any answers by then?"

"Shit," Devin groans as he flops down on the chair across from Nick. "I was holding off until Jordan could come up with something else. Security comes when she gives the final word. I don't think she's going to budge, so maybe I just need to get off her case and tell her to do what she's got to do. Bring in the damn landfill. At least that will get security here. Maybe they can catch some of Hoyle's men in the act and get them off the streets. Then we can keep working on the journal and try to get enough evidence to put him away for murder if he killed Brent. That's really what I came here for, to see him pay. I can still accomplish that."

"It still leaves you in the doghouse with Rebecca." Luke chimes in.

"I'm starting to think I could build Disneyland here in Clover and it still wouldn't fix us. We might be a lost cause." He drops his head and rubs at the tension in his temples.

"I think Jordan is going to come around," I say, leaning against the wall and crossing my arms.

"I think you've been compromised, kid," Luke replies, looking up from the book just long enough to raise an eyebrow at me.

"Excuse me?"

"You're looking at her like a love sick puppy dog. You don't want to see what's right in front of you. That girl isn't going to change her mind because it doesn't help her to do so. She's only looking out for herself. It's business."

"She's not like that." I shake my head and look down at my boots.

"Oh come on," Devin shouts, "seriously, you fell for her? You've got to be kidding me. I gave you one job: change her mind, by any means necessary. I saw her getting all doe-eyed for you, but I figured that was part of your plan. I didn't think you'd fall for her." Devin's disappointment cuts at me. I hate to fail at a job, but this wasn't really a fair expectation of anyone. I'm not in the business of swaying people through emotions.

"All you had to do was seduce or charm her and get her to change her mind," he repeats, shaking his head at my failure.

"Really?" I hear Jordan's voice and my head shoots up. I'm praying she didn't hear that, but I already know she did.

"Jordan, it's not like that," I insist, walking quickly toward her.

"Oh please, Click, if you think you're the first man to try to play me in order to get what you want, you're crazy. Don't flatter yourself. We stupid women, we'll do just about anything when our hearts get in the way. Yeah, right." Jordan pulls her coat from the hook and puts it on with fury.

"Don't go, Jordan, please let me try to explain. I really do—" My words are cut off by the slamming of a door in my face. She's leaving. I blew it.

"It's too dangerous for her to go off on her own right now. People know what she's in town for. If Hoyle doesn't get to her, someone not wanting that landfill might find her first," Nick calls, pointing at the door.

I pull open the door and chase after her. I call out her name, but she responds with just her middle finger. "You can't go off on your own. You can hate me and think I tried to screw you over, but that doesn't change the fact that it isn't safe out there. The men who already shot at you and the people who don't want the landfill, they'll all be gunning for you. You can't go."

"Do you even hear yourself? I *can't* go? As if I'm property or livestock, something you can control. Why don't you try talking to me like you care rather than you own me? Oh wait, you *don't* care, you just pretended to in order to get what you want." She points her finger in my face and scolds me, "If you even start to say that you really did care about me I will kick you so hard in the balls you won't be able to walk for a week. I don't want to hear it."

I use every ounce of willpower and military training to push back the emotions I'm feeling. With a stoic tone,

I try to reason with her. "There's a meeting tomorrow morning. People griping about the security not being here yet, mad about what's happening on their land. Hoyle's been breaking fences so cattle get loose, burning up crops, and pouring more of that stuff around to poison the area. They want answers, and you're the only one who can give them that. I think you should go. Tell them security is coming. Tell them the deal is what it is. But please just stay here tonight, stay where it's safe."

"If I get killed, you'd get another project manager, maybe one who'd fall for your bullshit."

"If you get killed, I couldn't live with myself." I stare into her face with such intensity that she looks away.

"I don't want to see you, any of you. I'm going upstairs and I'm staying there until morning. After the meeting, I'm gone. I'll pass the deal on to another project manager and put this whole ordeal behind me."

She storms past me and back into the house, slamming the door in my face a second time. I hear her boots, heavy on the stairs, as she stomps to the bedroom she'll be sleeping in tonight, alone.

"So wait, if I'm doing the math right, there are two women, one in each bedroom, and four of us with no place to sleep?" Nick asks and takes a long swig of his beer.

"Looks like it," Devin agrees and makes his way to the kitchen for his own beer.

"I call the couch," Luke interjects, looking up for only a moment from the book he's working on.

"You don't get to sleep until you get that book figured out and I get some answers. No beer for you either, just coffee."

I slump down in the chair next to Luke and rest my heavy head in my hand. "Can I help?"

"Yes," he answers, nodding his head vigorously. "I'll take a coffee with milk and two sugars."

I snarl at him, angry with them all for the position they've put me in. Angry at myself for blowing it with Jordan. For failing the job I've been given.

Chapter Fifteen

<u>Devin</u>

I believe the saying is: *Hell hath no fury like a woman scorned.* Well, multiply that by two and stuff it in a tiny house and you have a tinderbox of a situation, just waiting for a spark.

The ride over to town hall is one of silence, no one having the guts or desire to speak up. Rebecca is about to lose what she had been hanging onto: the hope that I could be the hero rather than the villain. Jordan seems on the verge of a fistfight with anyone who says the word landfill. They are angry, and with every second that ticks by, the anger seems to grow.

We all file out of the car looking like a motley crew of pissed-off, overtired strangers.

The small hall is full, with nearly every seat taken and people leaning against every available inch of wall space. There is grumbling amongst the people, a low hum of dissatisfaction. We make our way to the front of the room, with the exception of Jordan, who hangs back and stands by the door, looking ready to run. There are marshals around, trying to keep the meeting fairly safe, but I still am not sure if I should be more worried about Hoyle or the people in this town who I gave my word to, but up until this point, have not come through for. I know I exploited their desire to get rid of Hoyle. They read my agreement and saw how it included ousting him. They weighed it out, and in the moment, made the choice to vote for the landfill, but in reality they're likely having buyers' remorse. And the fact that we haven't come through on our end of the bargain, providing security, gives them every reason to be angry.

Our attention is drawn to the small podium in the front of the room where Mrs. Nettleton is the first to speak. She's a wide woman, shaped like a box dressed in a floral tent. She wobbles a bit when she walks, but now, as she readies herself to address the group, she looks perfectly sturdy. The crowd falls silent as she begins to speak.

"I was born here. Every second of my life has been spent here. My kids were born here. Everything I know, everything I believe, is here in Clover. I've put up with corruption, crime, the mill closing down, and my neighbors starving. All of those things I've faced with my back straight and my head held high, because we're not people to just back down when times get tough. We made a deal with the devil and signed off on a dump coming to our town, all because we wanted to be rid of the men running this place. That was what was promised. Freedom. Well, my last chance at feeding my family this year, the cattle that provide us with milk, and in turn money, are gone. Our fence was cut down at the farthest point of our property and we've had no luck bringing them home. Now what am I going to do? This is too much. Our backs can't take it. We'll break. You'll break us." She points a crooked finger in my direction and every head in the room spins my way. "You promised us security, you promised we'd be rid of him. Well, you lied."

I hear a shout from behind me and the tone is angry enough to have me turning around to make sure someone isn't coming my way swinging a shovel or something. "She's right," the man's voice booms. "All my livestock have been run off my land, too. My fences are all broken, and I don't have any money to rebuild. You promised us protection. Where is it?"

"I understand the frustration," I say, getting to my feet and trying to quiet the crowd. "I want you to know the reason for the delay is an attempt to find a more suitable fit for Clover than a landfill. That's not an easy process and unfortunately we haven't been able to alter the deal. But I thought you should know that is why security isn't here yet."

The rumble of the crowd grows so loud that I can't hear myself think. I can see shaking heads, body language turning from upset to completely irate. Rebecca, who is still sitting, reaches up to touch my arm, a gentle reminder that, even angry, she's still behind me. A shrill whistle comes from the back of the room and I scan the crowd until I find the source. It's Jordan, her fingers pressed between her lips, trying to draw everyone to silence. It works.

"Security is on its way. They'll be here by nightfall, and you and your land will be safe. My company will work to get your fences mended and your land cleaned of any chemicals that may have been spilled there." She looks regal, strong, and unwavering as she holds court in this large room. Until this point I've seen her as an adversary, and while I wouldn't consider myself sexist, I've sold her short. I can see this now as she speaks to this room.

"So that's it then? The landfill is a done deal? I mean, I get that this was voted in, but come on, we were desperate," a skinny woman holding two kids, one on each hip, asks.

The whole room falls silent once more, waiting to hear the answer, the answer I think I know. But judging by the look on Jordan's face, I feel like maybe I'm missing something.

"No," she says firmly. "No landfill." She lets the confused roar of the crowd rise and then fall before she tries to speak again. "I spoke to my boss this morning. My company has been working on a new idea and we've just been waiting for the right place to pilot it. I convinced my superiors this morning that Clover is the right place."

"What is it, a toxic pit?" a man next to me shouts sarcastically.

"No. It's a state-of-the-art recycling facility. I think the closed mill can be converted and the land we intended for the landfill can be used to construct the remaining facilities we'll need. But it's more than that. Clover won't just house the recycling plant, it will become one of the first completely energy-self-sufficient towns in the country. Solar panels, wind turbines, and so much more. I told my boss this morning that the town of Clover was the perfect spot to try this out, because the residents are as self-sufficient as they come. Nothing can knock them down and we'd be crazy to pilot this anywhere else." I watch as she makes eye contact with Click, and I can tell there truly is something there, something I stomped on. Another emotionally inept move on my part. Something else to add to my list of mistakes and missteps since coming back to Clover.

"So no trash?" an old man asks, cupping his ear to hear her better.

"No trash, sir. And this will put Clover on the map. Done right, it could be the blueprint for towns all across the country. It's going to pump life back into your economy for generations to come. But it's not going to be easy. Every single person in this town needs to be behind this in order to make the numbers work. I'll need everyone's support. It's going to be real work."

A man old enough to be Jordan's father stands and pulls his baseball cap from his head, tucking it respectfully under his arm. "Ma'am, work is something I've been looking for these last two years. I've skipped meals, given up on my broken-down truck, and lost more than a little sleep wondering how I'm gonna feed my family. If you got work, I'll be the first in line for it. I'll show up, every day, every hour, until you don't need me any more. And I know a hundred people in this town who feel the same way. You give us a chance, and we'll make this happen. We all want Clover back the way we remember it from years ago. And we're willing to work for that."

I hang my head slightly, feeling wholly selfish and inadequate. I don't have this type of conviction, this much passion for anything positive. Everything I push for is about me. Nothing I do is for a larger purpose than my own need for closure and revenge.

After a moment of hesitation a cheer breaks out, and Jordan is quickly surrounded by thrilled residents of Clover all trying to thank her. As their energy and exuberance escalate, Click jumps to his feet and cuts through the crowd to help Jordan make her way toward the door. I hook my arm in Rebecca's and slip out the side of the building just in time to see Jordan and Click hopping in the car and speeding away.

"There goes our ride." Rebecca smirks and shrugs up at me. "You think they're going to make up?"

"Who knows? I'm certainly no expert in that department."

"You got rid of the landfill, that's a good start."

"Jordan did that. I can't really take credit. If it weren't for me, the landfill never would have been a problem in the first place."

"And if it weren't for you, Clover wouldn't be about to change for the better." She leans into me, and I wrap my arm around her, pulling her to my body. We haven't kissed in far too long and I'm dying to feel her lips on mine again. Her face saddens a bit as she speaks. "Now I just need to get my little girl back here. Do you think once the security team is in place it will be safe?"

"I do." I turn her toward me and bend so I'm at her eye level. "Maybe we could stay at the hotel tonight? Pick her up in the morning?" Her reaction to my devilish smile reminds me how worth it she is.

"I think we could work that out." I feel her cold hand slip up the back of my shirt and she runs her nails down my spine. I lean in and kiss her. She pulls back slightly to whisper something to me, something she might not want to say any louder for fear of my reaction. "I'm glad about the landfill, Devin, but I'm still scared for us. I know that no relationship is easy, but something inside me keeps telling me we're playing with fire. We're trying to make something work and maybe it never will."

"I know," I whisper, pressing my lips against hers again. "I have no idea if I'll ever get this right, if I'll ever feel like I'm fixed enough to be with you. But I don't want to stop trying, or stop kissing you while I look for that answer."

"Do you love me, Devin?" she asks with a hopefulness in her eyes that's mixed with a dose of fear.

"I feel more for you than I have for anyone in my life. I'm happier with you than with anyone on this planet. I'm not sure I know how to be in love, but if I did I'd want it to be with you."

"That sounds like you're grading your feelings on a sliding scale. I'm the best pup in a bad litter? You don't like anyone but you hate me the least?"

"That's not what I'm saying. You're it for me, Rebecca. From the moment I saw you standing outside chemistry class you've monopolized my thoughts. You're the bar of expectation that I've set for the world, and so far there's been no one else out there who even comes close. I might not be throwing the word love around, but that has more to do with me than it does with you. I might love you with all my heart, but it might not be enough for you. All I can tell you is that I'm here. I'm not running off, I'm not leaving you behind. I want to become good enough for you." She's still tight against my body and the more I say the stronger her grip becomes.

"Well, well, the love birds reunited." I know the drawl and arrogance in his voice before I even look up. Hoyle is standing ten feet from us, his hand on his hip, just above his gun.

"Go inside," I say, spinning Rebecca back toward the door. She hesitates and I give her a look that speaks volumes. Once she's gone I cut the distance between Hoyle and me to an uncomfortable six inches. He might be able to draw a gun faster than me but I've got plenty of pounds of muscle on him. I want to be close enough for him to realize that.

"Get out of here. This town is moving on without you. Best thing you can do is head out of here before someone takes it upon themselves to find a more permanent solution for getting rid of you."

"I seem to remember getting rid of you for almost eleven years. I think I could arrange that again."

"That's exactly what you did, *arrange* it. Pulled all the strings to make that happen. All to cover up the truth. That's why I came back, to make you pay for it. The truth won't stay buried for much longer."

His hand shoots out and wraps tightly around my neck, squeezing as his eyes grow wide. "You best not mess around with me, boy. You dig up the past and you'll be sorry." I don't react to his hand on my neck. I just smile and ignore the discomfort. I don't make a move for him. I'm not giving the son of a bitch a reason to shoot me.

"Hoyle," I hear Nick's voice calling from behind me, "get your hands off him. I've got no problem charging you with assault." In reality I know Nick has no plans of arresting Hoyle unless he does something very dramatic. Whatever takes the old sheriff down needs to be something ironclad. But the threat is enough for now. Hoyle drops his hand from my neck and takes two steps backward.

"You think you're searching for justice? Hunting the man who killed my boy, thinking you're gonna make him pay for the time you lost? It's not gonna lighten your burden at all. You can chase that ghost all you want, you'll never get the answer you're looking for." He spins on his heels and disappears into the woods.

I hear Rebecca's boots on the gravel. "You okay?" she asks, running her hand across my neck.

"I'm fine." I lean down and press my lips to hers, an intense hunger in my kiss. "Let's get out of here," I whisper, brushing her bangs away from her face. "I can't take another minute of not being alone with you."

We hitch a ride with one of the very pleased residents of Clover and hop out in an excited frenzy, making our way through the entrance of the hotel. The moment the elevator doors slide closed we're on each other, kissing and pulling at clothes as the floors ding by. When the elevator comes to a stop, my hand is up Rebecca's shirt, her teeth in my neck. We break apart reluctantly and scurry to my room. It hasn't been long since we slept together, nothing compared to the eleven years prior, but it still feels too long. I slide the key in the door and push it open with my shoulder, pulling Rebecca in behind me. I spin and lower her down onto the large bed.

She's smiling up at me. The anticipation and excitement is flowing wildly between us. I unbutton her cotton shirt and she shrugs it off. With a quick motion I'm out of my shirt as she pulls at my belt buckle. When life is this fragile, this mixed up, it adds urgency to moments like this. I don't want my phone to ring with bad news; she probably doesn't want time to think about how much she misses Adeline. The faster we dive in, the better we'll both feel.

She makes quick work of my buckle and my pants fall to the ground. I step out of them and bring myself down on top of her. I slide her out of the rest of her clothes and stare at her beautiful body. I don't know if I believe in soul mates, in there just being one person in the world for each of us, but I know I've seen plenty of naked women in my day and none stir this much passion in me.

I sink my hand into her hair, and my teeth into her neck. I hear her let out a noise that's part pain, part pleasure and when I start to back off, unsure how she feels about this primal bite, she slides her hand up to my neck and holds me there, seeming to beg for more. Her other hand is braced tightly on my bicep, and every time I move and tense the muscle, she grasps it harder. I'm propped up above her and feeling too limited, my hands unable to explore her. I roll to her side, breaking my lips from her and smiling at the sad little dissatisfied moan she gives.

"Don't worry, you won't be disappointed for long." My hand slides down and I feel her legs part for me. My touch sends her back arching and she throws her head backward. The last time we were together was about finding again what brought her pleasure, now I know and it's all about taking her there over and over.

She grabs a handful of my hair, moaning louder and louder. Even though she isn't touching me excitement is coursing through me as I hear her voice grow more frantic. I lean over her, until our mouths line up as I pleasure her with my finger. She groans seductively into my lips as her body shudders. She swirls her tongue around mine and runs her hand through my hair.

Maybe on a different day, with a different woman, I'd pace myself by kissing my way up and down her body, but with Rebecca, I'm too out of my mind with anticipation. The only thing I can do is roll on top of her. She's still winded, her eyes barely open, when I slide inside her, finally feeling at home.

There is no child sleeping down the hall this time, no tentative dance of emotions. We won't exchange soft words or timid feelings. This is just us. Here alone. And I want all of her. Now.

I rock back and forth in her and watch her hands fly up, over her head, clutching at the pillow and sheets as if she's holding on for dear life. We ignore the sound the large oak headboard is making, rhythmically slamming against the wall. Our eyes meet, our faces so close together that we're urgently breathing the same air. I stare into her eyes. I see my future in her blue pools staring up at me, and as frightening as that is, I can't look away.

My breath grows more desperate and I hear hers matching mine. She's moaning my name, and I quicken my pace. I cover her lips with mine and swallow her words. Breaking the kiss, I sink my head down by hers, taking in the scent of her hair and rubbing the impossibly soft skin of her cheek against the roughness of mine.

The wave of euphoria rolls over both of us and I bury my face in her neck. She thrusts her nails into the muscle of my shoulder and quivers until she falls limp with contented exhaustion. A moment later I do the same, dropping my weight down onto her.

My cheek still pressed to hers, I feel her face curl into a smile. "We may not have everything figured out, but we sure as hell have *that* mastered."

I laugh, so relieved for the peace I find in her arms. If only I could bottle this, take a swig of it every time the plaguing voice in my mind pulls me to the past. If only she were enough to make me forget.

I roll off her, hating the sensation of being torn away, becoming separate from her again. I don't go far, just enough to take my weight off her and then draw her to me. Lying here like this, I realize in this moment I'd do just about anything she asked of me, and it makes me grateful that she hasn't. I'd be powerless.

I glance at the clock and remember it's the middle of the day. We should be eating lunch or helping Luke figure out the code in the notebook, but instead we're here. We're a knot of sheets and legs, sweat and kisses. Our problems aren't completely solved or fixed, but we had a victory today, and this was our celebration. She asked me not to destroy her town, and I obliged her request. That deserved some rewards, which we both just received.

I run my to-do list through my head: catch a killer, change the deal, fix things with Rebecca, and get rid of Hoyle for good—all in time to leave here with Luke tomorrow night. The deal has been changed: one down. I haven't wrapped my head around leaving for New York. I know I committed to Luke that I'd sell the company and, on paper, it's the right thing to do. If I had known I'd get my chance at revenge down here in Clover maybe I would have waited but the wheels are already in motion. It's a very lucrative offer and I'd be foolish to pass it up. That's all so easy to say right now, but when my ass hits that seat in the plane, I imagine I'll be wrestling with some powerful emotions.

Chapter Sixteen

<u>Click</u>

"I'm pretty sure we just stole Devin's car. Do you really think he's going to appreciate us taking off without him?" Jordan is turned in her seat, looking out the back window, seeming to expect sirens any minute.

"He'll understand," I retort flatly. "The crowd was a little over the top. I think it's better if you take a step back and let them process what you've told them."

"Have *you* processed it?" she asks, turning forward and staring straight ahead.

"It was a shock. I thought you'd be coming in today and just moving forward with the landfill."

"I'm exhausted." She unfastens the clip holding her hair up and rubs her fingers into her scalp, trying to work out the tension.

"You must have been up all night crunching the numbers, trying to figure it out."

"That's not what I mean." She leans her head against the cool glass of the window and closes her eyes. "I'm just so tired of fighting. Fighting to be seen as an equal in the face of making seventy cents on the dollar compared to every man at my company doing the same job. I'm tired of having to always explain why I'm good at what I do, prove myself. I hate hiding who I am, where I'm from. Last night I lay in that tiny little bed and stared up at the ceiling, and I swore that when this was all done I was going to drop everything and just be myself. Even if that doesn't mesh with my job, or my family. But you know what? When I tried to figure out what that would look like, I couldn't. I don't even know who my real self is anymore. I think she's gone."

"She's not gone, Jordan. She's the person who just changed the lives of everyone in Clover for the better. Stop competing and clawing your way through life. You might lose some people along the way, but odds are they weren't worth it anyway."

"I staked my career on this deal. That's how I got my boss to sign off. I told him if I couldn't pull this off, he could fire me. I think it's telling that he jumped at the opportunity."

"So we make it work. Everything you said about Clover is true. They're gritty and hardworking, and if this plan is going to happen anywhere, it will be here."

"And if it doesn't? If Hoyle and his men make it impossible or something else keeps it from working, then what?"

"Then you take stock, check out who's still standing with you, and keep moving forward."

"Are you still going to be standing there?" she asks, her eyes closed, her head still pressed against the window.

"Yes, if you want me there. You have to know what Devin said, that isn't what I was doing. I wanted you to fall in love with Clover, not—"

"I didn't fall in love with you," she shouts, her eyes shooting open as she sits up. "You're a good guy, and there's clearly something between us, but I wouldn't call it love. Are you saying you're in love, because that's going to freak me out?"

"Jordan," I reach my hand over and take hers, which is flailing as she speaks, "calm down. I assure you, I don't love you." I smile and pull her hand in for a kiss.

"Promise?" she asks, scanning my face, and I can't tell if she's serious or being sarcastic.

"You want me to promise you that I *don't* love you?"

"Yes, because if you *do* love me, then you are highly illogical and I can't really tolerate that."

"I can promise you I don't love you, and the more you talk, the easier you're making that." I pat her leg and smile, wondering how the hell I got caught up in her so fast. I pull the car over to a clearing on the side of the road and watch as she looks around, wondering what I'm doing. "I don't love you, but I am going to kiss you." I lean in toward her and move her long dark hair behind her ear.

"Well, that's not very spontaneous, just announcing it like that."

"Do you like spontaneity?"

"I hate it. Fail to plan, plan to fail." She's stuttering and I can see her nerves rising the closer I lean in to her.

"That's perfect; I *plan* to kiss you."

"Are you asking me?" she whispers when my lips are just inches from hers.

"No." I cup her face in my hand and close the gap between our mouths quickly, before she can come up with a smartass remark. I've kissed my share of women, so I'm shocked when I feel warmth spread across my chest as I kiss her. I feel like I'm kissing her with my whole body, all my senses. I can smell the flowery scent of her perfume, taste the fruitiness of her lip gloss. This kiss overtakes me in a way I've never experienced. Maybe it's the fact that we've been shot at together or that I've seen her cry, and change, and take a huge risk for a good reason. Whatever it is, it has me holding on tight and not letting her go.

She's kissing me back just as passionately and the world outside this car disappears. The center console is the only thing keeping any space at all between us. I slide my hand up from her knee to her thigh, her designer pants feeling like silk beneath my rough hands.

I don't see it coming, but in one confidently swift move Jordan crosses over to my side of the car, straddling me. She never breaks the kiss, just brings her body over to me, and I take full advantage of the better position. My hands are up the back of her shirt, sliding across the smooth perfection that is her espresso skin. She's rocking above me, moving against me in a way that has her moaning and me growling into her kiss. Her mouth pulls away from mine and I'm certain it's to tell me how illogical this is, but I'm wrong. She's kissing my neck and biting at my skin and I wrap my hands up in her hair, praying she never stops. I have no plan here. We're on the side of the road, a quiet road, but this isn't what I had in mind when I pulled over. If I thought this was an option, I'd have driven straight back to the hotel and spent the rest of the day trying to make her forget how much work she has ahead of her with this deal.

I feel her hand on the buckle of my belt, when a roaring eighteen-wheeler blows by us, laying on his air horn, and laughing I'm sure. He likely got a glimpse of us.

The blaring noise sends Jordan jumping and then clutching me so tightly I can hardly breathe. Her nails are in my skin and her mouth hovers over my neck as she tries to regain her composure.

"We should stop," she whispers, and I can't tell if it's a question or a statement. I contemplate suggesting the hotel, but I've never been that guy, the pushy one, even when a girl is grasping for my belt. With four sisters you come to realize the female heart is tied tightly to the female body, and it's not to be handled recklessly.

I nod and loosen my grip on her reluctantly. I feel the warmth of her body disappear as she slides back over to her side of the car. I shift in my seat, and take in a deep breath, trying to balance the need to drive the car with the raging desire coursing through me. This is where years of self-discipline come in handy.

"I need to get my stuff from Nick's house and make a few hundred phone calls. I'm about to call in every favor I have." Jordan straightens her shirt and flips down the mirror in the visor to wipe away her smeared lip gloss.

I put the car in gear and focus on the road ahead of me. I don't know exactly when the time will be right for Jordan and me, but if the way I'm feeling right now is any indication, when it does happen it will be incredible.

"Yes ma'am," I say, completely goading her on. I know how those words infuriate her.

She looks across at me with rage in her eyes. Once she sees my sly grin and knows I'm teasing her, she relaxes and shakes her head at me. That lighthearted smile, the one that makes her whole face glow, that's all I need. Now I can drive.

Chapter Seventeen

<u>Devin</u>

Pulling into Nick's driveway, I see everyone else is already here. Rebecca and I have been off the grid for a few hours and I'm just hoping we didn't miss anything important.

We head in the door to find everyone gathered in the living room, beers in hand looking pretty celebratory.

"Hey," they cheer at us, raising their glasses in our direction. You'd never know this morning we were all on the verge of throttling each other.

"Great work in there today," I say, pointing at Jordan.

"Thanks, that was the easy part, now I have to actually pull it off."

Nick crosses the room and hands a fresh beer to Jordan. "Listen," he starts as he pats her shoulder, "you don't know me from Adam so this might not mean much to you, but what you did today took guts and I'm proud of you." He tips the front of his hat down at her and I watch as she averts her eyes. I know that feeling, the intensity of a moment too much to look at full on.

"Thanks," Jordan musters. Click is leaning against the wall and he hasn't taken his eyes off her. Poor kid is caught up in her something fierce.

"Now the real work begins," Jordan continues. "I made some big commitments to my boss and it's going to take a lot to get this thing going. You're selling your company on Friday, Devin, so that means you're out of Clover? I'll be working with the new leadership?"

242

Every eye in the room comes my way, even Luke looks up from the journal he's been completely fixed on. "I'll be sticking around for a bit after the sale. I had that worked into the contract. I'll continue to be your contact here in Clover and, more than that, I'll help you anyway I can. You stuck your neck out today and I don't intend to leave you high and dry."

"Good, because one big part of my agreement with my boss was turning this into a PR dream come true. It has all the makings of one, turning a struggling town around, creating the blue print for the country as far as energy efficiency. It practically writes itself but I need a face for it. I'm going to be too busy working the numbers to worry about anything else. The problem is they're giving me no one. This is my project and mine alone. I can hire outside the company, but they're not giving me a team."

"That's not really my strength," I admit as I grab a beer from the fridge. "I'm never good in those moments." On my way by I slap Luke on the shoulder, because I know he'll have something to say about this. He's distracted but joins the conversation briefly.

"He's right, Jordan. If I had a dollar for every meeting that ended with cursing and on the verge of a fistfight, I'd be a billionaire. Devin is a great decision maker; he'll maneuver his way through the trickiest acquisition, and kick your ass in chess. But he isn't tactful or patient. That's what you need in a PR guy." He says this last line as he jots down more notes from the journal, not seeming to realize the door he just opened.

"He's right," I agree with a wide smile. "I'm not your guy. He is." Luke's nodding his head absentmindedly until he realizes what was just said.

"No I'm not. I stand to make a good chunk of change from the sale of the company on Friday. I'm taking that money and sitting my ass on a beach somewhere hot for the next month. Then, like I've always said, I'm reinvesting somewhere and starting up something new."

"Are you seriously telling me that you don't want to be the guy breaking this story? Traveling around town, shaking hands, kissing babies, doing the interviews? Think of all the great press you'll be a part of." I flop on the couch next to Jordan and Rebecca settles on my lap. Just the feel of her thigh in my hand gets me excited again. Why did we leave the damn hotel?

"No way," Luke insists as he stares down at the book. "I still haven't even heard how she's pulling this off. I've been living in the business world a long time. I can't see how she's going to turn a profit off this. I don't want my name on something that's going to go bust."

Jordan sits up a little straighter in her seat and I can tell Luke's words are met like a challenge to her. "It's not going to go bust. The eco-friendly side of it is going to get us a good amount of government subsidies, and in turn lower our cost for energy dramatically. The setup of these systems will create jobs and stimulate the economy in Clover. Factored into our original cost was the income we pay employees at our facilities up north. Cost of living is significantly lower here with no unions. People will get a very fair pay but our company will save tremendously versus the forecast. If most of the labor force comes right here from town we'll make out the best. A good PR guy could even round up some more investors, people who want their names on the pilot of this cutting-edge idea. If you guys can get Hoyle to stop messing with the land and causing problems, we should be able to rally everyone together and pull this off."

Luke makes a mildly impressed face, but I know him well enough to understand he likes what he hears. I don't push any more and neither does Jordan.

Widening his eyes and taking his nose out of that journal for the first time since we got back here, he asks, "What, so that's it? You aren't going to *make* me do it Devin? Tell me you won't sell the company unless I agree? Come on, let me save some face here at least and make it look like it was against my will?"

"Fine, if you don't take the job, I'll make your life a living hell," I shoot back unconvincingly.

"How can I say no to something that intimidating? I'll do it. But I'm only signing on for a short time. That beach is still calling my name." Luke dives right back into the book and begins jotting things down again.

"Well, security should be here soon," Jordan says, and I see her eyes dart up toward Click and then quickly away.

I jump at the chance to help bridge the gap of what I've broken. I'm starting to realize it's not an effort to drop the selfish myopic side of myself. It was more of an effort to live that way, to turn off the fact that I actually notice other people's pain, and that it affects me. Over time it became a habit, something I forced myself into, but I'll admit there is a sense of relief letting a little empathy back into my life. "You'll need someone to head them up. Someone who's spent a little time in Clover, proven his loyalty and skill."

"Sorry, Devin, I'm pretty happy as a marshal," Nick laughs as he shrugs his shoulders.

"I was talking about Click. I know it's your show now, Jordan, but I can't think of a better man to head your security."

"Well," she stutters, "that would be up to him." She takes a long drag off her beer and avoids turning toward Click.

"I'd be honored," Click says, clearly not sharing that wary feeling, as he looks right at her. He's trying to catch her eye, staring down at her, trying to connect.

"Okay then, so that covers security and PR, we need a plan for getting rid of Hoyle. You find anything in that book to incriminate him?" Jordan brushes right over any potential for emotions with Click. Maybe I'm not the only damaged person in this room.

"I'm working on it," Luke says and I know him well enough to see a few of his nervous ticks showing. He's worried about something, maybe even hiding something.

"Well I hate to break it to y'all," Nick says as he gets to his feet, "but if you plan on staying in Clover long-term, there ain't no room at this inn. Y'all are gonna need a more permanent solution. If you've got security coming today, I'm going to get my wife and boys. That means this house is going to be full tonight. Sorry."

Rebecca shoots off my lap and claps her hands together. "Nick, can I go with you to pick up the kids? I want to see Adeline as soon as I can."

"Sure, I've got room in that big ol' Suburban for you."

"I'm just going to freshen up."

"Take your time, I've got two car seats and a booster seat to wrestle into place." Nick dips the front of his hat again. "Just remember folks, you don't have to go home but y'all can't stay here." He heads out the door and I catch Rebecca's wrist.

"I've got a ton of phone calls to make still," Jordan says as she reads the scene and heads upstairs. Click takes her cue and heads out the back door toward the fire pit. Luke doesn't move, but he seems so engrossed in what he's doing I don't even care that he's here.

"You excited to see Adeline?" I ask, knowing the answer but just wanting her close to me for another minute.

"I feel like I'm going to bust. I can't wait to have her back in Clover. Though I'm not sure where we'll stay. You burned a bridge at my daddy's house and I'm pretty sure I've been fired from both my jobs by now."

"No matter what happens you never have to work at either of those places again. As long as I'm around, you and Adeline will want for nothing. I'll find us a good place to stay in Clover."

"All of us?" she gestures toward the back door and at the stairs, indicating I might need a place for Jordan and Click too.

"They're adults, I'm sure they can make their own arrangements," I say coldly and she touches my cheek, reminding me that my blustery exterior will get me nowhere. "I'll help them find something too." I lean in to kiss her.

Before our lips meet, she whispers, "It's not so bad being a nice guy, is it?"

I don't feel like a nice guy. I feel like the same guy who's making slightly different choices.

"We're going to work this out, Rebecca. We're going to find a way to get *us* right."

Danielle Stewart

"I just need you to keep trying, Devin. If you don't give up, I won't either," she says, running her hand through my hair affectionately. "I'm going to get my little girl. You make sure we have a place to lay our heads tonight. I don't care where as long as we're together, as long as we're safe."

She hustles up the stairs, grabs her things and is heading out the front door when I hear Click tap lightly on the glass of the back door. He's trying to draw our attention without making too much of a scene. I can only see the profile of his face, but I can tell there is a seriousness in his expression that is speaking volumes.

I snag Rebecca's arm and press my fingers to my lips, gesturing for her to be quiet. Luke stands and peers around the corner trying to get a better look at what Click is doing. "What is it?" he mouths at Click and is met with a hand signal indicating we should all get down. I pull Rebecca backward against the nearest wall and then slide down with her.

"What about Nick?" Luke whispers as he crouches down as well. "If it's serious we should warn him. He's probably strapping those seats in, with his back hanging out of the truck. And what about Jordan upstairs?"

I look down at Rebecca and realize I'd shield her, take any number of bullets for her without a moment's hesitation. If, in any minute, someone crashed through this door, every ounce of life would need to be stolen from my body before I'd let a hair on her head be touched. In this moment, I realize I don't want to live a second without her.

"Can you get upstairs to warn Jordan?" I ask Luke, and he nods as he makes his way, staying low to the stairs. He breaks into a sprint and disappears up them.

"Nick?" Rebecca whispers, her brows furrowed in worry. "Jeannie and the kids, if anything happens to Nick, what would they do?"

"I'm not leaving you here," I say sternly. Before I can say anymore, Luke's head appears at the top of the stairs. "Go over to Luke, get upstairs and stay." She laces her hand in mine and pulls it up to her lips. The warmth of her breath on my hand makes me ache to hold her tight until the danger is gone. She kisses the back of my hand and runs her soft fingers across my rough cheek. "Be careful."

She makes her way quickly over to Luke. They disappear up the stairs and I suck in a deep centering breath, wishing she were back with me.

I stay low as I make my way to the front door. When I look toward the back door, Click is gone. I don't know what he saw, what he heard, but I know leaving Nick out there without a warning is dangerous. I peer out the lace curtains of the front door and see Nick looking pretty oblivious as he loads the last car seat into the back of his large Suburban. I knock on the glass to try to get his attention but he doesn't hear me. I can hear the bumping of his music and I know he'll only be able to hear me if I go out there.

I pull open the door and survey the front yard. I let out a loud whistle and watch as Nick's head pops out of his truck. I wave him over quickly as I keep my eyes darting from one side of the yard to the other. There is no sign of Click, but also no sign of danger that I can see.

He drops what he's doing and rushes over to the door. I step aside and shut it quickly behind him.

"What is it?" he asks, his hand resting above his holstered weapon.

"Click told us all to get down, I think maybe he saw or heard something out back. I don't know where he is now."

Nick unholsters his weapon and heads for the back door. "Stay here. You know where my gun safe is upstairs. Use it if you need it." Before his hand can hit the back door a loud pop rings out. The shattering of glass sends both Nick and me to the floor. At least five more shots ring out and I can hear debris hitting the floor, pieces of Nick's house being shot up and destroyed.

The only sound worse than the cracking of wood and breaking of glass are the screams coming from upstairs. I crawl on my stomach to the bottom of the stairs and get a glimpse of Click flashing by the back door. I hear one more shot and then everything falls silent. I hesitate, stopping on the first step, waiting for something else to happen.

Nick is on his feet, his weapon poised for action as he peeks out to his backyard. He yanks the door open and breaks into a run, obviously seeing something that warrants it. I look up the stairs and see Rebecca standing there with a shotgun in her hand. "Take it," she says and tosses it down into my hands. "We're okay up here."

"I love you," I say as I step down off the stairs and cock the gun. I'm out the door before I can hear if she replies with the same words. I see Click pummeling a man I can't make out. He's throwing punches and jabs with such precision I almost can't believe this is the same quiet guy who's been *taking it all in.* The other man is like a rag doll now as he falls backward to the ground. Nick is there, yanking cuffs from his belt. He's slamming the man down and I can hear expletives flying from his mouth.

As I approach, even through the bloodied nose and swollen eyes, I can tell who this is. "Collin," I say as I sink a kick into his ribs.

"Trust me, guys, no one wants to kill this piece of shit more than I do. He just shot up my damn house, but I think he's had enough." Nick yanks him to his feet and I go nose to nose with him.

"Hoyle put you up to this?" I snap, burying my finger in his chest. "Did he promise you another fix or something?"

"You're gonna end up dead. This is bigger than you know. You think this is just about you trying to mess with him. You're messing with something much bigger. I might have missed you today, but someone is going to pop you, and anyone else trying to build on the land. They'll keep trying until that company backs out. You don't know what you're into here."

"And what about Rebecca and Adeline, what if one of your bullets would have hit them?"

"I could give a shit. If they're dumb enough to be with you then they deserve whatever they get."

I heard Nick's words, I know he told us to lay off, but I can't. I cock my fist back and hit him so hard that the life instantly leaves his body. He goes limp in Nick's arms, unconscious and hunched over.

"Sorry," I say to Nick as I shake the ache out of my hand.

"If you didn't do it, I would have," Click says, leaning down and grabbing Collin's legs, helping Nick lug him to the house.

I can see Rebecca's face looking out the upstairs window, Luke and Jordan over her shoulder. All I can think is, what have I started and how many people will get hurt in the process?

Chapter Eighteen

<u>Devin</u>

"We won't be hearing from him for a while," Nick says as he steps back in the front door. The commotion is starting to settle down. We've all given our statements to the other marshals Nick called in. Rebecca tried, rather unsuccessfully, to make the shot up kitchen look halfway presentable for Jeannie's return.

"Are you still thinking of picking up the kids?" Luke asks, sitting back in front of the book he's supposed to be deciphering.

"Security has landed," Jordan says, checking her phone. "You'll all have people assigned to you directly."

"My buddies are on high alert now, too," Nick chimes in and points to the few men out surveying the yard.

"I don't even want to think about what would have happened if Click hadn't given us some warning when he heard someone out there. We would have all been just sitting here." Rebecca gestures to the seats that could have been covered with blood now if not for Click. She's still tucked under my arm. I haven't let her go since I came back in the house and saw with my own eyes she was not hurt.

"That's the truth. Nice work, kid," Nick says, slapping Click's shoulder. "You've got some impressive skills."

"Thank you." Click nods and falls right back to being his quiet self.

"I'm just sorry I brought this on all of you. I don't know how I'll face Jeannie, after what Collin did to your house."

"Rebecca, Collin wasn't here for you. Hoyle sent him," Nick says, trying to make her feel better.

"And he alluded to something more going on here. Something bigger. Any ideas Nick?" I ask, rubbing Rebecca's back in support.

"No. But I'm sure as hell going to find out. He said the land was what this is all about. I'm guessing maybe there is something more going on. I'm going to put some of my most trusted guys on it. After this," he gestures to the damage, "I want answers."

"I'd still like to go with you to get Adeline." Rebecca finally pulls away from me and it feels like my own skin tearing away. She steps on her toes to kiss me, and I cup her face, making it last a few extra seconds. I don't know why, but I have this sinking feeling in my chest, like that kiss might be the last one I get from her for a while. I shake off the sensation and pull up a chair next to Luke at the table.

Nick and Rebecca say the rest of their goodbyes and head for the door. I notice Click and Jordan haven't said much to each other, but their eyes keep meeting.

"I really need to get back on the phone," Jordan says, and heads quietly up the stairs. I expect Click to go with her, to say something, but he doesn't.

"I've got to talk to you, Devin," Luke says but stops abruptly as Click pulls up a chair next to us.

"Go ahead," I say, folding my arms over my chest, trying to shake the weird mood that's come over me. I can tell by his tone that Luke has something on his mind.

"It's of a sensitive nature, we can chat later."

"Is it about Click?" I ask, too tired and distracted to wait until later to go over whatever Luke needs.

"No, but . . ."

"Then I don't care if he hears it. I trust him."

"Okay, well I found Brent's case in this book."

"What? Why didn't you tell me when I got here? We could have gotten Nick on it right away."

"I don't have the whole thing decoded yet. But the section of it I have worked out is enough to make me think we might not want to get Nick involved yet."

"Why?"

"Brent wasn't killed by blunt force trauma and smoke inhalation like the medical examiner officially reported. It was a gun shot."

A rush of excitement and hope courses through me. "That's perfect. That's what Nick needs to know. It could be enough to get the case reopened."

"There's more." He looks from me to Click one more time, giving me the chance to clear the room. When I don't, he throws down his pen and comes out with it. "Rebecca's name is in here. As best as I can tell, her blood was found at the scene. I think Macready was pointing to her as a suspect."

"What?" I twist my face in disbelief that Luke is even considering this as truth. "Rebecca didn't kill Brent," I say, leaning backward and shooting him a *stop screwing around* glare.

"I'm not saying she did, I'm saying her name is in the report, and I think her blood was found at the scene. If there is even the slightest chance she had something to do with Brent's murder, I don't think we should get Nick involved. He'd be obligated to pursue it."

"She didn't do it." I bang the table adamantly.

"Does she have an alibi for that night?" Luke asks calmly.

"I didn't, but it doesn't mean I killed him. She was at home, painting."

"That would be easy for someone to challenge. She was alone in her room? Did she leave for the hour it would have taken to kill Brent, who knows?"

"I know she didn't do it. That isn't who she is."

"Let's just look at the facts, Devin. Since you got here and started pursuing all this, how has she acted? She keeps telling you to leave it alone, stop digging. Could that be because she doesn't want you to uncover anything? I'm just playing devil's advocate here."

"No, she wants a fresh start, she's earned that. We've both been through hell on our own and we're finally in a place where we might be able to make this work." Luke has instantly turned into my enemy. He's still the same guy I've worked with for two years, the man I silently respect, but in this moment, I hate him.

"She sat right at this table and said *someone should just shoot Hoyle*, get rid of him."

"That was a figure of speech, she was just frustrated with me. She'd never kill anyone. And why would Hoyle pin it on me if Rebecca did it. He has no reason to protect her."

"You don't know the circumstances. Maybe in protecting her, he was hiding why his son was killed. You told me in the past he'd threatened her, maybe she acted in self-defense. Maybe Hoyle didn't want that story coming out."

"She would have told me."

"When? In the nine years she lied to you through letters?"

"Go to hell." I toss my head back, completely exasperated by this conversation. Luke is making rational levelheaded arguments like he always does, but he doesn't know Rebecca like I do.

"I can't figure out the rest of this, Devin. It's like Macready knew this was something that needed extra encryption. Maybe Jordan can help me. Once we get an answer you can decide how to move forward. I'll support you either way. I just wanted to give you a heads up about not getting Nick involved yet."

"Give me the book," I say, my lips pursed and my face deadly serious. I watch his hand press down on it harder.

"Why?"

"Give me the book, Luke. You're not showing it to anyone else, not Jordan, not anyone. Give me the book, or I swear to God I'll beat the shit out of you if I have to."

I see Click put his body on the ready, stiffen slightly, his senses pulsing in case he needs to jump in. "Click, if you draw your gun on me you'll regret it," I snap, narrowing my eyes at him.

"You dug the thing up," he says, shrugging his shoulders. "As far as I see it, it's yours to do what you want with."

I can't tell if he means that or he's playing me, ready to tackle me if I make a move for Luke.

"Devin." There it is, that soft kid-glove voice Luke uses on me when I'm on the edge. "The answers you've always wanted are right here. Don't you want to know the truth? It doesn't mean we'll be calling in the troops to take Rebecca away. I told you, once we know we'll do whatever you want, but can you really trash this book and never know what actually happened?"

Danielle Stewart

My head is spinning and sweat gathers on my forehead. I've never had a panic attack, but I imagine the thudding of my heart and the weight on my chest is pretty close. I jump to my feet and Luke brings the book to his chest to protect it. My chair goes flying backward and hits hard against the old wood floors.

"Devin," Luke shouts, pleading with me to use my head. I blow past him and head for the back door toward the yard. There's a dim fire burning, something Click probably built earlier in the afternoon.

I pace around it, scratching my head anxiously, trying to make it work better, to kick-start the answer I need to come out of it.

I hear the door slide open and I'm ready to slug Luke, who's probably hidden the book somewhere in the house. I'm sure he's about to tell me it's for my own good. I look up to see I'm wrong. It's Click, not Luke, and he's holding the book in his hand.

He tosses it down on the bench and starts adding logs to the fire, stoking it and making it snap and roar.

"What are you doing?" I ask, my voice like nails, full to the brim with anger.

"It's your book, Devin. This isn't a game, it's your life."

"Should I go see if Luke is beaten half to death in there?"

"He's worried. He considers you a friend and he wants you to use your head."

"He doesn't get it. Nobody does."

"I think I do," he says, sitting on the stump across from me, the fire lighting his face as I huff out my disbelief in his comment.

"I was eighteen when I left home for the service. Right into a war. Scared out of my mind. You had a cell and I had a whole desert, but trust me, I know what it takes to survive, what you have to do to yourself to just keep moving. Some guys drink, some guys gamble. But, guys like us, we plan. We convince ourselves that we can fix all the broken. Steal back everything we're missing, as long as we can follow the plan. You came here a week ago thinking you'd be able to make everything right in your head again if you could just put this plan in motion."

I've never even considered comparing Click and me. Mostly because I thought of him as everything I wasn't, everything I could have been. The good Marine, the years of service.

"She wasn't supposed to be here," I say, shaking my head and staring into the woods behind Click. "Everything I needed to do is crumbling. I've spent years telling myself I could have my life back if I just finished all this, came here and made people pay." I look down at the journal and feel the rage returning. "I should be back in New York by now starting my life over. That's what I told myself. When I got back there, after all this was over, I'd stop being such an asshole. I'd feel better. I'd be better. I'd let people in again. Now if Rebecca really did . . ." I trail off; I will not say the words. I will not make it *that* real. "If she did it, I don't want to know. I don't want to live in that world. The world where I lost her, because of her. I can't get right with that in my head."

"You'd have served her time."

"It's not even that. I would have served a lifetime for her and never blinked an eye if I had known she did it. But now I'm on this hunt. I'm chasing this ghost, and I've pinned any hope for the rest of my life on finding the person to blame. I need that person to be someone I can crush, someone I can destroy. If not, I'll have this weight on me the rest of my life." I feel the thudding of my heart growing louder and my hands are balled into fists. "I had a plan."

I take a seat on the bench, the book sitting right next to me. I lift it and am shocked it doesn't weigh a ton; with all it holds I expect it to be heavier.

"I had a plan," Click says, and I change my focus from the book to him, wondering if maybe he really can relate to me. I've felt like this drifting broken boat for so long, telling myself that no one could ever imagine what it feels like to walk in my shoes.

"I was going to come home. Spend time with my sisters, all their kids. See my mom and dad and go right back to the old life. The laughing, the fun of it all. But no one was where they were supposed to be, where I told myself they'd be. Everyone was seven years older, seven years further into their lives, but not me. I was just stuck in a strange, timeless void. Whatever spot I thought I'd fit back into was gone. I was home twenty-nine hours. That's it. I packed up my duffel bag and left without saying a word. I called my CO and asked him to tell my family I was fine, but wouldn't be back for a while. I had a plan. It was to go home, but no one seemed to be reading the same script as me. So I left, got a call for this job, and haven't seen any of them since. Gone seven years, finally free, and I leave again just over a day later."

I let his words sink in; he's a kid who lost a long period of his life and came out of it different. He's trying to fit back into this world, just like I am. Trying to figure out how much of his old self is gone for good, and how much he might be able to salvage.

I look down at the book and then into the fire. I think about the permanence of fire's destruction. Burned is burned, there is no fixing that. Is that the same for me?

"Would I be crazy to toss this in the fire? To never find out if she did it?"

"My mom used to say crazy is only crazy if everyone can see it. I don't see a crowd out here. I say you do whatever you think is best."

"What would you do?"

"I don't think I've ever had what you and Rebecca have. How could I, really? I've spent so long ducking bullets and trying to keep sand out of my eyes. Hard to fall in love under those circumstances. So I can't really say what I would do."

This damn kid is throwing me for a loop. I had him pegged all wrong. I assumed he had the emotional depth of a cereal bowl. Here he is making me actually stop and think. I hate that.

"What are you going to do? Your plan to go home fell apart. Now what?"

"I didn't know what I needed, and now I have it. I've got a new plan."

"What's that?"

"I'm still going to go home. Just not right now. I thought after all I've seen, after the things I've done and can't undo, that the only thing that would make me forget would be jumping back in to my old life. Pretending. Ignoring. Now I'm here and I realize what I really needed was to take some control. Clover's its own little war. I did a lot of fighting over there, and I'm not sure it made much difference. Here, I might be able to actually help. For me, I think that's what I need. I can't erase the things that haunt me. But I think I need a war I can win. Then maybe I can go home."

"I thought I knew where my war was. Who my enemy was. I've been eating, sleeping, breathing my revenge for so long, and now this book, this stupid cryptic book might tell me none of it matters."

"Or it might tell you that Hoyle really did kill his kid. It might put him away for the rest of his life."

I look down at the tattered blue cover one more time. I close my eyes and toss the book, feeling the pull of it on my soul as it leaves my hand. I regret it and feel relieved all at once. I don't know if I've got this right, but sitting out here, letting it tear me apart, isn't the answer.

The book lands with a slap in Click's hands. "No one else gets that. No one. You keep it safe. I don't want that answer today, but I'd like to know it's there if I'm ever ready for it."

"No problem," he says, slipping it inside his coat. "Devin, you might think you're no good to anyone, that your only purpose is to hold people accountable for what they've done, but you're putting things in motion here that have potential for more than you know. For me. For Jordan. For everyone here. Maybe that's a byproduct of what you thought you were doing, but it's still something to think about."

"Yeah, I'm a real hero, Click," I mutter, heading back for the door. "Listen, I know I gave you shit about the Jordan thing, but if there is even the slightest chance that you love her or could love her, do me a favor."

"What's that?"

"Don't let this place crush the shot you have. I've got a feeling the next few months here in Clover are going to be messy. If you have to choose between her and this place, grab her and get the hell out of here. I wish Rebecca and I had."

"Are you going to say anything to Rebecca? Ask her more about what happened that night?"

"No. I'm going to try to salvage whatever is left of my plan and try to focus on getting Hoyle put away. Maybe it won't come from that book but he'll slip up."

As I pull the sliding door open, I consider thanking the kid, but I'm too caught up in my own train wreck of a mind to say anything else. I hear his words trailing in the house behind me and instead of closing the door to cut them off, I hesitate for a second, wanting to hear what he has to say.

"Devin, find a war you can win."

End of Change My Heart

Continue Devin and Rebecca's story in All My Heart

Books by Danielle Stewart

Piper Anderson Series
Book 1: Chasing Justice
Book 2: Cutting Ties
Book 3: Changing Fate
Book 4: Finding Freedom
Book 5: Settling Scores
Book 6: Battling Destiny
Book 7: Chris & Sydney Collection – Choosing
Christmas & Saving Love
Betty's Journal - Bonus Material (suggested to be read
after Book 4 to avoid spoilers)

Edenville Series – A Piper Anderson Spin Off
Book 1: Flowers in the Snow
Book 2: Kiss in the Wind
Book 3: Stars in a Bottle

The Clover Series
Hearts of Clover - Novella & Book 2: (Half My Heart &
Change My Heart)
Book 3: All My Heart
Book 4: Facing Home

Rough Waters Series
Book 1: The Goodbye Storm
Book 2: The Runaway Storm
Book 3: The Rising Storm

Midnight Magic Series
Amelia

The Barrington Billionaires Series
Book 1: Fierce Love
Book 2: Wild Eyes
Book 3: Crazy Nights

Danielle Stewart

Sign up for Danielle Stewart's Mailing List

www.authordaniellestewart.com

One random newsletter subscriber will be chosen every month this year. The chosen subscriber will receive a $25 eGift Card! Sign up today by clicking the link above.

Author Contact
Website: AuthorDanielleStewart.com
Email: AuthorDanielleStewart@Gmail.com
Facebook: Author Danielle Stewart
Twitter: @DStewartAuthor